I0633699

Liza

Shelley Munro

Munro Press

Liza

E-book ISBN: 978-0-9951395-0-3
Print ISBN: 978-1-99-106366-3

Editor: Evil Eye Editing
Cover: Kim Killion, The Killion Group, Inc.

Munro Press, New Zealand.

First Munro Press electronic publication September 2020
First Munro Press print publication November 2024

DEDICATION

For Paul, my husband, partner in crime, and fellow adventurer.
Every day is a good day.

Introduction

A dragon shifter and a human woman meet...

...Two worlds collide.

The encounter shouldn't have occurred, and the dragon species must battle the consequences.

Elizabeth Carrington: single-mother with a daughter and an obnoxious ex who refuses to leave without a chunk of her inheritance. An aspiring writer, she glimpses the unbelievable during a research trip, and when she awakens after the resulting car crash, she isn't in England any longer. Not that she understands this calamity because a knock to the head has stripped her memories. She is a woman with no past and no perception of dragons or their danger to her.

Dragon shifter Leonidas, Champion of the Skies, is the youngest son, and his parents have arranged a betrothal for him with

Nandag, The Strongminded. He rejects this match his parents insist will bring peace and cement bonds between the Dragon Isles.

Once Liza crashes into Leo's life, everything changes. While his family, friends, and neighbors are baying for her death, instinct propels Leo to protect this attractive stranger.

Their friendship deepens from respect to love as they attempt to discover how and why they met. What they learn will rip apart the dragon world and propel the inhabitants of the Dragon Isles into an unknown future.

You will love this first book in the Dragon Isles trilogy because it introduces a courageous and sexy dragon, a feisty human battler, and a new world full of mystery, magic, and mayhem. Plus one or two dragon-caused infernos when tempers race out of control.

Author's Note to Readers

The idea behind the Dragon Isles series was two-fold. First, I spotted a pre-made cover designed by . It featured a woman with a land and sea view behind her. The clouds above were in the shape of a dragon, and the title was *The Mystery of Dragon Island*. I fell in love with the cover and purchased it even though I didn't have a story ready to go with it.

Many months later, I was watching one of my favorite programs, *Escape to the Country*. They always have a special interest item on the show, and the particular one I saw was about Newcastle Emlyn, the village where the last dragon in Wales supposedly died. I immediately thought of my cover, waiting for its story and blended the two ideas.

This trilogy wasn't a story that came easily. The three books are interconnected, and I struggled to pull the threads together. But I'm stubborn and determined, and although I grappled with my characters and plot, the romances proved the perfect way to occupy myself during our COVID lockdown here in New Zealand.

The setting

I adore England, and each time I visit, it's like coming home. The story concept I visualized suited an English setting, but it took a long time to decide where to place my islands. To those readers who live in Northumberland or those who are familiar with the area, please forgive me. I have played fast and loose with the geography of the region. Some of my setting is real and is what you'll find in the area while in other places, I've used artistic license. There are cliffs in my story, while in reality, the area is much flatter. I have placed trees where there are none.

Just go with it, okay? Enjoy the romance, and please forgive me for my writer's imagination because I couldn't find everything I needed in the way of a setting to keep things real.

I hope you enjoy the adventure and soar with the dragons. And, if you'd like to keep up with my upcoming releases and news, please subscribe to my newsletter. (https://shelleymunro.com/newsletter/)

CHAPTER 1

The Last Dragon

Castlenew Emlyn, Northumberland, England

*L**ate, again.***

Elizabeth Carrington—Liza to her friends and family—grabbed her handbag from the passenger seat and exited her car. The heels of her boots *tap-tap-tapped* the pavement as she hustled onto High Street and scanned for the teashop Mrs. Manson had mentioned during their last phone call.

Her bloody ex. If he were within reach, she'd loosen the ties on her temper and strangle the selfish, calculating, cheating—

Ah! She hot-footed it to a brick building with a bay window and a bright red awning. A sign in the shape of a woman announced this was Barbara's Café.

Liza spotted the elderly couple, her stress leaving her shoulders. Mrs. Manson had informed her they'd sit in their usual corner. She'd suggested Liza buy them a cuppa, and they'd tell her the tale of the last dragon spotted in the region.

"Mr. and Mrs. Manson?" she asked, forcing brightness and enthusiasm into her voice. The eager part was simple. The sunny happiness proved more difficult since her ex-husband had dropped a bombshell this morning and disrupted her routine.

Bastard.

She hated Tony Richards. Detested that he'd tricked her into thinking he was decent while he'd hidden the greedy and corrupt man beneath his handsome shell. Tony refused to leave her alone, refused to let her and their daughter move on with their lives, refused to grant her a divorce.

Gritting her teeth against a snarl, she shoved her personal drama back to focus on her book of dragon myths and legends. Far more exciting and inspiring. Her new work-in-progress, *The Magic of Dragons*, fueled her creativity. Her gut told her this book would galvanize publishers. Liza pinned on a smile—stiff and uncomfortable but enough to show the couple polite interest.

"Tom and Miriam, dear." Mrs. Manson beamed, interest flashing in her brown eyes. A cream hat, adorned with brown and orange flowers, perched on her gray curls while she wore a cream twinset and a tweed skirt. A string of lustrous pearls circled her neck.

Mr. Manson—Tom—appeared uncomfortable in his white shirt and paisley tie. His thin hair lay in neat strands across his head, the comb marks still in evidence. Liza couldn't see his trousers from where she stood, but his shirt buttons strained over his belly.

"I'm Liza Carrington. I'm so sorry I'm late. Can I order you a tea or coffee? Something to eat?"

"We'll have a cream tea," Miriam told her with a decisive nod.

Liza held back her amusement. "I'll be right back."

With their orders placed, Liza joined Tom and Miriam at the table. She pulled out her notebook and her phone. Her pen hid at the bottom of her handbag, but she finally plucked it free. One day, she'd Marie Kondo her handbag into neatness and practicality.

One day.

"Is it true you're writing a book of dragon tales?" Tom demanded.

"Yes, dragons have always fascinated me. I figured with the rise in popularity of the fantasy-based movies and television shows, now was the perfect time to write my book."

"Are you published?" Miriam asked.

"Not yet," Liza said. "But I'm motivated to change that with this book."

A plump, height-challenged woman, wearing black clothes and a scarlet apron, bustled over with a tray of cups and a teapot. After setting them on the table, she retreated and reappeared with a plate of sandwiches, two scones, a dish of jam, and another of clotted cream.

With the arrival of the tea, Tom relaxed. It was apparent Miriam had bullied him into his best clothes to meet the lady author. A little polite chatter and Miriam might calm too instead of behaving like a Regency dowager and crooking her little finger as she sipped her tea.

"Have you lived in the village long?" Liza asked.

Miriam picked up her napkin and leaned closer to her husband to dab a spot of cream off the corner of his mouth. "We were both born in Castlenew Emlyn."

"Aye, our families settled here four generations ago." Tom rolled his eyes at his wife in affection. "My older brother lives in the original cottage, although the family has added to the building's footprint over the years."

"June and Alf modernized the kitchen and the bathroom last year," Miriam shared. "George, our eldest son, works with Tom at the manor house. June and Alf's children have left. I doubt they'll be back. Joy is engaged to a boy from New Zealand. Imagine that."

Liza grinned. "My mother is a New Zealander. I went to school over there."

"What made you come to England?" Miriam asked, diverted, curiosity sparkling in her lined features.

"I wanted to know my father. He's English. My parents divorced when I was four and I never saw much of him. My mother died in a motor vehicle accident five years ago. I didn't have other family in New Zealand, so it wasn't a tough decision to move to England." And she'd thought she'd escape Tony. Unfortunately, her husband had learned her father possessed money and he'd clung to their wedding vows and followed her to the UK. It was a pity he hadn't behaved that way during their years together. His constant cheating, the last time with her friend, had been the impetus for her to kick him out and make changes.

"Do you enjoy living over here?" Tom asked.

"I do. My daughter loves it, and we've made friends in the village where we live."

"You have a daughter?" Miriam asked.

"Joanna. She's six years old."

Liza reached for a sandwich and caught Tom's furtive gaze on her plate. He'd finished his scone, his plate holding mere crumbs. "Have a ham sandwich, Tom. I doubt I'll get through them." She nudged the plate in his direction. "Now, this dragon. Describe him to me."

Tom and Miriam exchanged a glance.

"You color the scene, Tom," Miriam prompted and added. "This tale has passed down through generations of Tom's family, even though this encounter supposedly occurred hundreds of years ago."

Tom lifted his cup and swallowed a mouthful of tea. "The

dragon was black as midnight. A gigantic beast. I heard his teeth were half an arm in length, but folks might've exaggerated. The villagers spotted him flying through the sky long before he reached the castle walls—such was his massive wingspan. Soldiers shot arrows at him. The creature roared, and its fiery breath rippled over a wheat field, setting the crop on fire. For a while, the villagers feared the dragon might retaliate and attack, for he was a ferocious beast. His black scales sparkled under the sun, and malice glittered in the creature's red eyes. Aye, a formidable sight, this demon beast. While the villagers raced to put out the fire, the dragon landed on the castle battlements."

"The castle on the village outskirts?" Liza asked, recalling the ruins she'd driven past before entering the village center.

"The very one." Miriam leaned nearer, caught up in the tale. "Can you imagine the shock of an enormous dragon turning up without warning?"

"You said the dragon had red eyes? That sounds unusual."

"My grandfather told me what his grandfather told him," Tom said. "The creature had irises the color of green gemstones, but when his mood worsened, the dragon's eyes turned red. At the height of his rage, the dragon's eyes resembled rubies."

"An estimate of his wingspan?"

Tom scratched his chin. "From what I've heard, the creature cast a massive shadow. I was told the dragon wielded his tail, knocking a dozen men to the ground as they attempted to creep up behind him."

"The dragon most likely smelled them. Our ancestors weren't as keen on bathing as us." Liza jotted notes in her standard shorthand. "Did any of the arrows pierce his body or was his hide too thick?"

"That I don't know," Tom said.

"If the dragon grew angry and attacked in return," Miriam said. "My guess is at least one arrow struck the beast. I understand the local museum has a handwritten account of the attack. A priest witnessed the dragon's arrival and mentioned the excitement in his monthly update to his superior. The museum curator opens several days a week."

Tom scratched his chin. "I'm uncertain of today's hours."

"I'll check once we're finished. What happened after the dragon perched on the castle walls?"

A chuckle burst from Tom. "You'll never guess. He only went to sleep."

"He had a snooze." Miriam chortled. "You'd think the dragon might've wanted to find food or wreak revenge, but no. He went to sleep."

Liza tapped her pen on her notebook. "From what I've learned, dragons were intelligent creatures and misunderstood. In those days, people feared what they didn't understand. Perhaps the dragon required a haven."

"Mayhap," Tom said. "But you're right about the villagers being afeared. The most important thing on their minds was getting the dragon to leave or, even better, killing the creature. They were holding a market day. Drovers had driven livestock into the village—sheep, pigs, goats, and horses to sell. There were jugglers to entertain the people, fortune-tellers for the lassies, a pie merchant, a bread vendor. Old crones hawking apples and others embroidered handkerchiefs. The dragon's arrival spoiled their fun while the drovers worried the beast might seize their livestock for a snack."

"What did they do?" Liza asked.

As always, Liza experienced a sneaking sympathy for the mythical dragon. Humans had misunderstood and underappreciated the legendary creatures, the tales she'd researched full of knights and locals who'd bested the magnificent beasts. She imagined meeting a dragon if she'd been alive hundreds of years ago, and the questions she might ask if the creature could communicate with her. Was it exhilarating soaring through the sky? What was their favorite snack? Was there a dragon language? Was it easy to learn? Yes, so many questions. A grin curled across her lips. Her father had told Liza her thirst for knowledge could drive a man to drink. Curiosity hadn't worked with Tony. He'd hit her whenever he'd decided she needed to cease her chatter.

"Well, one of the castle soldiers was a wily, battle-hardened man. He picked up his bow and arrow and a bright red shawl," Tom said.

"You'll never guess what he did next," Miriam said, her brown eyes wide with anticipation.

"What?" Liza asked, content to let the expectation build.

"This soldier waded into the river that ran past the castle walls. Once he stood in the middle, he shot the dragon with an arrow. An extraordinary shot since the arrow hit the dragon on his vulnerable belly. The beast awoke with a mighty bellow and spied the man in the river. The soldier draped the red shawl over his head and dived beneath the surface of the water. He swam underwater until he reached the far bank of the river and crawled into the trees.

"Meanwhile," Tom continued, "the dragon was furious. The arrow dug into the dragon's stomach, and it was in agony. He spotted the soldier with his red shawl and flew from the castle walls in a fury. Fatally wounded, the dragon swooped and attacked the floating red shawl, seizing it with its talons and destroying it during the last moments of his life. The beast succumbed to death, sank below the surface, and vanished. The people crept from their hiding places and cheered the brave soldier since they'd had a lucky escape. And to this day, the residents of Castlenew Emlyn—indeed, the entire country—have never spotted another dragon."

Liza's pen raced across the page. "Wow! The last dragon ever seen in England."

Tom nodded. "Dragons are extinct now. It's sad, even though they caused fear and chaos during their time."

"Do you believe dragons were real rather than fictional beasts?"

Tom smiled. "You tell me. You're the one who's doing the research and listening to the tales. Is there an element of truth in the stories?"

"I'd like to presume so," Liza said. "I imagine seeing a dragon might change a person."

"Aye," Tom said with amusement. "It might put the fear of God into you too."

"Do you have everything you need for your book?" Miriam asked once the teapot was dry, and crumbs littered their plates. "I thought I'd take this opportunity to clothes shop for the family wedding next month."

Tom grumbled under his breath, and Liza grinned.

"Thank you so much for meeting me. Apart from the museum, is there anywhere else I should visit while I'm in Castlenew Emlyn?"

"A wander through the castle ruins might help you get an idea of how things were when the dragon arrived," Tom suggested. "The outer wall is intact and a true replica of back in the day. The river, too."

"Excellent," Liza said. "I have a camera. Thanks again. It was lovely meeting you. Which way will I find the museum?"

"Turn right on leaving the café," Miriam said. "Walk along High Street until you come to the secondhand book store and turn right. You'll find the museum at the end of that street."

"Thanks," Liza said.

Miriam rose and dragged a still-grumbling Tom from the café. Liza took a moment to jot a few more notes and impressions before she packed away her notebook and phone. She'd check out the museum opening hours first before she visited the castle and snapped photos to go in her book. Her best friend, Cherry, had told her she'd pick up Joanna from school if Liza were running late. If necessary, she'd call Cherry to organize a pick up once she'd determined her plan of attack.

After a brief walk, Liza studied the notice in the museum window. She smiled with satisfaction. Serendipity. She could wander the village and the castle ruins while she waited for the museum to open. Although she'd check in with Cherry, she'd have plenty of time to drive home via the coast road. A special treat for completing her last interview and collecting everything she required to finish her book of dragon myths.

Eagerness pulsed through her as she set off to explore and photograph the castle ruins.

Leonidas, Champion of the Skies, youngest son of Tudoarreo, The Dragon Lord, and Qille, The Taker of Life, stomped from his father's study. He fervently wished he were someone else's son.

Perhaps the son of Red, The Cloth Weaver, or Deon, The Grumpy.

As their son, he'd mate with a female of his choosing. No ending up the sacrificial dragon. His parents had summoned him and ordered him to enter a betrothal. His intended—Nandag, The Strongminded, a dragon from a highborn clan on Smoking Isle. Avoiding his family and living at his isolated property had *not* saved him. Now that it suited his parents, they'd recalled their youngest son and expected him to jump to attention and follow their orders.

Nan, The Strongminded.

Her name *did not* inspire a happy mating.

Leo stalked along the tiled passage and slammed through the thick wooden door that led to his old chamber. Once inside, he shoved the door closed and stripped off his footwear and clothing. He retrieved a pack from a carved wooden chest. With economical movements, he folded and packed his possessions inside before opening the double door to the balcony. No matter his parents' dictates, he refused to stay. Leo vaulted onto the balcony ledge and placed his pack within easy reach.

Cool wind caressed his naked limbs. He caught a whiff of pine and wild herbs coming from the mountains. His mother had ordered him to attend the dinner party she'd arranged with the local nobility, but he'd refused and left his parents' presence without seeking permission.

They'd already stolen his freedom to choose his mate.

He'd be damned if he'd let them rob him of his remaining time before his betrothed arrived and the formal courtship began.

Leo summoned his dragon, the shift from man to beast faster than most. He'd trained hard, kept his body fit, his mental faculties sharp to become the best. He'd worked to earn his sobriquet and transform from Leonidas, The Younger to Leonidas, Champion of the Skies. Instead of wasting his prize money and jewels, he'd purchased a property and built a home. As a youngster, he'd trained with a jeweler, taking his fascination with precious stones and turning the interest into a means of making money.

His older brothers might scoff at the modest dwelling. Still, Leo valued his independence, and he'd discovered personal satisfaction in earning his way instead of living off his parents at the clan castle.

Now, with one easy blow, his parents had stolen his dream and foisted Nan, The Strongminded, on him. They'd insisted he must be the son to take this burden because they didn't approve of him grubbing in the dirt or raising stock to sell for food. It didn't matter that in his spare time, he crafted exquisite jewelry. In truth, he hadn't thought admitting he was the mystery master jeweler behind the Marquess brand could earn him freedom from this trap.

They'd decided, and that was that.

He had two weeks plus the time it took for the betrothal formalities to plan and execute his escape.

Rising fury turned his vision red. With a screech of rage, Leo grabbed his pack in his talons and lifted into the air. Powerful beats of his wings had him departing the castle stronghold. As he flew over the bailey and courtyard, several dragons and humans lifted their heads in curiosity, but given his anger, he arrowed through the sky and over the ridge before they could do more than blink.

A human village nestled in the next valley. Whitewashed cottages perched on the hillside and overlooked the sea. The residents were the descendants of Viking explorers, lost fishermen, and smugglers who now made their home on Hissing Isle.

Hissing Isle, so named for two reasons. Caves littered the coastline. Visible if the tide was low, they created a distinct hiss as the incoming water refilled them. Instead of the sand of the other islands, small rounded pebbles covered the beaches here. They rattled and hissed as the waves churned them back and forth. Hissing Isle comprised one large island and two smaller ones, uninhabited because of their rocky terrain.

Mountains thrust upward from the largest island, their slopes covered with fresh-scented pines. The alpine meadows grew nutritious grasses for livestock and valuable herbs, prized by humans and dragons alike. Two principal towns—one inhabited by dragons and the other by humans—hugged the coast where the temperatures remained moderate during the depths of winter.

Leo flew onward, the familiar scents and the natural terrain releasing his stress. Familiarity and pride settled in his gut as he glided over his plot of land, high in the mountain region on the east of the island. Few dragons flew this far east, but it was Leo's favorite spot. He settled on a rocky outcrop. From here, Leo gazed over the North Sea. Perfume Isle and a faint smudge of volcanic smoke from Smoking Isle were visible on the horizon.

Nan, The Strongminded, came from the clan who lived on Smoking Isle. Perfume Isle, which was closer, was home to a third dragon clan. The druids who powered the protective magic that shielded their world lived in an isolated corner of the same island as Nandag.

"We are not mating with The Strongminded dragon," his dragon informed him. *"I refuse."*

"We require a plan," Leo stated aloud, his mind buzzing with anger.

"I will help to think of a scheme to rid ourselves of this Strongminded female."

Fury pulsed anew at his parents' highhandedness. For years, they'd ignored him and now they decided he was useful to their plans. Leo spat out a frustrated curse and surveyed his surroundings. The wind changed, and a whiff of death carried to him. He scowled, knowing he should investigate. He lifted off, immense wings beating fast.

His bloody parents.

Once he'd mated with Nandag, they'd expect him to dwell in the castle. He'd lose everything he valued. Leo shrieked his frustration, a blast of hot flames punctuating his vexation. He soared on the airwaves, letting them draw him down and over the sea toward the other islands instead of investigating the death stench. Mindful of intrusion into the neighboring clan's airspace, he veered until he flew parallel to the mainland. Although he couldn't see it, he sensed the mass of land and heard the whisper of the waves as they struck the shore.

His great maw opened to taste the wind, and his giant wings slowed to a less frenzied beat. His body dropped lower until he skimmed the sea, and for a moment, he could've sworn he heard a woman singing.

CHAPTER 2

She Wanted a New York Times Bestseller, Dammit

L iza drove along the coast path—a B road—and since it was midweek, she passed few cars. The roiling North Sea reached to the horizon, calmer than usual, sparkling under the afternoon sun. She caught glimpses of Lindisfarne or Holy Island, as it was referred to by locals. The island's castle dominated the landscape silhouette. One day, she'd arrange a trip to the island, accessed via a causeway from the mainland. Maybe, once she finished her book. A visit would be inspirational. She could imagine a dragon living near that castle...

Since the afternoon was sunny, she'd rolled down the roof of her sporty Mazda and drove with the wind whipping her ponytail and an enormous smile on her face. She belted out the words of an old rock ballad about a lover who'd shaken her world the entire night long.

Halfway through the chorus, her phone rang, and she ceased singing to answer the call using hands-free.

"Hey!"

"Liza, it's Cherry. Are you driving?"

"I am, but the hands-free is working fine. My research visit took longer than I'd hoped. Can you still collect Joanna from school? If you're busy, I can get Rena to meet her for me."

Her younger half-sister enjoyed time with Joanna. Meeting Rena had been the second magnificent thing to come from her move to the UK. Family was important to Liza, and she wanted this support for her daughter. Here in England, she had her father, a half-sister, and in Cherry, a loyal friend. She also had a psychotic husband who refused to release her from their marriage and wanted interaction with Joanna, not because he loved his daughter, but because he thrived on harassing Liza for daring to grow a spine and leave him.

"Rena called me." Cherry hesitated.

"What?" Liza demanded, her warning antenna alerting her to trouble.

"Tony rang the school and informed them you'd agreed to let him pick up Joanna after classes finished. Joanna told the headmistress this wasn't true, and that you were doing book research today." When she spoke again, Liza heard her friend's admiration. "Joanna told them Liza had authorized Cherry and Rena to take her home, and the headmistress should ring us to confirm. She got hold of Rena first."

"Popsicles," Liza muttered instead of a more suitable pithy Anglo-Saxon curse. She tried to keep her swearing down on account of her daughter. "I'm still an hour from home."

"Rena and I have got this. We're both collecting Joanna, and the headmistress agreed to let us wait in the staff car park. We should avoid Tony since he'll be loitering out the front with the other parents."

"Thank you." Liza gripped the steering wheel, her gaze on the road while her mind struggled with a way to get rid of Tony Richards, short of paying him off. "I hate that you and Rena are getting dragged into this mess."

"That's what friends and sisters do." Cherry's airy reply raised gratitude in Liza. "Rena suggested we fashion a doll in the image of Tony and stick pins in it."

Liza barked out a laugh as she scanned the glorious beach to her left with its white stretch of sand and the rocky cliffs. The road followed the line of the cliff, and on this portion, a guardrail created a protective, if somewhat flimsy barrier. She drove up a hill, and the panorama from the top stole her breath. Blue sea. Blue sky. She could still see the outline of the castle. The odd white cap on the waves. A boat. Probably a cargo ship heading to Dover or another port on this coast.

"Cherry, we should drive up here for a weekend and visit Lindisfarne. It's gorgeous here today. I have the top down."

"Lindisfarne? The island with the abbey? Holy Island? Rena was muttering something about weird dreams and robe-wearing monks when I spoke to her earlier."

"Monks?" Liza chuckled. "Give me a naked sex dream anytime. Robed figures sound creepy. Oh, Cherry. You should see the view. Not a cloud in the sky. It's a dazzling blue that's too exquisite to describe. The air is fresh with the tang of the sea."

"Stop, you're making me envious. The strongest aroma here is dusty books."

"You love your bookstore," Liza countered.

Cherry's chuckle rolled from her, and Liza grinned in concert.

The air took on a strange shimmer that grabbed her attention. She gaped, her smile fading. The atmosphere resembled fabric, and it was ripping. A giant green head stabbed through the shimmer.

Liza gasped, trying to make sense of what she was seeing. The air-fabric ripped further to expose a colossal body. Wings. Talons. Red eyes.

And they were staring at her.

W-was that a dragon?

A shocked cry forced up her tight throat.

"Liza?" Cherry spoke in a sharp tone.

Liza continued to stare until the jolt of her car jerked her back to the present. She'd driven off the road. Before she could correct her steering, her vehicle collided with the protective barrier. She screamed and fought the wheel, struggling to return to the tarmac, but it was too late. Her car flipped, and the last thing she heard was Cherry's frantic shouts, demanding to know what was happening.

The airbag exploded, jamming her against the seat. She screamed again as her car flew over the edge of the cliff. A glimpse of green snagged her attention. *Huh!* Something was very wrong with her eyes.

That *was* a dragon.

The creature darted past her car and disappeared because the airbag blocked her gaze.

Then her car struck the sea—the sound explosive and the collision shocking her from head to toe. Her head smashed against the car side as she struggled to release the seatbelt. The airbag held her fast, and the vehicle began to sink.

Her last thought before blackness claimed her was that she didn't want to die. Dragons existed, and she wanted a *New York Times* bestseller, dammit.

CHAPTER 3

Rescue From the Lidless Box

L eo read the astonishment in the woman's eyes. The same disbelief speared him in the chest, stealing his breath.

Impossible.

He wasn't meant to see her. Nor she him.

None of this should be happening.

Her red metal box roared and thumped into the shiny barrier edging the cliff. Sparks flew from the point of contact, filling the air with a pungent metallic stench. Momentum kept the lidless box flying, and Leo beat his wings to avoid a collision. The box slid across the rocky ground. It balanced on the edge of the cliff before it tipped and toppled.

The instant the box fell, Leo snapped from his shocked trance. He darted after the steel box, flapping his wings faster to keep up.

A scream rippled from the woman, but the terror-filled cry ceased. Concerned, he directed his body closer, maneuvering with his wings. The woman slumped and blood trickled down her cheek.

The box struck the water with an enormous splash, the icy wave that pummeled Leo knocking a hole through his bewilderment. His thoughts slotted into proper order.

The woman.

She'd die beneath the water if he failed to act fast.

Already, the box had sunk under the waves. Air bubbles shot to the surface. Leo filled his dragon lungs with air, dropped his pack of belongings, and dived into the sea. The box settled on the seafloor, stirring mud and silt and obscuring his vision. Leo kicked his legs and propelled with his wings, instinct guiding him.

By sheer fortune, his right talon grazed the woman's arm. He tugged. He yanked harder. Something held the woman in place. He slashed at it with his free claw, his chest constricting as he fought his desire to breathe.

By Lodar, God of Torture! He must save this woman. Every instinct propelled him to rescue her. He increased his speed, frantic to breathe air, frantic to pull her free, frantic to escape this situation.

Lodar, please.

He couldn't last much longer. Already, the chilly water was sapping his energy. Leo hacked at the bindings restricting her, and at last, she popped free. With his wings, he propelled upward until he broke the surface. His lungs burned as he greedily sucked in air.

Leo couldn't take to the sky now that he trod water, so he swam to the nearest beach, thankful he'd learned the skill as a youngster. Once he felt solid ground beneath his feet, he stood and carried the woman up onto the narrow sandy shore tucked between two massive guardian rocks.

Two rocks on the mainland.

A mystery he did *not* comprehend.

He and his people had left the mainland hundreds of years ago after the slaughter of their prophet. Thanks to their deal with the druids, their island homes were invisible to those on the English mainland, while the dragon kind couldn't see the enormous landmass either. They sensed it, but thanks to druid magic could not interact with the humans there in any manner. For the safety of the dragon kind.

Concerned at the implications, Leo set the woman on her side. Her features were pale and blood seeped from the wound on her head. A second, smaller cut turned her hairline red. He recalled an animal that had almost drowned. An elder had saved it by laying the animal on its side and breathing warm air into the creature's mouth.

He leaned closer, ready to blow air at her mouth when he recalled the elder had mentioned he must wear human form at this stage. Dragon breath burned animals and humans.

Leo summoned his skin, the change rolling over his scales slower than usual because of his fatigue. With his transformation complete, he squatted beside the woman's still form and fitted his mouth to hers. He blew his breath into her three times before he pulled back to observe the results. Nothing. He repeated the action, letting his breath come deep in his chest, whence his dragon-fire grew. This time his exhalation was warmer. Not, he hoped, hot enough to burn her fragile throat, but sufficient to jolt her awake.

While he waited, he ran his fingers through her long brown hair. Her clothes clung to her body, revealing sleek muscles and full breasts. Her apparel was unlike anything the dragon women wore on Hissing Isle. Not even the humans who lived with them wore clothes akin to the ones clinging to this woman. They showed her form in an indecent yet alluring manner.

"Awaken," he demanded of the woman, impatient with her continuing slumber. It was time to discuss the reason for this impossible meeting.

Then he recalled that along with the breathing, the elder had rubbed the animal's chest.

Leo nudged the woman onto her back and stared at the swell of her breasts. Some women—no matter what their race—became agitated if a male touched their curves without permission. He hesitated. No, better for her to harangue him and live rather than remain still as death.

Leo placed his hands in the middle of the woman's chest and pressed down in a rhythmic pumping action. At the same time, he inhaled into her mouth, part of him aware of the velvet texture of her lips. A frisson of pleasure raced through his limbs. *By Lodar!* He ignored the lengthening of his masculine parts.

Examine those possibilities later. Instinct told him this woman was important, and this drove him to continue breathing for the woman, urging her back to life.

She made a sound—a kind of splutter—and hope bloomed in his chest.

He pressed her torso again, taking care to curb his full strength. Leo breathed into her mouth, using a smidgeon of his dragon-fire.

The woman spluttered again, this time louder. He lifted his head an instant before water gurgled from her mouth. Leo shifted her onto her side, so she didn't choke on the emerging liquid. She coughed, a ragged exit of breath and more water.

Leo scrutinized her, willing her to breathe on her own. Instead, she coughed and coughed, vomiting. Uncertain of how to help, Leo sheltered her from the sea breeze.

Beneath the fetid stench of vomit and the salty tang of the sea, he caught a lighter and more attractive scent of herbs and flowers. The fragrance enticed him closer, and he used the waiting time to tend the wounds on her head. He licked across her temple, cleaning away the watery blood before he found the source.

The woman ceased her coughing, yet she never spoke or stirred. She was breathing on her own now. Excellent.

Soon, he'd cleansed the wound. While the edges were jagged, the scarring would be minimal. Such things worried females.

Leo lifted his head to stare across the sea. A hazy shimmer shrouded the chain of islands protected by the druid's magic. Alarmed, he sprang to his feet. The islands were fading.

He must leave.

Now.

Leo summoned his dragon without taking his attention off his blurry island home. He glanced at the woman and hesitated. Leaving her here was a death sentence. Soon the tide would cover this sliver of sand. He could fly her to the clifftop, but what if he encountered humans with weapons? A bow and arrow capable of piercing his dragon scales?

He scanned the sea again, fear at the dimming view propelling him to action. He'd take the woman with him and doctor her at his cottage. Once he discovered how or why they'd met, he'd return her to the mainland. Somehow.

Leo lifted her with his talons, taking care not to pierce her pale skin or her strange clothes. He leaped, his wings catching the air, and headed for home.

He flew fast, anxiety propelling him to speed. The islands grew fuzzier. He shot into a cloud, his body striking air so dense he barrel-rolled. He veered left where the misty haze shimmered with extra light. While he still struggled through the thickness, the air didn't drag as hard against his wings. Without warning, he burst through the invisible barrier, his speed picking up as if he'd flung his body from a catapult.

A trace of fear nipped at him until he spotted Hissing Isle in front of him and the thrust of familiar mountains. Curious, he turned his head, his blood running cold since he could no longer see the mainland. It was as if it had popped from existence.

Leo slowed his wingbeats and set a course to his mountain cottage. He had no explanation for what had happened, yet a sense of satisfaction and excitement pulsed within his chest. He'd saved the woman, which pleased his dragon.

The human skin side of him with his more complicated thoughts and ideas experienced a sliver of fear. The woman's presence heralded danger.

She was an unexpected impediment, and he'd need to consider what to do with her.

CHAPTER 4

Gwenyth, The Beautiful

She woke, her head throbbing. She lifted her hand to her skull, and her arm muscles ached too. The gloom in the room and the weird quietness had her tension rising. Her breath caught. Aided by the moonlight slipping through the large picture windows beyond the bed, her gaze flitted from square shapes to rounded objects.

She struggled to remove the tight band from her waist. A masculine arm! She froze, not recalling going to bed. Was she sick? She struggled to remember.

"Go back to sleep," a masculine voice rumbled.

Excellent idea.

Exhaustion weighted her eyelids, her body. She smiled drowsily. Marriage and family were important, and she was lucky to have a wonderful man who held her protectively during the night.

When she woke again, daylight spilled through the window and the view beyond stole her breath. She stared at the mountain meadow and the distant trees—mainly pine. A stream meandered through the clearing, and chestnut cattle with sweeping horns grazed, their tails lazily flicking their contentment.

She pushed to an upright position and groaned at the pulse in her head. Gingerly, she lifted her hand and probed the sore spots with her fingers.

"Ouch!" she muttered, puzzled by the bandage she encountered.

She tried to recall the reason a drummer thumped inside her head. Not a single answer presented itself.

A faint murmur drew her attention, and she smiled. Her husband, with his beautiful green eyes and his too-long black hair, stood in the doorway. The sexy black stubble shading his jawline and framing his sensual mouth had her pulse racing. Her fingers itched to touch.

"Morning…" She hesitated, her mind blank when she attempted to summon his name. "Sweetheart, why is my head so sore?"

His face softened, and he prowled the distance between them. Stunned she could win such a beautiful man, she threaded her fingers in his callused ones.

"Why can't I remember your name?" She pushed at her mind,

at her memories. What was her name? Panic roared through her, and her hand tightened, her nails digging into his flesh.

"Shush, do not fear," he whispered.

Something in his stunning eyes reassured her and stomped on the burst of distress that shouted at her to flee. Kindness.

"You fell and hit your head. I am Leo. You are Gwenyth, The Beautiful."

He'd doctored her wounds and called her beautiful. She relaxed a fraction more, curiosity taking precedence over her initial reaction. An image of a wedding flitted through her mind, dimming the throb for a welcome instant. A darkly handsome groom. A bride. Happiness. Guests waving farewell. The honeymoon...

"Gwenyth?" Leo prompted.

The name didn't seem familiar, so she latched onto another part of his sentence. "I fell?"

"You did. The bleeding has stopped. I have made you a potion to reduce the ache of your head. You stay there while I get it for you."

"No, Leo." The pressure on her lower stomach informed her of an urgent need of a restroom. "I need the bathroom."

His brows drew together, and he opened a chest to retrieve a robe. He helped her stand and don it, his gaze strumming her naked body for an instant before he gifted her with a gentle smile. "This way."

"It's crazy, I can't remember. Sweetheart, I'm sorry to spoil our honeymoon." Heat flushed her cheeks. "I can't even remember if we made love. Did we?" Her body told her nothing, but her head... Her skull throbbed and ached with each shuffling step, the pain arrowing downward to pool behind her eyes. She turned her head, attempting to focus on his sexy features, and once again wondered how she'd won such a man. Just looking at him made her heart race, her body soften with urgent need.

Leo wore black trousers and nothing else to cover the muscular, tattooed goodness of his chest. A magnificent, mainly green, dragon tattoo that stretched from shoulder to lower belly. Aware she was staring, she prodded again at her confused mind.

Leo hesitated, and her swift glance didn't aid her in reading him. "You were hurt," he said. "There's plenty of time."

She blinked against the brighter light as her husband gestured at a pair of clogs. Once she donned them, he guided her outdoors. Strange, his accent didn't strike notes of recognition either, and it should, given how the rough sexiness made her shiver and imagine interminable nights of decadent passion.

"Have we been here before?" She frowned, searching her memories, finding emptiness. A deep, endless vacuum. "What happened? How did I injure my head?"

Leo tucked his arm around her shoulders when she teetered, his wintergreen scent filling her gasping breaths. "Easy there with the questions, my lodestone."

My lodestone. Had she heard the particular endearment before? Puzzled, she let him guide her along a short path, their footsteps muffled by pine needles. They halted before a small building, not much bigger than an old phone box. This one was constructed of logs and matched the main dwelling.

"The long-drop is in there."

She wrinkled her nose.

"You could pick a tree." Humor glinted in him, and his smile took him from handsome to breathtaking.

"I'll use the restroom. At least it doesn't smell."

"A friend from a neighboring island designed it to become one with nature. Should I wait for you?"

"Please. I feel as weak as a kitten."

"Once you're done here, I'll get you the potion to help your headache. I was lucky to have the correct herbs on hand."

Herbs? Gwenyth wanted to ask questions, but the pressure on her bladder urged her to speed. She took care of business and washed her hands using a thick, soapy substance and the warm water running into the scooped-out center of a rock. After drying her hands on a thick chocolate-brown towel, she exited the restroom.

"That wasn't so bad, my lodestone?"

Her heart melted at the gentle teasing. She shook her head and moaned, the dart of pain almost bringing her to her knees.

Leo scooped her off her feet, his rapid steps carrying them back to the cottage. Inside, Leo removed the clogs and set her on the bed. "Wait there while I get you the potion for your head. Are you hungry?"

This time, she knew better than to communicate with the nod of her head. "No, I don't want food."

"Get into bed. I won't be long."

She slipped beneath the covers, exhausted after her trip outside. Why couldn't she remember the accident? Crazy as it was, she hadn't even recalled her husband's name. Leo. She stared at the green meadow, the bright color bringing a hazy memory of...something. When she tugged at it, the recollection dissipated, leaving a yawning hole.

She focused on the bedroom, and certainty blazed through her. She hadn't visited here before. Positivity filled her, although she couldn't say why.

The second Leo appeared carrying a steaming pottery cup, she asked for confirmation. "Have I been here before?"

"To my cottage? No, this is the first time."

"I thought so," she said with satisfaction.

"We haven't known each other long," he said as he handed her the potion. "Drink this. It should help with the pain in your head."

She sipped the liquid with suspicion. It tasted sweet rather than tart, and for a potion, it wasn't objectionable. "We had a whirlwind courtship?"

He smiled. "We did."

She stared at the crinkles that formed at the corners of his eyes. He was still bare-chested, and her gaze took in the dragon tattoo. As she studied the beast, it winked at her, and a puff of tattoo smoke formed rings above its head. She gasped.

"What's wrong?"

"Your tattoo moved." She blinked before focusing on his chest again. This time, the tattooed dragon waved and swished its tail.

Leo glanced down, then back at her. He rolled his eyes. "He is my other half. My dragon likes you. In fact, he saw you first."

"A dragon?" she whispered, her gaze connecting with his. "I-I like dragons."

"Which is lucky for me."

"Have I seen your dragon?"

"Of course." He glided the tips of his fingers over her cheek. "Have you finished your tonic?"

"Yes."

Leo took the cup from her. "Then stop worrying about dragons and everything else. Sleep."

"But I should remember you," she protested. Everything in this situation seemed new, but he'd admitted they hadn't known each other for long. Sighing, she reclined and let him cover her with a cozy woolen blanket. Sleep might clear the fuzziness in her head. She'd puzzle over everything later, and once her headache faded, she'd indulge herself and explore her husband's gorgeous, sexy body.

CHAPTER 5

No Ceremonial Ring

L eo checked on the woman several times during the next two hours. His dragon insisted on it, and after remembering his old nurse shaking one of his older brothers awake after a head wound, he'd done the same thing. Gwenyth's eyes had fluttered open; she'd frowned at him as she answered his questions and tumbled back into sleep.

She believed she was his wife.

It wasn't unknown for a dragon to take a human as a mate. Not common, but it had happened. His dragon had prompted him to agree with the woman, and once he had, he'd seen the possibilities. If he told everyone he was married and acted as if it were so, he might wriggle out of this betrothal his parents had forced on him.

Leo pondered the problems, mindspoke about them with his dragon. His parents for one, and then there was Nan, herself. "My parents will wonder why I didn't tell them about my marriage."

"We didn't have a chance to speak."

"But they'll ask if I informed the head butler after their decree."

"Bah! He smirked at us and left the audience chamber as quickly as your parents. When did he offer an opportunity? They told us. They ordered. We must try this scheme," his dragon declared. *"I find our wife desirable."*

"Me too," Leo murmured.

"Then we keep her."

"We know nothing of her origins. What if she is responsible for the tear in the barrier shielding us from the mainland?"

"What if she isn't, and she's an innocent?" his dragon countered.

"I should contact my friends on the other islands and ask if they've flown their boundaries recently."

"Yes."

"What if her memory returns and she remembers everything? What if she has a man?"

"Bah! What man would let his woman travel without protection? I say we wait, and meantime, we court her. Every time I gaze upon her, I yearn to taste her beautiful mouth. I ache for this. Gwenyth's conviction will persuade everyone we can no longer become betrothed to this Nan dragon. Your parents must accept our marriage."

A shudder worked through Leo. He'd tried not to dwell on her, but the woman he'd named Gwenyth had worked her magic on him too. It was her appearance and her intoxicating scent of exotic herbs and a hint of flowers. Her immediate acceptance of him and his dragon. "What if my parents attempt to injure her, or worse, kill her so the betrothal can advance?"

"We protect our mate."

"She is so beautiful. How could she not already belong to another?" His dragon had called her their mate, and Leo wanted this to be true.

"She wears no ceremonial ring."

"No." He could make her a ring, one fit for a woman such as her.

"We are agreed? Treat her as our mate and use her to escape Nan, The Strongminded?"

"Aye," Leo said. "We can't go to the castle. I can't trust anyone to have my back there."

"We hire men to watch over her. Men who will be loyal to us, to her. We must face our parents soon before the plans go too far."

"True. My friends might offer help, one of the tutors at the battlegrounds. I need to contact them to ask about the magic failure anyway. My gut is uneasy with this discovery. You know what happened the last time we had open borders. The humans on the mainland tricked us, used us, killed us whenever they found us in our dragon forms. I doubt much has changed during the intervening years."

"Some humans accept us."

"We can't risk a repeat of the massacres. Our population is only now recovering and flourishing."

"Leo?"

Leo hustled into the bedroom at Gwenyth's call.

"Who are you talking to?"

"My dragon."

"He talks?"

"I bite sassy human females," his dragon muttered.

"We mindspeak—our common language. Sometimes, I speak aloud because it helps me mull over weighty problems." Leo felt his dragon stir and saw Gwenyth's eyes widen.

"He appears grumpy."

"You insulted him," Leo said.

"I'm sorry." She wrinkled her nose. "My lack of memory is at fault. It's most disconcerting having a black hole inside my recollections."

"Awww," his dragon sighed. *"She's adorable."*

"Once you're feeling better, we'll visit my parents," Leo said, his lips twitching because he'd never, ever heard his dragon utter the word *adorable*. The thought of the battle he must fight with his parents dampened his burst of humor.

Gwenyth's brows rose, and Leo sought an explanation that would answer her questions yet reveal little.

"We'll tell them of our marriage once we reach the castle." Leo concealed his grimace.

"She must hold our scent first." His dragon's words held relish and apparent anticipation.

Leo's body tightened, his mind traveling the same route as his dragon's—touching and kissing and rutting to combine their signature scents. His fresh with her herby floral. He shook his head hard to divert his brain. He was turning as foolish as his dragon.

"Your parents live in a castle?" she asked after a brief hesitation, a widening of her brown eyes.

"Don't worry. My parents will like you. So will my older brothers."

His dragon snorted so hard a puff of smoke exited Leo's nostrils. *"Keep on saying that and we might both believe it."*

"Will your parents approve of me?" she persisted.

"No," Leo admitted. "But you shouldn't worry. We'll have little to do with them. I spend most of my time here or with friends on the neighboring isles."

"Oh, joy," she murmured, her wry tone making Leo laugh. "I'll have a fire-breathing mother-in-law."

"Honestly," he said, his lips twitching yet again, "it will be fine. I will protect you."

"Protect me?"

"You are our mate, and we guard what is ours." Leo made the promise, intending to stand by his words.

She fascinated him, and he wanted her as much as his dragon.

Lust. He experienced a jolt each time he took in her slender body, her brown eyes, and her shiny brown hair. Surely, an excellent start in a relationship when he and his dragon craved her so strongly. It was the stuff of the old legends his nursemaid used to tell him of drakes who discovered their true mates. He'd thought the tales just that—stories spun to fascinate young dragons and to lull their active minds to sleep.

But this magnetic pull he was experiencing had Leo beginning to wonder if the bedtime tales held a sliver of truth.

Giving up the possibility of a true mate for whatever he could expect from Nan, The Strongminded, was ludicrous and shortsighted on his part.

"We cannot give her up," his dragon snapped.

"What if Nan decides the blow to her pride is too much, and she demands a blood apology?" Leo asked in mindspeak. He gave into temptation and brushed a lock of Gwenyth's long hair away from her face. It was lustrous and smelled of the salty brine of the sea.

"How is your head?" he asked.

"Better," she said, fingering the wound at her temple. "The ache has receded."

"Are you hungry?"

"Yes."

"Come and talk to me while I prepare food," he said. "I've put out a shirt and a pair of trews for you to wear.

"She needs to keep warm," his dragon pointed out.

Leo rifled through his wooden chest and pulled out a plaid, woven by women who lived on the farthest island north. Long ago, the women's ancestors had lived in the Highlands of Scotland, and they continued with the traditional crafts of weaving. He strode to her side and draped the plaid over her shoulders.

"Thank you. I'm lucky to have such a thoughtful husband. Where did we meet?" She slipped out of bed and tugged on the shirt to cover her nakedness.

Leo stared at his feet, hating to lie more than necessary and guilt surging to the fore. He couldn't help but study her, his fingers itching to test the softness of her skin. *What do I tell her?* he mindspoke to his dragon.

"Tell her you think it'd be better for her memories to return on their own, that we shouldn't fill in the gaps for her."

"My dragon and I think you should remember on your own rather than us filling your mind with information that will wedge together like an ill-fitting puzzle."

Her brow creased as she frowned at him, and Leo stilled, wondering if she might snap and snarl and show her teeth. Many a male dragon bore scars from temperamental females. He studied her, fascinated as her brow cleared, and a rueful smile grew. She edged closer, and every one of his muscles tensed; his inner dragon also alert to danger. Her fingers curled around his biceps, and she rose on her toes and pressed a kiss to his cheek.

His dragon gave a tiny moan, undone by her sweetness, while

Leo froze, the spot where her lips caressed firing salvos of heat through every muscle in his body.

Before he could kiss her in return, she stepped back and sat on the edge of the bed to tug on the trews. They were too big, but she folded them at the waistband and the legs.

Next, she draped the plaid around her shoulders before gazing at him in expectation. "What are you making me to eat? What can I do to help?"

Leo shook away the stupid while his dragon shifted his position on Leo's torso and peered around Leo's ribs to better see Gwenyth. "A beef-and-vegetable pie. While that is cooking, you can snack on fresh bread and cheese. And perhaps some apple juice."

Her brows rose, and her forehead creased again as if something worried her.

"Is there a problem?"

"You cook pies?"

"My dragon and I enjoy eating. If we don't cook, we don't nourish our body and remain strong. The younger dragons snap at our heels, planning to steal our title."

"Your title?"

"Everyone in the Dragon Isles has a title they have won through their behavior or their endeavors. I am Leonidas, Champion of the Skies."

"What does that mean?"

"My title tells other dragons I am the fastest and strongest at aerial battle. I have other lesser titles, such as the one I was born with. Leo, The Youngest Son, or another I acquired is Leo, The Landowner. My older brothers and parents call me Leo, The Land Grubber." Leo forced a grin despite the internal ache that accompanied this confession. "They have no conception of the personal satisfaction of a day's labor or my contentment once I relax and enjoy the peace of my mountain home."

Her mouth opened and closed without sounds emerging while her gaze darted to the old battle scars on his chest and back. The one on his thigh. Finally, she said, "I don't think I like your family."

"They have their moments." Leo removed the cheese and butter from the chiller and the fresh bread he'd obtained at the human village. He'd found shopping there meant he didn't encounter dragons connected with the castle. Best that way since less gossip regarding him made its way to his parents' ears.

He cut two bread slices with a sharp knife and placed them on a blue platter before nudging them toward Gwenyth. Leo shunted the butter and cheese closer to her. "Would you prefer strawberry jam?"

His dragon grumbled a complaint because he had a sweet tooth and hated to share.

"Cheese is fine," she said, accepting the knife he handed her. "Tell me about this aerial fighting. It sounds...interesting."

"Her words do not match her expression," his dragon said, bristling with disapproval. *"She is like other females who say one*

thing and mean another."

"Did you receive your scars from these battles?"

"Yes," Leo said.

"Hmm, I suppose it is no different from men or women pummeling each other on the rugby field or in the boxing ring. They also receive injuries."

Leo wasn't sure who her words were meant for, nor did he understand their meaning.

"Is this aerial fighting a sport?" she continued.

"A sport?"

"Yes," she said. "Entertainment for other dragons to watch. Is there prize money or a special status that comes with winning the aerial battles? Apart from the title, I mean."

"I have my title, and I used the prize money to purchase my land," Leo said.

"That makes sense," Gwenyth said and popped a piece of cheese into her mouth.

Mesmerized, Leo watched her eyes close and her lips purse as she savored the tidbit.

"This is excellent cheese."

"She confuses me. Intrigues me," his dragon said.

Leo agreed and set about gathering the ingredients to make his pastry. During his younger years, before his growth spurt, he'd spent as many hours hiding in the kitchen as he had learning to fabricate jewelry. The cook had set Leo to work, teaching him skills to become self-sufficient.

"Tell me more about your battles," Gwenyth said. "Is that topic allowable?"

"It is." Leo settled into the familiar routine of cooking. It relaxed him and his dragon after a tense day or a demand visit to his family. "We have smaller, less prestigious aerial battles on this island and the other islands also host battles. I trained and won several of the smaller ones to earn enough for the entrance fee of the more important yearly aerial combat battle. Growing up, I was the runt, and my older brothers bullied me. After one particularly nasty encounter, I sought an older, retired champion to train me."

Gwenyth cocked her head, interest sparkling in her brown eyes. "Did he help?"

"Not at first. He recognized me as a son of the ruling family and assumed I was a spoiled brat. Outsiders don't always understand the castle dynamics. When I persisted, he told me I had to start at the bottom. Later, he confessed he thought I'd give up in a week. He and his champions wagered on how long I'd last."

"They lost their money," Gwenyth stated, delight shining on her face.

"They did. All the physical grunt work I completed strengthened my muscles and Alfric demonstrated other exercises I could use to increase my fitness. I went on training flights with Alfric and his men. Instead of hiding in the castle to avoid my brothers, I visited Perfume Isle and Smoking Isle. On those islands, the dragons didn't recognize me. While they knew of me, they never matched my face with my position. After working hard for over a year, I won my bouts instead of receiving the first blood. My reputation grew until I earned enough to enter the biggest and most important battle."

"Did your parents not wonder where you were? Worry about why you weren't at home?"

"No," Leo said. "I told them I was staying with my friends and wanted to attend school on Perfume Isle." He shrugged. "They didn't care since I was the youngest, and they had three other sons should something happen to me."

"That's terrible. I would never treat my child so," Gwenyth snapped.

"How would you handle a child?" Leo asked.

"I would love them, support them, and try to help them get ahead in the world. I would teach them right from wrong and show them by deed they have worth. Your parents—they sound selfish and irresponsible. I'm not excited to meet them. Or have we already met?"

"No, you haven't met my family." He flashed a grin. "Your lecture is not something I'd tell them to their faces," Leo said, even as he sought the meaning and veracity of her words. Did she speak the truth, or was she merely saying that to win him around?

"Your parents might have ignored you and treated you as disposable, but they've taught you there is a better way to raise and nurture children. You will raise your offspring differently and not in the way they behaved with you."

Warmth squeezed his heart as he floured the marble counter and tipped out his pastry. She sounded angry on his behalf. Indignant because his parents had been hands-off in their child-rearing. He and his brothers had possessed material advantages and had plenty of food to fill their bellies. Despite the bullying, he'd had many advantages others of his age lacked.

"How long have we been married?" she asked. "I can ask that question?"

His parents would ask. "Almost one week," he said.

"Why don't I have any clothes or possessions with me?"

"How are you going to answer that one?" his dragon queried with an air of smartarse.

"You traveled to Hissing Isle by boat. There was a storm." Leo shrugged. "The North Sea is unpredictable and punishing. You almost drowned. I will wash the clothes you were wearing later."

"Not bad," his dragon purred. *"You should publish a fairy tale."*

"Is that how I hurt my head and lost my memories?"

"I couldn't get to you fast enough." The truth as far as it went. He'd been so shocked to see her, and he hadn't acted with his usual speed and clear thinking.

"But you did get to me," she said. "Was anyone else hurt?"

"No, everyone is safe."

"I'm glad," she said with a yawn. "Maybe I'll go to sleep now. I don't think I can wait for the pie."

"I'll save you some," Leo promised and wiped his hands.

"Is there a toothbrush I can use?"

"I have tooth cleanser. Swish it around your mouth. No brushing required."

She nodded, wincing as she climbed off the stool.

"Take a quick shower to warm your muscles," he said. "I'd recommend a soak, but I worry you might fall asleep in the middle of your bathing."

"My skin is itchy. I presume it is from my dip in the sea. A shower would be most welcome." She limped to the kitchen doorway and hesitated. "I don't remember which way to go."

Leo placed the pie inside the cooking square and set a timer to remind himself to check on it later. He wiped his hands and strode over to her. "This way, my lodestone."

Leo guided her past his bedroom and through a connected tunnel that led to a hot pool. He bypassed the steaming pool and directed her to the water drop he'd designed. It was much like a shower, but it ran continually and emptied into an underground stream that emerged lower down in a valley.

"I need to check my cattle. Will you be all right on your own? I won't take long."

"I'll be fine," she said, reaching over to squeeze his forearm.

"Once the pie is cooked, and you're tucked in bed for your nap, I'll leave."

She smiled. "This is an amazing area. I can't believe I have no memory of this." She set the wrap on a wall peg and started unbuttoning her shirt.

Leo blinked as she let his shirt drop over one shoulder and drift to the insulation mat. His dragon purred so hard, Leo's skin vibrated, yet he couldn't remove his gaze from her pale skin and rounded buttocks. "You're mesmerizing," he murmured.

She turned to him with an impish grin, giving him a glimpse of her breasts. "You think so even with all these scrapes and bruises?"

"I do," Leo said firmly, entranced by her feminine curves. While she wasn't as robust as most female dragons, her humor and smiles more than made up for her differences. Some might call them deficiencies. Her inability to fly. Her lack of fire. "I'll get you a towel and a robe."

"Thanks," she said.

"We're keeping her," his dragon stated as Leo made good on his promise. He returned to his bedroom for the robe and pulled a towel from a storage cupboard.

"What if she belongs to another?" Or worse, his parents drove her away. As rulers of the clan on Hissing Isle, they had the power to make his life uncomfortable if he continued with this lie.

"We are Champion of the Skies," his dragon retorted. *"We're smart and battle hard. If we have to, we will fight for the right to keep her."*

"You make it sound easy. The tear in the magical fabric between us and the mainland worries me. We pay our annual tithe to the druids. There should be no issue. No interruption to our protective barrier. As soon as Gwenyth recovers, we'll travel to visit my friends on Perfume Isle. We must learn if they have seen or experienced this phenomenon."

"After facing the ogre-parents, a visit to our friends would be most welcome."

"I agree." Leo returned and discovered Gwenyth sitting on one of the stone seats he'd carved into the rock wall. Her face, when she glanced in his direction, had lost every hint of color. He scooped her off the rough seat and held her upright while he wrapped the towel around her wet torso.

"Sorry," she whispered.

"Why are you apologizing?" he demanded, his voice rough with concern.

"I'm spoiling our honeymoon with my weakness. This should be a time of fun and laughter and copious amounts of fulfilling sex."

His brows rose, and he glanced down at her pale face. "Copious?"

She huffed. "You're gorgeous. Every time I glance your way, I want to lick you all over and trace each of your bulging muscles with my mouth."

Leo stared, pleasure at her heartfelt words reverberating through him.

"*Keep. Keep. Keeping her,*" his dragon chanted. "*Copious sex would be good for us. I'd like it. You'd enjoy it. We're keeping her.*"

"*Yes,*" Leo replied. Nan, The Strongminded, was not the woman he wanted at his side or in his bed.

In his room, he set Gwenyth on her feet.

"You're exhausted," he said. "Let me dry you properly." Leo patted away droplets of water, working fast because she required her rest. Even so, he took delight in touching her smooth skin and watching the way her body reacted. Her breathing quickened while her pink nipples pulled to tight buds. She watched him through glittering eyes, her expression telling him she enjoyed his attentions. When he kneeled to dry her legs, he scented her sweet arousal, and it pulled an answering response from him. A tightening of his body. He ignored this and wiped her feet. She'd painted her toenails a delicate pink. His dragon purred again while Leo's lips twitched.

Leo set aside the damp towel and tugged one of his clean shirts over her head. An instant later, he guided her to his bed.

"The linens smell of you," she murmured, her eyelids fluttering closed. "It's like being in your embrace."

Leo smiled so wide, his mouth hurt, but she'd already succumbed to slumber.

"*Aw, she's so cute,*" his dragon said. "*You like her as much as I do.*"

"Yes." Leo scooped up the damp towel and left his bedroom. He removed the pie from the oven and left it on the counter to cool.

"We'll check the stock and investigate the death stench. I should've checked earlier—"

"Your parents angered us. We cannot bring the dead to life, so waiting for a time won't hurt."

"The scent has made me uneasy. I feel we must investigate."

"Will Gwenyth be safe here alone?"

"As long as we do not delay." Leo removed his clothes and tossed them over the back of his favored chair. He padded outside and halted in the middle of his large terrace before he called his dragon to the surface.

As always, his transformation was quick, his dragon exploding from him in a rush of exhilaration. An instant later, his sturdy hind legs arrowed him upward while his giant emerald-green wings aided his lift into the air. Rapid strokes took him farther up the mountain to his high pastures. The distinct, coppery scent of blood filled his nostrils, and Leo glided on the airstreams instead of flapping his wings. His intent gaze scanned the landscape.

A pack of wolves roamed the area where he grazed his cattle. They'd never taken one of his animals before, but there was always a first time.

His mind raced ahead while he considered possibilities. He'd thought he had an unspoken truce with the wolves, and although they couldn't communicate, he'd tried to make them understand his cattle were out of bounds. During the hard winters, he often left food for the wolves so they didn't kill his more valuable animals.

Once Leo reached the pasture, he landed and shifted. He scanned his cattle, doing a rapid count. They were here—all thirty-seven of them—and they milled together at the far end of the pasture near one of the mountain streams that ran through his property. At least the offensive stench wasn't from one of his animals.

Perplexed, Leo followed the death trail. It led through the top of his meadow and into the pines.

Foreboding stalked him as the odor grew more substantial. Now that he was closer, the wild, gamey aroma of wolf combined with the blood along with another scent he didn't recognize. Uncertain of what he might find, he strode nearer.

A young wolf of around three months old lay on its side, a spear protruding through its shoulder. Blood pooled around the pup with a larger amount of blood nearby. Where was the pup's mother? The rest of its pack?

A soft whine came from a thicket, and Leo lifted his head, his eyes narrowing while he focused his senses. He spotted a black nose. A second pup. Somehow this one had escaped the death that had claimed its sibling and probably its mother.

Leo crooned to the wolf but remained still. He didn't know what had happened to the pack, but he couldn't leave this pup alone to die. Even worse, someone had trespassed on his land and killed at least two wolves. He had no idea why.

The area bordering his belonged to Ulrim, Protector of the Forest. Ulrim valued the acres left to him by his grandfather, and he gained his title after he refused to sell any portion of his property to Myndunth, The Banker. Rumors had circulated for months regarding a gambling den and luxurious accommodation. The speculation had died a gradual death, since Ulrim refused to comment, other than to confirm his land was not for sale.

Now Leo wondered if something more sinister was afoot. The other side of Hissing Isle contained fewer green spaces and more luxurious homes belonging to wealthy dragons. Some made their fortunes in jewel mines while others traded in leather, wool, foodstuffs, or construction.

Leo wasn't confident of his suspicions, but he'd hate for the wolves to end up driven from their natural home. While he'd been pondering potential scenarios, the wolf-pup crept from concealment. Leo's scent would be familiar to the pup. All he knew was he couldn't leave the creature alone, and he didn't have time to track the pack since he ached to return to Gwenyth.

"I guess we should follow the scent trail," his dragon stated, sounding a trifle grumpy.

"Later," Leo replied. *"With that amount of blood, I doubt the wolf is alive. I'll take the pup home and feed him, look after him while we decide what to do next. I would follow the trail, but I don't wish to leave Gwenyth alone for too much longer."*

His dragon perked up at the decision. *"Darkness will fall soon.*

Best, we follow the trail during daylight."

The pup came closer, and Leo remained unmoving until it nudged his hand with its cold, black nose. Leo still waited and let the animal come to him. He murmured encouragement and ran his hand over the pup's matted fur. The wolf trembled but cuddled closer. It allowed Leo to pick it up, and he carried the cub toward the steel storage chest where he kept necessary supplies—natural remedies in case any of his animals were sick or injured. A lead for his boss cow. Wherever he led his boss cow, the rest of the herd followed, which was handy if he wished to move his cattle to a lower pasture. It also contained empty hessian bags he used to ferry supplies while in dragon form. He plucked one of these from the chest and placed the wolf-pup inside.

Before he left, Leo studied his cattle. They hovered in a tight bunch, acting skittish. He'd shift them tomorrow or the next day to one of the lower pastures where it was easier to watch over them along with the yearling cattle already there.

Leo transformed to dragon and carefully picked up the bag containing the pup. This time he scanned his land as he flew, searching for anything out of the ordinary. Nothing jumped out at him, and he soon landed on his balcony.

When he removed the wolf-pup from the bag, it was shuddering even harder. He cuddled the pup to his chest and strode inside. All was quiet, and when he peeked into his bedroom, he found Gwenyth sound asleep. He figured he'd let her rest.

He grabbed a towel and wrapped the pup in it. The temperature had dropped, and Leo partially shifted to breathe over the kindling he'd laid in preparation. With the fire going, he set the pup down, and once he'd satisfied himself, the wolf would stay put, he went in search of something for it to eat.

"Not too much food," his dragon cautioned. *"I don't want to clean up after it gets sick."*

Leo snorted. "I'd be the one doing the cleaning. You'd use my fingers and thumbs as the reason I'd be better suited for the job."

"Do I look stupid? I am a wise and clever dragon."

Leo snorted again, entirely unimpressed by his dragon's logic. He heated a portion of beef stew—the meat he'd had over after making his pie—and placed it on a dish. The pup had wriggled free of the towel and savored the radiant heat from the fire. It lifted its head at Leo's approach.

"Here you go, fellow." Leo nudged the dish of meat closer and stood back while the pup sniffed and investigated. Finally, he stuck his nose into the bowl and ate a chunk of meat.

"Where did the pup come from?" Gwenyth asked, her husky voice startling the wolf.

He gave a panicked yap and crowded against Leo, seeking protection. Leo smoothed his hand over the pup's back and crooned nonsensical words to him until the wolf calmed enough to return to his food.

"I found him when I went to check on my cattle. Someone killed his mother and sibling."

"That's terrible," Gwenyth whispered. "Is he okay?"

"He's uninjured, and he's eating, so that's an excellent sign. How is your head?"

"Better," she said. "I'm feeling hungry again."

Leo rose from his crouch near the pup and closed the distance between him and Gwenyth. Unable to help himself, he slid his arm around her midriff and dragged her against his side. Without hesitation, Gwenyth curled closer.

"You make me feel safe." She squeezed him.

Leo's big heart seized for a second, before giving a thump and racing faster than average. "You make me happy," he said gruffly. "Let's have pie."

"I think your wolf is a she," Gwenyth said.

Leo glanced in the pup's direction. She stretched out in slumber after sating his appetite.

"We're collecting females," his dragon chirped. *"How fun."*

Leo grunted. "Dinner," he repeated.

Gwenyth poked Leo in the chest. "Did you snort at me?"

"My dragon is making smart-arse comments."

"I wish I could hear him."

"That might happen one day," Leo said, yet guilt filled him. What if she had a husband? He knew nothing of her previous life. Besides, he needed to investigate the failing barrier. He must send a message to his friends on the other Dragon Isles on the morrow.

Although he hated to leave Gwenyth alone, he'd have to bury the wolf and investigate the mysterious slaying, drive his cattle home.

"How will that happen?"

"Sometimes, the dragon part will recognize his true mate and wish to bond. I've heard it feels as if a bracelet snaps into place. Not every dragon ends up with a genuine mate bond."

She cocked her head, curiosity and intrigue fighting for supremacy within her gaze. "When does this happen?"

Normally during the first time a dragon made love with his woman, but he could hardly tell her that. "I'm uncertain," he replied. "I've never met a dragon with a true mate."

Gwenyth frowned. "Well, that pops the fairy tale of true love."

"She sounds tetchy. You'd better feed her."

Leo agreed with his dragon. "I'll serve dinner."

"You know me so well," she said, her brow smoothing. "I get grumpy if I'm hungry. Will the puppy be all right there?"

"She will. Dragons have excellent hearing skills. I'll know if she's in distress."

"You're a caring man." She gave him a quick squeeze before aiming a kiss at his lips.

The instant their mouths met, he groaned. His dragon groaned.

"Kiss her back, numbskull. This is our opportunity to romance her."

Leo didn't hesitate further. He dragged her close, his pulse racing in exhilaration, and kissed her. Her mouth opened to him when he ran his tongue along the seam of her lips. Sweet darts of pleasure surged the length of his body. Her lips were soft. Decadent, and he wanted to feast on them for hours. Their tongues twirled together as she plastered herself against him.

Sweet, sweet lodestone.

He groaned again. His dragon echoed the sentiment, and they dived back into a second kiss. Finally, he pulled away and pressed their foreheads together. His lungs labored while her taste lingered on his tongue. Her scent wrapped around him—memorable and so intimately *her*. His natural scent added a piquancy that thrilled him.

"Mine. Mine. Mine."

"Ours," Leo corrected silently.

"We're not giving her back."

"We might have to if she has a man."

"Stop mentioning a man. I get it. Either way, we will fight for her. We are The Champion of the Skies. We will not fail."

Gwenyth's belly let out a rumble, tearing Leo from his unpalatable thoughts.

"I'd better feed you before you nibble on me," he quipped.

Gwenyth laughed and twirled away from him. He caught her audacious wink before she sashayed to his kitchen. "I might enjoy nibbling on you."

"By Lodar," his dragon breathed. *"Let her nibble."*

Leo had to agree.

CHAPTER 6

I Want to Kiss and Make Love to You

"This pie is delicious." Gwenyth added a moan of appreciation as the savory, meaty flavors burst across her tongue. "I can cook, but I don't think I'm this good."

"Are you trying to saddle me with cooking duties?"

Humor burst inside Gwenyth, and she arched a brow. "Has it worked?"

"We'll need to judge your skills first. If you're feeling up to it, you can take over the duties for tomorrow."

"Smart," she acknowledged, enjoying the natural flow of their conversation. Every time she focused on his powerful features and dark stubble, his piercing green eyes, his sensual mouth, she wanted to cheer. She was so lucky to have Leo as her husband. Not only was he handsome and pleasing to her eye, but he was also kind and strong. How many dragons would've saved the wolf cub? Few, she suspected. Many would've left it as too much trouble, or worse, eaten the pup for a snack.

"That's settled then." His eyes glittered with an otherworldly glow and a faint hint of gold. His inner dragon? She should recall this stuff. The critical, intimate details. Instead, this hole in her memory made everything fresh.

Gwenyth pushed away her empty plate even as she wished manners allowed her to lick the remnants of the gravy. A yawn escaped, forcing her mouth wide. She clapped her hand over her lower face.

"You're tired," Leo said. "You should go to bed. Let me clear the dishes."

Gentleness and understanding instead of chiding her for poor etiquette as Tony—

She frowned as her brain cut off the thought and supplied no further information. Who was Tony? Gwenyth shook herself and focused on Leo. "No, I've slept most of the day. I'll help to clean up, and we'll go to bed together. My headache has gone, and the bump on my head has ceased hurting, unless I knock it by mistake."

"What if I pounce on you the minute we step into the

bedroom?"

She winked. "I'm counting on it."

His intent study and the flit of his gaze had her body heating. He growled and stood. "I hope I make it through the dishes."

"We could always do them tomorrow."

"Tempting," he said. "But I need to fix the wolf-pup a bed and take her for a walk."

Thoughtful. Yes, she approved. "Why don't you do that while I start the dishes?"

She stood and collected their plates. A glance at her fingers as she stacked them brought a frown. She wasn't wearing a ring, although it looked as if she had in the past since a pale indentation showed on her finger. Another puzzle to consider. Perhaps they'd argued, although she couldn't fathom why. And this mysterious Tony. Should she mention him to Leo? No, she'd wait and hopefully remember more about how he'd fitted into her life. It wasn't as if she could picture the man. He could be anyone.

In the lounge, Leo chattered to the pup, and the wolf yipped in response. Anyone who cared for and respected weaker beings was a keeper.

Gwenyth hustled over to the sink and started the dishes. Leo had cleaned the kitchen after he'd cooked, and she soon had the few dishes draining in the dish rack. She wiped the surfaces, and after a final check to determine everything appeared tidy, wandered to the bedroom.

Her preparations were minimal. She cleaned her teeth and washed her face, and this felt natural. Normal for her. It looked as if she might have a black eye by the morning, and the knot on her head ached, although she'd not admit it.

Tonight, she intended to get her hands on her husband's delectable physique, and nothing would halt her from following this plan. She ached for him, her body twitchy as if she hadn't been with a man for a long time. Although she was sure this wasn't true, it was weird how the knock on her head had changed her reality.

A door opened and closed, and she stripped. She discarded the soft shirt Leo had given her to sleep in and slid beneath the covers.

Leo entered the bedroom ten minutes later—time for her to picture those big hands of his gliding over her back and her bottom. Time for her to ponder how his mouth would caress her breasts and suck on her nipples. And time for her to imagine how it would feel as he pierced her with his cock and massaged the sensitive spots that would give her pleasure.

"I thought you might be asleep."

"No."

"Every time I glimpse you, I want to kiss and make love to you." He cleared his throat. "I'm not sure I should. You injured yourself. You require rest to recover."

"Have you considered your hesitation is scaring me? I wonder if we were estranged if there was someone else or a problem within our marriage. I don't have a wedding ring. None of my clothes are here, apart from what I was wearing, although you explained their loss. I can't remember much about you or our life together. It-it makes me nervous."

"We're meant to be together," Leo stated, the hint of gold shining in his eyes, giving him an unworldly presence.

"Prove it," Gwenyth said.

"I don't want you to have regrets."

"So we *were* having trouble with our marriage. You told me we hadn't been married for long, so that doesn't bode well."

"There are difficulties," he agreed. "But they're not with us. Outside problems. My parents, for instance. They wanted me to marry another dragon. They'd arranged the marriage without any consultation with me."

Truth rang in his words. "So, it was external difficulties that left this strain between us?"

"Yes." Leo stripped off his clothes and turned off the lantern before she could study the lines of his massive body. He slipped into bed but didn't reach for her.

A spurt of temper flashed through Gwenyth. This would never do, and especially not since she feared her jitters might shake her free from her skin. "Leo, I'll make this clear, so there is no misunderstanding," she stated, surprised her voice lacked a tremor. This asking for what she wanted seemed uncharacteristic.

"What?" he asked, and caution screamed in his tone.

"I want you. I want to celebrate our love."

"But you're injured."

"I've lost my memory. Physically, I'm fine." She ignored the twinge at her eye and the accompanying thud of her head. She was confident she'd feel one hundred percent once their marriage stood on more solid ground. "Please."

"If we do this, you're mine," he stated. "I'm keeping you."

His words cut and dug at her temper. "That's what I want, but I'm already yours. We're married, remember, so we should act like a wedded couple."

He rolled without warning, his solid frame caging her against the mattress. "Be certain."

"I want this." Gwenyth meant every word.

Leo sought her mouth, their lips crashing together before he gentled the contact and seduced rather than took. Not that he had to worry because she was a sure thing. Her hands curled around his shoulders, then she ran one down his back. A puckered scar interrupted the smooth glide of her fingers, and she hesitated before telling herself this dragon-man held immense strength and the skills to survive aerial battles. Her husband showed intelligence, and one day, he'd retire and let another take his place.

She was safe.

He would keep her safe.

Her brow puckered at the anxiety that crept into her, the sense of danger.

Leo lifted his head. "Have you changed your mind?"

"What?" She stared at him, her pulse racing. "No. I touched one of your scars, and it pushed my thoughts in a weird direction. Was I in danger? Had someone threatened me?"

"You hadn't mentioned anything of that nature." His features tightened, his green gaze bleeding into red. "Have you remembered something?"

Her flash of fear passed, yet it left her unsettled. "No, I'm solidly here in the present and naked with my husband. If I promise not to let my mind wander again, can we make love?"

"Anything, my lodestone."

He rolled without warning, and she found herself draped over his massive chest. "You explore me. No more mind-traveling."

"Hey!" She pinched one of his flat nipples. "That was rude of me. I hope I don't make a habit of drifting in the middle of our sexy times."

He laughed, and Gwenyth gaped at his sparkling eyes, his kissable lips, and warm expression. "Next time you do that, I promise to put you across my knee and spank you."

"Let's not do that," she murmured. "Now changing the subject. Is your dragon ticklish? If I wriggle my fingers over your tattoo like this." She skimmed her fingers over his skin and tried not to grin when she spotted the way Leo's tattoo shifted and cocked his dragon head. He jumped at the tickle of her fingers and retreated, stretching away from her touch.

Leo chuckled, even as he wriggled to escape her teasing caress.

"Ah!" She made tickly motions in the air with her fingers.

"We are ticklish," Leo admitted, his mouth wreathed in a grin. "Please stop."

"It'll be my secret weapon."

Leo snorted, and everything in her softened. She leaned closer to kiss him, enjoying the slide of her breasts against his pecs. The instant their lips met, something clicked inside her, almost like a key sliding into a lock. Everything about this moment seemed right. Perfect. She sighed against his mouth and explored his lips with her tongue.

Leo took over the kiss, and she let him, instead focusing on the heat of his mouth, the way his touch propelled sensual flames through her veins. The solid strength of him and the way he excited her made her happy. So happy, but strangely, this emotion seemed fresh and unusual as if everything was new. But, given the short duration of their marriage, she supposed it was a novelty.

Her hands roved his muscles—his arms and pecs—before she wriggled down his body. Smiling, she ran her fingers over his belly, using a firm pressure rather than seeking to tease. His nostrils flared, his regard steady as she lifted off him.

"You must train a lot to maintain your fitness and strength." Gwenyth pulled a face. "It pains me to ask because I know this stuff, but every time I try to access the information, my head aches."

His big hand landed on her thigh. "It's not important, my

lodestone. Your memories will return in time."

"You hope," she retorted.

"I hope," he agreed. "But it's not so bad getting to know me—us—again, is it?"

"I'm worried you'll get impatient." The words emerged without thought, and they shocked her. Leo didn't seem the intolerant type. He had given no irritated comebacks, not a hint of exasperation. Yet a sense of discord troubled her.

A mystery something lurked in the depths of her mind.

Something worrying.

This Tony?

She had no idea.

"Never, my lodestone. Never."

His words should've reassured her, yet an instinct gnawed and worried at the black hole in her mind. Confusion fluttered in her stomach and tightened her chest. Her thoughts froze—the ones she could still access, at least.

He'd shown her nothing except support and kindness and...and love.

"My lodestone, as much as I'd enjoy making love with you, why don't we wait? Your mind is elsewhere. I'm here. You're here. We have all the time in the world."

Leo's tone was soothing and full of empathy. Not a trace of aggravation oozed from him, yet her tension rose. A memory of a blow. A slap across the face.

Gwenyth forced a smile. "Maybe you're right. My head is aching again."

"Don't let your apprehension win. Think of this as an opportunity for us to fall in love a second time."

She melted as Leo drew her into his brawny arms. He kissed her with a gentleness that had her mind returning to sex.

She wanted him.

Fact.

Which made her hesitation and wandering mind more puzzling.

She yawned without warning, and Leo laughed—the sound low and musical.

"And you're also exhausted. You've had an eventful day. Try to sleep."

Gwenyth wanted to object, yet she couldn't stop her eyes from closing and another yawn escaping. She wasn't sure whether it was the blow to her head or something else, but everything about Leo seemed unfamiliar. It was part of the reason she'd wanted to make love with him—to reconnect, or at least to reestablish the bonds they'd enjoyed before her accident had jolted her out of her standard groove.

Although her eyes were closed, she strained to recall the boat capsizing and came up blank. Even thinking about this mystery Tony propelled shards of pain through her skull. She frowned into her pillow because nothing made sense. Trying to force the memories hurt, so she released her worry and let sleep take her.

By the time she woke, night had turned to morning. She rolled over and discovered she was alone in the gigantic bed. The sheets on the far side held no body warmth. Where was Leo? Unaccountably, his absence bothered her.

She slid off the bed and dressed in the stack of clothes she found on the dresser—a pair of tight-fitting black trousers—slightly too big for her—and a warm shirt that hung to mid-thigh. In the kitchen, she discovered a note from Leo, which she skimmed. At least he'd left a note. His thoughtfulness counteracted her pique.

A yip sounded from behind her, the pup pleased to see her.

She smiled and crouched beside the wolf to scratch behind her ears. "It looks as if we're on our own, pup." At least for the morning while Leo took care of shifting his cattle. "Let's find something for you to eat."

By the time she'd fed the wolf, and herself and cleaned up, the morning was well advanced. The pup followed her around, and Gwenyth even took her for a brief walk outside.

Gwenyth made a pot of tea and settled to enjoy the view of the valley. With the warm sun shining on her face, she drifted close to sleep.

A loud thump jerked her upright. The wolf-pup darted behind her legs and growled. Gwenyth bolted upright to gape at the scarlet dragon hovering before her. The creature sat on the balcony, his wings wafting the air.

The dragon wasn't as big as Leo in his beast form, but the red creature loomed. Its narrowed eyes and pissed attitude raised her hackles.

"Who are you?" she demanded. "What do you want?" She eyed the dragon and frowned at his enormous maw. Sharp white teeth sparkled in the light, and Gwenyth swallowed her alarm.

Belatedly, she noticed the dragon carried a leather pouch. The bag dropped at her feet with another noisy thud. Gwenyth started. She edged away, fear growing as the dragon's eyes glowed red to match its scaly hide.

The creature's scales shimmered, and it shifted in front of her to reveal an older man. A naked older man with an irritated expression. After one quick peek, she kept her gaze at face level.

"Who are you?" the man demanded. "Where is Leonidas?"

"I asked first," Gwenyth snapped.

The man drew himself up, his raised chin displaying arrogance and disinterest. "I am the butler to Tudoarreo, The Dragon Lord, and Qille, The Taker of Life, the parents of Leonidas, Champion of the Skies." With this pronouncement, he scooped up the leather pouch and opened it. Seconds later, he produced a paper tube. A ruby-red seal ensured tampering wouldn't go unnoticed. "Where is Leonidas?"

"He is busy shifting his cattle," Gwenyth said.

"You are?"

"I'm Leo's wife," Gwenyth said. If he was Leo's parents' butler, shouldn't he know her identity already, or at least know of her?

"Leo doesn't have a wife," the butler spoke in a harsh voice, and wily amusement seeped into his features. "Ah, I understand now. He's a sly one. You refused to sleep with him, so now he's stringing you along."

"That's not true," Gwenyth said, stung at the dragon's implications.

"Whatever," the butler said with a shrug. "Make sure Leonidas gets this communication from the castle. It is most important."

"Of course," Gwenyth said, accepting the tube.

Indignant heat flushed her cheeks. Angry words tickled the tip of her tongue, but she bit them back, not wanting to give this arrogant naked butler the satisfaction. The cruel twist of his lips told her, he didn't care if he'd hurt her. He reveled in the pain and confusion she hadn't hidden.

She lifted her chin. "If that's all, you can go now. I'll make sure Leo receives this."

The butler sniffed, even as he shifted forms and increased in size. A puff of smoke drifted toward her, and the butler curled his upper lip a few seconds before he spread his wings and used his back legs to spring from the deck.

Gwenyth watched the red dragon until he vanished.

Not married.

The butler had spoken with certainty. Gwenyth paced, her agitation increasing instead of reducing. On realizing she was crushing the correspondence, she took it inside and flung the tube onto the counter. She scowled at it for a long moment before stomping back outside. The wolf-pup released an anxious yip, sensing her unease.

"Shush, sweetie." Gwenyth squatted beside the pup and scratched her behind the ears. "We need to give you a name. That will give me something to think about instead of wanting to yell and shriek." As she continued to pat the wolf, her ring finger caught her attention. That faint white indentation she'd noticed earlier. Her list of questions continued to grow.

She walked to the end of the deck, her gaze gliding over tree-covered hills as far as she could see. Sunlight glinted on the water in the stream. She scanned the sky and was relieved to find it free of dragons. The last thing she needed was more unexpected visits from dragons who were big enough to eat her in two or three bites.

Funny, but Leo didn't scare her in the manner of this mystery butler. He hadn't given her his name, just his position. Another question for Leo. Did she have a title? Everyone else seemed to have one.

The hours passed, and she and Jenny—the wolf-pup—went inside to think about cooking dinner. She found herbs and spices and other ingredients plus utensils and pots by trial and error. Frustration bubbled up when it took several attempts to locate a wooden spoon. These were tiny things, yet her lack of familiarity filled her with irritation. She and Leo spent a lot of time here and minimal at his parents' castle, so shouldn't she recall where she stored things? Nothing about this situation was logical. Nothing slid into her memory with a relaxed awareness. Nothing screamed routine.

Right now, her world comprised of a blank, and it was the most vexing thing.

CHAPTER 7

The Truth Comes Knocking

Leo hated leaving Gwenyth alone, but he'd had no option. Not with the tasks he needed to complete. He'd woken Gwenyth twice during the long night. She'd grumbled at him and gone back to sleep, her irritation reassuring him of her health.

He flew directly to the kill site and buried the dead wolf. With that grisly task done, he followed the trail. It ended in a large clearing, which pointed the finger at a dragon killing the wolves. Although he had the scent in his mind now, nothing about the pungent aroma triggered a clue of the culprit's identity.

His dragon, who had remained quiet to this point, let out a

yawn. *"I don't understand why a dragon would kill a wolf and remove the carcass. If they were hungry, why not steal one of your cows? That's what I'd do. They'd be much tastier than a stringy wolf."*

"Unless it's a message," Leo said. "The rest of the wolf pack has left the area. I have seen no footprints or smelled fresh territory marking since we arrived. The place stinks of fear."

"Yes," his dragon agreed.

"I'm shifting this herd of cattle to the pastures below the cottage. Safer for my sanity."

"We intended to move them to the lower pastures soon, anyway. Let's hurry so we can get back to Gwenyth. I like her," his dragon purred.

Leo did too, and he wished his conscience hadn't talked him into forgoing lovemaking the previous night. Holding Gwenyth in his arms had turned into pure torture. Of the sweetest kind—certainly—but he ached to claim her.

His integrity chose that moment to kick him in the butt. He should tell her the truth—they weren't married, but he craved that tie to her. She'd started asking questions, and his excuse that she should recover her memories on her own held shades of murky gray.

"I need to confess," he whispered.

"It's been one day. Can't we wait a little longer?" his dragon pleaded. *"We haven't made love to her yet. She smells sooooo good."*

"Our saving grace is we haven't reached that point."

His dragon's snort rippled through his mind. *"You're too honorable. Considering your parents and your older brothers, it's unique. You're nothing like the rest of your family."*

"I left and made my own way. Had I stayed, my character might've formed differently. Having another dragon pummeling me focused my mind, and any deluded notions of privilege bled out of me with my blood."

"I miss those days."

"Me too," Leo said. "Fighting in the competitions was less complicated. Now, we fight through a quagmire of intrigue. Danger lurks each time we set foot in the castle. The bloody walls have eyes. All that posturing to earn favors. There's scarcely an honest dragon amongst them. My family, the nobles, and the common shifters."

Leo approached his lead cow and ran his hand along her back.

"Home," he stated and slapped her on the rump.

Soon, the cattle massed and ambled toward the lower pastures.

"There's one missing." Leo counted his cows and calves. He scanned the pasture and went hunting. His cattle seldom wandered alone, preferring to stick close to each other. He scented the air, allowing his dragon to take more control.

"Nothing," his dragon said.

"We'll take to the air." Leo released full control, and the transformation slid across his skin. An instant later, he sprang upward, the powerful beat of his wings taking him airborne.

He flew over the pasture then skimmed the treetops, using his nose and eyes as he searched for his missing animal. Leo's reconnoiter took him over the two other grazing pastures, and when he reached the third, a death scent prickled his nostrils. He landed, shifted to his human form, and followed his nose.

"Slaughter site," his dragon murmured.

Something—probably wolves—had fed on the entrails, but the remains were enough to tell Leo his beast hadn't died of natural causes. "What the hell is going on here?"

A slaughtered wolf and pup. A cow butchered overnight.

Every instinct screamed trouble, yet he wasn't certain of precisely what the danger was or from which direction it approached.

"I don't like this," his dragon muttered.

"Me neither. We can't afford to lose more cows."

Shifting the cattle took longer than Leo had expected because his small herd shied at every shadow and noise. The sight of his dragon upset them, so Leo trailed the cattle in his human form.

"A dragon did this," his dragon stated the obvious after witnessing his herd's skittishness.

"If I catch them, they'll be sorry." Understatement. Anger roared through him, but he tamped it down. Leo checked the area for footprints and scent trails. The interloper's stench contaminated the kill site. "It's the same dragon who killed the wolves." Not familiar, but a reek he'd remember in case he met the culprit during his next castle visit.

It was four hours later when Leo landed on his balcony and shifted from dragon to man. Dirt and mud coated his lower legs, and exhaustion tugged at his muscles. At least his cattle were safer. He could do a visual count from his balcony.

He inhaled and caught a hint of Gwenyth and... He froze.

Someone—another dragon—had stood on this balcony.

"Gwenyth!" A note of panic shaded his shout. If anyone had hurt her, he'd turn berserker on their arse. "Gwenyth."

Alarmed when she didn't answer, he stomped inside, his dragon senses on high-alert. She lay on his bed, curled up with the wolf-pup. A cute snore escaped her, and his tension dispersed. Safe.

Leo retreated to wash and find a set of fresh clothes. By the time he walked into the kitchen, he'd relaxed. The castle communication sitting on the counter shoved his mood back to high-alert. Unusual creases marred the tube as if someone had squeezed it hard.

Trepidation curdled his stomach. Leo picked up the tube and sniffed. The mysterious scent came from the delivery dragon. With resignation, he broke the seal and scanned the message. A note from his mother, ordering him to greet Nan, The Strongminded, on her arrival. His mother had arranged a betrothal party, so he should plan on staying.

The scuttle of claws on the floor dragged his attention from his mother's note. *His mother's command performance.* In this, he refused to falter. He rejected Nan, no matter what prestige or wealth she brought with her. Gwenyth was the one his dragon craved, and the sole woman to snare his interest in years.

The wolf-pup ran to him, and Leo crouched to pet the animal. Greeting completed, the pup nudged the food bowl in a hint.

"You're back."

Gwenyth's flat voice had Leo straightening. "Something wrong?"

"The butler dragon who delivered the tube sneered and informed me we weren't married."

"Telus, The Organized?"

"We didn't do formal introductions. He told me he was your parents' butler. Horrid dragon. He was rude, snooty, and dismissive. Are we married? Where is my ring?" She thrust out her hand, temper in the curl of her top lip, her sharp inhalations.

"Before me, you were with another man. He treated you shoddily, and you left him." Leo gave her a partial truth put together from clues he'd garnered. Her bare ring finger for one. "You're with me now." He prowled closer, desperate to offer comfort, to resolve her fears. Leo settled his hands on her shoulders, prepared to fight for her. "Please, Gwenyth."

She huffed out a breath and leaned in, relaxing against his chest. Leo bent his head and breathed in her scent. Green herbs. Flowers. *Her.*

"Tell me about our wedding," she whispered.

Leo was glad he couldn't see her face, nor she view his. Guilt slithered like a serpent—destructive and poisonous. Should he tell her the truth?

"We have to tell her something," his dragon said, his tone unhappy.

"I can't ignore the summons. My parents have arranged a betrothal for me."

She yanked away from him, angry color pooling in her cheeks. "A betrothal? Was the butler dude telling me the truth? Are you stringing me along with lies to get me into your bed?"

"If that were the truth, I would've pushed harder for sex last night," Leo snapped. "You are my one. *Our one.*" A plan formed. "I must go to the castle if only to inform my parents I have no intention of committing to their betrothal plans. Come with me. We'll stop at the human village to purchase clothes and visit the church. We will marry there."

Her brow puckered. "So, we're not married."

"Not according to our dragon laws." He chose his words with care. "I make jewelry in my spare time. A hobby for the chilly winters. I wanted to design and make your ring, which is why you do not have one now."

Truth.

"Where did we marry?"

Leo avoided her question. "If we produce a certificate from the human church, there will be no doubts."

"Do you love me?"

These lies became deeper and murkier. Leo loathed this, but he was committed to keeping Gwenyth safe. His dragon wanted her—had claimed her in truth. She intrigued Leo, and he found her attractive—easy to topple into love with her, despite their short acquaintance.

"I didn't want you to face this pressure while your memories remain absent. This emotional stress won't help. I'm sorry, my lodestone. My parents are ambitious, and they expect me to follow their orders. This time I refuse to obey them. You're in my life, and no other woman can or will take your place. We'll spend one night before returning here. You need clothes anyway. I'm serious about marriage. What do you say?"

"You're not telling me the truth."

"Do you refuse to marry me?" he asked, maintaining her gaze, his heart aching. He was fighting for something—someone—he and his dragon wanted. Unfortunately, their lack of history made this situation tricky. "If you don't wish to go through with the ceremony, I'll find somewhere else for you to stay. Perhaps on one of the other Dragon Isles. I must visit my friends to consult on a security matter, anyway."

"You'd palm me off on someone else?" Her voice was sharp, the flash in her eyes echoing her pain.

"Not willingly. Let me be clear. My dragon and I want you. Your spirit calls us, and we think of you even if we're apart. We wish to marry and strengthen the bonds between us."

"But you're not telling me everything," she said, this time with a trace of frustration.

"You've lost your memory," he countered. *Please let her surrender.* Every instinct told him the moment they joined their bodies, the mate bonds would snap into place.

She was theirs.

They belonged to her too.

Gwenyth held his gaze, and sensual heat exploded in his chest. It started from a spark near his big dragon heart and grew until he ached to hold her.

"Gwenyth?" he whispered.

Her gaze pierced him, searching, but reading her mind was impossible.

After a soul-destroying pause that had fear and panic roaring to life in him, she spoke. "You truly want to marry me?"

His breath stuttered before he formed words.

"Tell her yes. Yes. Yes. Yes!"

"Quit the racket! I can't think." Leo took Gwenyth's hands in his.

"This is important. Don't mess up," his dragon ordered.

"Marriage to you will make me happy. My dragon happy and fulfilled. I'd intended to ask you, had hinted at it, but I wanted to craft a ring worthy of you, my lodestone."

The hint part was an embellishment since they'd met the day

before, but from the moment he'd lifted her from the tin box, he'd wanted her. That was the truth. Another truth—marriage would protect them both, and he could claim her body with a clear conscience.

A mostly clear conscience.

"Do you love me?"

"My dragon and I believe you are our true mate. We both believe the mating bonds will snap into place between us."

"Numbskull," his dragon spat. *"Won't she ask if we've mated before?"*

"How long have we known each other?" she asked.

"I told you so," his dragon said, his brawny tattooed arms rising up Leo's chest in a display of disgust.

By Lodar! His dragon was right. He'd stuck his foot-claws in his mouth this time. Leo frantically sought to escape this mire.

"Truth," his dragon stated. *"Give her truth and pray she forgives us."*

Leo tightened his grip. "We've known each other for two days. I rescued you from the sea and brought you here."

"You let me think we were married." Accusation shimmered in her voice. Irritation. Gwenyth lifted her chin as she blasted him with her outrage.

"She has courage," his dragon stated with pride. *"We could snap her like a twig."*

"You couldn't remember anything, and when you mentioned

89

our marriage, I decided not to disabuse you of the situation. The knowledge comforted you."

"And the betrothal?"

Leo couldn't read her expression, although her mood still screamed irked. His dragon remained silent, so Leo gave Gwenyth more truth. "I'd met with my parents. They issued their orders and left before I could refuse. Telus, The Organized, who was also present at the meeting, never gave me a chance to speak either. As the youngest and the runt, my brothers bullied me while my parents ignored my presence. Now that I'm useful, my parents issue commands and expect me to jump. I left the castle in a mood, intending to go home. But I was agitated, furious with my parents, and I flew over the sea to settle my mind with exercise. That's when we found you. You almost died."

"So that part is true." Gwenyth frowned. "You saved me."

"Yes."

"But you'd never met me before?"

"No. It is my belief you came from the mainland."

Her eyes flashed, and eagerness lifted her expression. "So we can go to the mainland and discover where I came from. My name."

Leo shook his head. "You don't understand. Once dragons played in the skies over the mainland, but the humans feared us. Whenever the opportunity arose, they'd kill our kind. To save our species, we withdrew to the Dragon Isles. The remaining dragons cut a deal with the druids who live on Smoking Isle.

The magic-men conjured a spell to keep humans from seeing our territory. An invisible barrier separates the isles from the mainland, so we cannot trespass either."

Gwenyth blinked. She frowned. "If that's the case, then how did I get here?"

He shrugged. "Most days, we can sense the mainland, but it is invisible. Yesterday, the protective barrier was absent, and I flew along the mainland coast. You were in a tin box. You spotted me before the tin box jumped over the cliff and toppled into the sea. I plucked you out and brought you to my home. While I was cutting you from the box, the barrier reformed. We almost didn't make it back."

Gwenyth nodded. "You've told me everything?"

"I swear, my lodestone. That is the absolute truth."

"Thank you." Gwenyth tugged her hands free of his and marched off.

"Where are you going?"

"I must think."

"Don't let her leave," his dragon ordered.

Gwenyth halted. "Is it safe for me to walk in the meadow?"

"If you stay within sight of my home."

"No! She mustn't leave."

"I wish to walk."

The wolf-pup jumped at Gwenyth.

"Can I take Jenny with me?"

"Jenny?"

"The pup."

Leo gestured at the door. "You will find steps at the end of the path. If you require me, shout. Do not overexert yourself."

"I won't." Gwenyth ushered Jenny outside and left.

"You shouldn't have let her leave," his dragon snapped and stomped his foot hard against Leo's ribs. Leo grunted and pressed his fingers against the throbbing spot.

"She is not our prisoner. That is not the way to win her."

The tension bled from his dragon. *"You have a plan?"*

"The same one we came up with before. We woo her. At least there is honesty between us now. Lies aren't a solid foundation for a relationship."

His dragon released a derisive hoot. *"You've been listening to humans. We require quality dragon time. Immediately!"*

"Soon," Leo muttered, offended by his inner beast. "You experience the magnetic pull toward her. When we make love, magic will fill the air. I wish to savor every moment. We will *not* force ourselves on Gwenyth. We will—"

"If you continue this chatter, you'll scare her away," his dragon snapped. *"I'll never forgive you."*

Leo refrained from comment, but Gwenyth enticed his dragon and seduced his human side. They'd work together to win the fair maiden, which was as it should be. The two parts desiring the same outcome.

"How will we court her?"

"We will begin by cooking her a tasty meal," Leo said.

"I could eat," his dragon said. *"What of the parental summons?"*

"We must go." Leo scowled. "This is my fault. Instead of seeking my family's respect, I should've made my independence clear. They never see me as anything other than a tool."

"You were wise not to tell them you're the creator of the Marquess brand."

"My family has no inkling of our wealth or our network of friends. To them, I am still a weakling. A child."

"You have a plan."

Leo snatched one last lingering glance at the woman who'd given him the impetus and the reason for the coming family confrontation. Gwenyth's musical laughter floated on the air as she played with the pup.

His dragon issued a lengthy sigh, echoing his awe and admiration. *"She's beautiful."*

"After dinner, we will ask Gwenyth if she'd enjoy a walk."

"We start our wooing?"

"We'll make her a special ring. The one I started a few days ago will be perfect."

"For our marriage," his dragon said with such eagerness, Leo's lips twitched.

"Gwenyth may say no."

"We must point out marriage to us will offer her protection."

"As long as none of my family nor those in their circle get close enough to hurt Gwenyth."

"Let them try," his dragon snapped.

"They will," Leo said, certainty in his gut. The sudden betrothal arrangements raised his suspicions. He was missing facts of which his family was aware. "Our castle network might yield results. We should've consulted our contacts before leaving the castle."

"We wouldn't have met Gwenyth," his dragon pointed out.

Leo strode indoors, his mind full of the tasks he needed to complete. Unfortunately, he'd have to delay his trip to Perfume Isle. Once he reached the castle, he'd send a message via a trusted friend. That would have to suffice until he could speak to his friends in person.

"We're not going to have sex with her."

His dragon's accusation focused Leo on the present. "That bit about wooing Gwenyth instead of forcing her—that applies until Gwenyth signals us otherwise."

"But—"

"Gwenyth's wishes are paramount. We are not my parents, my selfish brothers, nor the sly courtiers. Gwenyth will signal if she wants us as much as we desire her. That is my last word on the matter."

"Are we certain of our parentage?" his dragon asked.

Leo barked out a rich laugh, full of understanding and amusement. "No, but everyone accepts us as the youngest in the family. We are stuck with our lot."

"Which begs the question—why are the parents pushing Nan, The Strongminded, at us? Why not one of our older brothers? All of them remain single. They would make better matches than us."

"An excellent point. I should've asked questions, demanded answers."

"Our parents carry arrogance as an extra layer of clothing. They never gave us a chance to object."

"Which is why our disobedience will shock them," Leo said in a dry voice.

"Are you talking to yourself again?" Gwenyth said.

"My dragon and I are discussing the betrothal our parents are attempting to force on us. We wondered why Nan, The Strongminded, would accept the youngest son."

"You're not inferior," Gwenyth snapped.

"She likes us. I knew it. I can't wait for the sex part."

Leo grinned. "Thank you."

"Do you have a plan?" Gwenyth asked.

"Your best protection is to wed us at the human church. Then, we'll drop by my parents and tell them a betrothal is impossible."

"If the snooty butler is indicative, your parents won't believe you."

"I won't lie. The benefits of marriage are greater for me. I'm uncertain why they are pushing this betrothal, but their actions speak of determination. Our marriage will both protect and endanger you."

"I could remain here," Gwenyth suggested.

"Two reasons that is a terrible idea. After Telus's visit, my parents are aware of your presence. If they consider you an obstacle, they might send an assassin to destroy you."

Gwenyth winced, then arched a brow. "The second reason?"

"Someone butchered one of my cows and also killed the pup's mother and littermate. This concerns me."

Gwenyth bit her lip, silent as she considered his words. "Do you have friends, ones you trust whom I could stay with while you're busy with your parents?"

"I have trusted friends amongst the commoners," Leo said.

Gwenyth nodded. "That's what we'll do then."

"And the marriage?"

"Are you certain marriage is necessary?"

"Yes."

Gwenyth held out her left hand. "It looks as if I'm already married or have been. What if my ring came off in the sea?"

"No," his dragon snapped.

Leo ignored his other half. "We will have a marriage certificate to present to my parents, which will save me from the betrothal."

"And place me in danger," Gwenyth pointed out.

"You were at risk the moment I brought you to Hissing Isle," Leo countered. "If anyone learns you're from the mainland, pandemonium will follow. The humans live here in safety, as did their ancestors. They're useful since they produce clothing and food. They trade with dragons and are a known entity. Most dragons will assume mainlanders mean to butcher them as they did in the past."

Gwenyth's brow furrowed. "Your words resonate with me. The part about killing dragons. It's as if my brain contains this knowledge. Do you think my memory is returning?"

"Does she have a man?" his dragon demanded.

"Shush. Let me communicate with Gwenyth."

Leo studied her familiar face: her straight brown hair, her solemn dark brown eyes, and the lush mouth that drew his gaze whenever she tipped her lips into a smile. He fought his sudden rapid breathing, the trace of panic his dragon had communicated. He—they'd known her for such a brief time, but she'd become important to them. Each physical touch soothed his typical restlessness while she fascinated his dragon half. Every instinct told Leo this woman—whatever her actual name—was essential to their wellbeing. Despite the arranged marriages prevalent in the dragon world, he had no wish to follow traditions, nor did he covet the riches a marriage to another wealthy dragon might bring.

Since the day long ago, when his older brothers had beaten him bloody and laughed before they'd run off to play with their friends, he'd embraced his desires. Leo, Champion of the Skies, marched to his personal drummer. Even so, since Gwenyth's appearance, his drummer had developed a stutter in his beat.

"Have you remembered other parts of your past?" He and his dragon waited in trepidation for her reply.

Her brow wrinkled as she shook her head. "Not a thing. I get flashes, but the second I tug at them, the memory fades. What happens if I never—"

"Worrying won't fix the problem," Leo interrupted, not wanting her to complete her sentence. "We travel to the human village and marry. Then we go to the castle. Once I've spoken with my parents and canceled the betrothal, we'll journey to Perfume Isle to visit my friends and investigate the mystery of our meeting. Are you agreeable?"

"A fair plan," she said, decisive in her agreement. "The truth is you are my sole option. I have no means of support, I'm an unknown quantity, and my memory of my former life is nil. Without you, my chances of survival are low."

"Did you have to give us a hearty dose of truth?" his dragon grumbled.

An equal amount of irritation, apprehension, and despondency thumped Leo in the chest. They wanted Gwenyth to stay with them, but not for the reasons she'd spelled out with harsh reality. He forced a smile and focused on projecting a calm exterior.

"We will keep you safe," Leo promised. "Although you are not an obligation. My dragon and I like you, and while our marriage might be fake, we want more. We would court you with a view to a genuine relationship."

"You've known me for two days," Gwenyth whispered, her eyes big rounds of surprise.

"We are decisive."

"I can see that." Gwenyth raised her chin and straightened her shoulders. She stuck out her hand. "I agree with your plan. Let's do this."

Chapter 8

Flying Attracts Bugs

I t was a relief to arrive at the human village. Flying clutched in a dragon's claws did not lend one dignity. Nope, it was plain scary. Leo had informed her he carried items inside woven bags or sacks, and that was how they transported Jenny since the wolf-pup wasn't old enough to fend for herself.

Gwenyth vetoed the bag transportation for herself, and Leo had clutched her in his right talon, which was how, according to him, he'd carried her after her rescue. Every bug they passed leaped at her mouth, and her hair flew into her face while terror kept her eyes squeezed shut. Somehow, an airplane seemed safer. Her frantic panic slowed enough for her to recognize she'd remembered something from her past. The instant she tugged the snippet, it dispersed like a puff of Leo's smoke.

Leo settled onto the ground, and she scrambled from his hold, relieved to have her feet on a solid surface. She swiped the back of her hand over her mouth and pulled a bug free. *Eek!*

"Not a favored way to travel?" Leo asked, amusement lighting his handsome features once he'd shifted. He pulled on black trews, a shirt, and footwear.

Her head jerked up, and she glowered at him. "Is there an alternative? I think you hit every squadron of flying bugs between your house and the village."

His sharp canines screamed danger. "I have two ideas we can try, but I must consult Saffron, The Leather Master, first."

"We should do that ASAP."

Leo grinned, a mischievous quirk of his lips that enticed her to touch. Before she could act, he crouched to free Jenny. The pup licked him on the face and ran in a circle, sniffing everything in her path. Leo rose and extended his hand to Gwenyth.

Unable to resist, she curled her fingers around his and ambled at his side. Quaint stone cottages hugged the hillside while a salty sea tang rode on the air. Leo led her toward a cobblestone street that sloped down the hill to the sea. Three small boats bobbed in the harbor, sails furled, the vessel's owners nowhere in view. The rush and retreat of gentle waves on a beach created a pleasing rhythmic hiss.

Jenny trotted at their heels. Several men nodded to Leo, and a woman pushing a baby in a stroller lifted her hand in a wave before she disappeared into a butcher shop.

"Good morning, Mr. Leo," a girl said.

Her younger brother toddled straight to him and raised his arms for Leo to lift him. "Mister. Mister. Mister!" he cried.

Laughing, Leo situated the boy on his shoulders and eyed his older sister. "Where are you off to today, Marcie?"

The girl skipped beside them. "Ma wants a loaf of bread from the baker. Is that your dog?"

"It is," Leo said. "This is Gwenyth. She's my special lady."

Gwenyth bit back a grin while Marcie ran her gaze over Gwenyth.

"She's pretty."

"Thank you," Gwenyth said.

Leo led her through the village, past the butcher, and a shop that appeared to sell cheese and butter. She sniffed as they approached the baker's shop.

Leo let the boy down. Marcie took her brother's hand, and they waved goodbye before disappearing into the bakery.

Glossy fruit tarts cozied up to beautiful pies with intricate lattice tops. Another shelf contained small cakes, big cakes, layered cakes, and others with unique shapes. Each caught her gaze, tempted her. A plate of delicate cookies in pastel colors sat beside a larger dish of more robust chocolate-flecked ones. The appetizing scent of bread and spices had her tummy rumbling while her eyes delighted in the edible bounty.

"I think I have a sweet tooth," she said. "I have an urgent craving for a cake."

"Why don't we return and purchase something for our midday meal once we have our marriage certificate in hand?" Leo suggested and urged her onward with a hand in the small of her back. "My dragon and I favor honeyed foods too, although we don't indulge ourselves often. We restrict sweets if we're training for our aerial battles."

Gwenyth's brows rose, and she poked his hard belly, humor spilling from her in a giggle. "You don't need to worry."

Leo shook his head and reclaimed her hand. He checked that the wolf-pup was following and headed farther down the cobblestone road. "If we put on weight and get flabby, we'd lose our title."

"We couldn't have that," Gwenyth said, her tone dry. "I and the dozens of others wouldn't enjoy studying your backside if you turned to fat." She jerked her chin toward the group of whispering women to their right.

Another two younger women joined them, and one—a dark-haired woman—almost tripped over a cobblestone since she was ogling Leo so hard.

"Huh," Leo said. "I've never noticed before."

Gwenyth held back a snort of disbelief. A man as sexy as Leo? She'd bet the local women enjoyed the spectacle every time he visited. How could he not detect their interest? "Have you not dated any of the humans before?"

"Dated?"

"Courted them?" Hadn't Leo intimated dragons didn't choose their partners? "Had a meal or spent time with a human. Slept with them." Heat collected in her cheeks when those words popped free, and she clapped a hand over her mouth.

Wow. *Just wow.*

What was wrong with her today? Men never rattled her. Calm and mature were her middle name. The information sprang into her brain, gave her pause. She strained to follow more of the logic but slammed into a brick wall of nothing. Gwenyth pushed at the darkness, and a jolt of pain warned her to cease.

"Sometimes, we visited the house of women who specialize in sex. If I'm at home, I remain on my land and only leave to purchase supplies. I visit the castle if my parents insist."

"What about sex?" she blurted. Oops, there went her filter failure again.

"Sex is healthy, and while I enjoy a female's body, neither my dragon nor I wish for complications. We are saving ourselves for you."

"But I offered myself the other night, and you encouraged me to sleep."

Leo ceased walking, a frown digging deep on his forehead. "You had a head injury and needed to recover from your dip in the sea.

We want you to enjoy yourself, not consider us a responsibility."

"I understand." *Lie.* Didn't all men accept an offer of no-strings sex? Once again, she followed the strand of remembrance before striking a wall.

"Ah, here is the church. Hopefully, Allen is present and can wed us straightaway."

"What about a marriage license and the rules and regulations?" Somehow, Gwenyth understood these were necessary to ensure the legalities.

"I'm hoping the minister will understand the difficulty we face if this marriage does not go ahead. Jenny!" Leo clicked his fingers to signal the wolf-pup. She trotted over to Leo, and he scooped her into his arms.

"Why are you carrying her?" Gwenyth asked.

"The humans are nervous of her. The women we pass are pushing their children behind them as if Jenny might bite."

"Do they have problems with wolves?"

"It's possible those who farm struggle to keep their livestock safe from wolves. We'll keep Jenny close to err on the safe side."

"What will we do with her while we visit the castle? I don't expect a wolf roaming the halls will excite your parents."

"I'd considered that already," Leo said. "Allen and his family might keep her. They fenced their yard to keep the children safe, which would work for Jenny. If not, one of my friends will mind her. This is the church," Leo said, ushering her onto another cobblestone road.

"Are we sure the minister will keep our secret?" Gwenyth asked. "What if one of your family questions him? If they discover our lies, everything we've done will be for naught."

"The minister is my friend. I did him a favor several years ago, and if we explain, I believe he'll help."

Gwenyth sucked in a quick breath, her imagination conjuring the minister's appalled reaction and worse... "What if your parents kill me? They could. Right?"

Leo's jaw tightened. "They might try," he conceded. "Which is why I'll never leave you alone while we're inside the castle. If I'm unable to protect you, I'll leave you with a trusted friend."

"What if your friends disapprove of me?"

"It's none of their business." Leo grasped her arm and led her through a hip-high wooden gate.

The church was a stone building and similar to many of the English churches on the mainland with a bell tower and stained glass windows. Its square angles and towers reminded her of the medieval era.

"Have the humans been here as long as the dragons?"

"Most are descendants of the original humans. Some of them come from Viking stock, and others descend from sailors who wrecked their ships during smuggling runs. Once the Druids helped us to protect our islands and made them invisible, the humans became trapped here."

"Didn't that worry them?"

"Most were outlaws in their own countries or ran businesses outside of the law," Leo said. "From my experience, the humans seem happy with their lot. There is plenty for them to do and keep busy. Most of them work hard."

"Could the human sector have anything to do with the break in the invisibility?"

"I've pondered reasons. It was a small window." He frowned. "At least, that's my supposition. The break might have existed for some time, or it might have occurred for mere minutes, and my finding you was sheer luck."

"Excellent for me." An involuntary shudder shook Gwenyth's shoulders. "I would've drowned. You said I was unconscious."

"Maybe we're meant to be together. Fate." Leo knocked on the large wooden double doors. When nothing happened, he opened the door on the right and tugged Gwenyth inside.

The interior of the church seemed dark, and it took seconds for her eyes to adjust enough to spot the altar. Her gaze lifted to the colorful rose window in teal, blue, and violet with a yellow center depicting a robed woman.

"Allen, are you here?" Leo called.

Footsteps sounded, somewhere from her left, and a tall, thin man appeared from a doorway. He wore black trousers, a plain white shirt, and a minister's collar. "Leo? What are you doing here?"

"This is Gwenyth Jones, my fiancée," Leo said, giving her a surname without a blink. "If you have time, we'd like you to marry us."

Allen cocked his head and stared from Gwenyth to Leo. "Rumor says you're betrothed to a dragon from Smoking Isle."

"Rumor is wrong. Gwenyth and I met, and that was it for me. I've always scoffed at love at first sight, but Gwenyth..." Leo's face softened, and even she believed he adored her. "We fell in love, and we'd like to formalize our relationship."

The furrows in Allen's forehead deepened. "We haven't called the banns."

"I'm a dragon," Leo countered. "We don't adhere to human rules."

The minister turned to Gwenyth, his gaze drilling into her as if to ascertain her genuine opinion. "What say you about the banns business? You are a human, are you not?"

Gwenyth straightened. "I love Leo. I'm no longer a youthful woman, and until Leo came along, I'd almost given up on finding Mr. Right. Leo is an admirable man. He's honest and hardworking. He's a decent dragon who never treats humans as if they're inferior. I'd need to search a long time to discover a man of Leo's equal."

Respect gleamed in the minister's eyes. "You're right. Leo has many excellent qualities, and he treats humans as equals. He's unfailingly polite and gives of himself to help those in need."

"So you'll marry us?" Gwenyth asked, her breath catching as she waited for the minister's reply.

"Others might question the validity of the marriage," the minister cautioned.

"I love Gwenyth, and the marriage will be real to me, to Gwenyth. We are the ones who matter," Leo said.

"Your family will not feel the same. They'll be furious."

"Plead ignorance should any of them accuse you of helping me to get out of the betrothal they arranged for me."

"Your parents are formidable foes," the minister said, still hesitating.

"I will donate to the church," Leo said. "My friends and I support many in the village by purchasing our goods here rather than from the dragons."

Allen grinned. "Blackmail, it is then. Let the ceremony begin."

CHAPTER 9

Lots of Kissing

"I pronounce you man and wife," Allen said, his bearded face one big beam of happiness and satisfaction. "You may now kiss your bride."

Leo winked at her, his broad and happy smile punching her right in the chest. Gwenyth found her lips curving with the same awe and exhilaration. Leo's excitement at their marriage was difficult to resist. While she liked Leo—heck, she'd fallen for the handsome, caring dragon—reservations swirled in her. Her lack of recollections worried her because monsters might swim in her forgotten memories. Was she even a decent person?

Who knew? She didn't.

Gwenyth stared at the sparkling ring he'd slid onto her finger. The red-and-blue stone picked up the light while the rose-gold band glowed, even inside the church. It was breathtakingly gorgeous.

"Hey." Leo clicked his fingers in front of her face. "Something wrong?"

"No, everything is perfect." Gwenyth leaned closer and offered her lips.

Leo's mouth closed over hers, and he drew her nearer. Everything in her current world faded to the background while her new husband tasted her, seduced her, and left her weak-kneed with his kiss.

"Ahem," a voice trespassed into their private world. "Ahem!"

Leo drew back without haste as if he hated to release her.

"This is a church, a place of god," Allen chided, although his eyes twinkled. "Where are you going now? To the castle?"

"Not straight away, no. I have a surprise in store for my darling wife."

Leo drew her against his side. His warm strength and familiar scent brought a sense of comfort—a welcome.

"Congratulations," Mary-Anne, Allen's wife, said. "You couldn't have a better dragon for a husband. Let me see your ring. Oh, it's gorgeous. A Marquess, by the look of it. You lucky woman. A handsome husband *and* a generous one."

"A Marquess?"

"The most highly skilled and sought-after jewelry designer in the Dragon Isles. The identity behind the brand is a cosmic mystery. No one knows who he or she is," Mary-Anne gushed. "Your husband is spoiling you already with a unique Marquess ring."

Gwenyth slid a glance at Leo, a breathless lightness taking her by storm. "I am lucky. It's a wonder a clever woman hasn't snapped him up earlier."

"From what I hear, many have tried," Mary-Anne said. "Isn't that true, Faith?"

Faith, their other witness, had said little either before or since the marriage ceremony, but now she nodded with enthusiasm. "Congratulations to both of you."

The door to the church opened, and Allen's three children spilled inside with Jenny chasing them. The wolf-pup skidded into a pew and released a surprised yelp.

Leo chuckled and scooped up the pup.

"Dad, can we keep her?" the oldest of Allen's children asked.

"No," Allen said. "She belongs to Leo and Gwenyth."

"Would you consider looking after her for us?" Leo murmured to Allen in an inaudible voice, so the children didn't overhear. "It will be difficult to keep her safe where we're traveling. Gwenyth and I need to journey to Perfume Isle. It might be up to three weeks."

Allen summoned his children with a wave. "Leo has asked if we can mind Jenny. Would you like that?"

"Yes, please," the three kids chorused.

Allen grinned at his wife. "Well, we'll do that then."

"Thank you," Leo said. "That is a weight off my mind. It will be better for Jenny here."

Leo shook Allen's hand and kissed Mary-Anne's cheek. Gwenyth hugged them both since they'd welcomed her without reservation.

Soon, she and Leo were on their way.

"Where are we going?" Gwenyth asked.

"We have a few hours. I've arranged an outing to a friend's property. He has a private beach where we can swim and enjoy the sun. I thought we'd visit the bakery on the way there and buy a few supplies. We'll also make a quick stop at the seamstress's parlor. How does that sound?"

"Perfect. Do we need to fly?"

His lips twitched. "No, the cottage is within walking distance."

He offered his hand, and when she entwined their fingers, a frisson of pleasure seeped deep into her. After their requisite stops at the bakery, the grocery, and the seamstress where they arranged to collect clothes on their return journey. Leo led her down a narrow cobblestone alley. They traversed a set of stone steps, the scent of the sea growing stronger with each stride. The walkway gave way to sand and a tiny beach.

"Is this it?"

"No." Leo smiled, his green eyes alight with contentment. "We need to walk along the beach and into those trees. It's the next bay where we're spending our time."

The gentle swish of the waves relaxed her and seemed familiar, although she hadn't visited this area before. Tiny pebbles crunched under their feet, and an audible hissing came from the shingle shifting with the wave action. Leo led her into the trees—a grove of pine. She sniffed the fragrance and smiled. At this end of the beach, she could no longer hear the village noises or voices.

She followed Leo down a trail that wove through the pine trees. The path rose upward until they exited the trees. The tiny beach consisted of white sand instead of the regular hissing pebbles.

"It's beautiful."

"A fisherman friend owns the property. I helped him build his cottage and lent him the money to purchase the land."

"That was nice of you."

"He's a decent man who works hard. He was having problems finding the money, and I wanted to return the favor he did for me."

"What did he do?" Gwenyth asked.

"He is a talented artist and designer, and he helped me with the interiors of my home. Are you hungry, or would you like to go swimming?"

"I don't have a swimsuit," she said, disappointed since she loved swimming. She frowned at that because, during her recent experience of the sea, she'd almost drowned.

Leo grinned. "No special clothes necessary. I'm swimming in my skin." He winked at her. "What do you say, wife? Do you want to go swimming?" His words held a dare along with the sensual purr.

"Of course." Gwenyth followed Leo down the slight incline and onto the sand.

Leo led the way to a spot where a tree draped its shadow over the sand.

"Are we setting up camp here?" she asked.

Leo's gaze burned hot, his green eyes almost golden with heat and something else. Perhaps longing.

Her hands went to the laces on her tunic. Without haste, she tugged them free and whooshed the garment over her head. Beneath, she wore her lingerie, the two pieces she'd been wearing when Leo found her. Cream and black with lace of both colors. She dropped her trews next, the removal easy since they were too big for her.

She peeked at Leo and saw he'd frozen in position, his eyes wide as his gaze measured her curves in a visual caress.

While he'd stripped off her clothes and helped her to dress when she was too weak to do it herself, he hadn't seen her when she'd donned her underwear. Now, she wanted to flirt and tease. She smiled—no, beamed—inside, but she didn't let him see her humor.

Gwenyth reached behind her to unfasten her bra. Already, her nipples had become taut, her body achy and wanting him. Had she felt this way before? The thought shoved past her joy. A frown wrinkled her forehead—she felt the tension trying to swipe away everything right in her life. *No!* She refused to spoil this moment.

Without letting another notion surface, she let her bra fall away and down her arms.

"Gwenyth," Leo murmured, and he sounded entranced and strained too.

Impishly, she winked at him before stripping her panties down her legs. "Last one in is a rotten egg."

She turned from her stunned husband and sprinted across the sand to the water. She kept running, not even hesitating at the splash of cool waves against her calves.

Gwenyth swore Leo's gaze singed her backside, and she desperately needed the chill to douse the ardor heating her skin. Gwenyth ceased walking once the water reached her breasts. Only then did she turn to see what Leo was doing.

A tremendous splash filled her eyes and mouth with water. She spluttered, and an instant later, Leo's arms wrapped around her, drawing her against his hard chest.

"You're a tease," he murmured seconds before he crushed his mouth against hers.

The kiss held desperation, their teeth and noses clashing until they managed the perfect fit. His breath was hot, his flesh under her cold hands just as searing. Tongues stroked, licked, tasted.

Desire roared through Gwenyth. She moaned in enjoyment, his skin beneath her fingertips hot. Leo's hands caressed the skin of her arse. He was burning her alive, yet there was no visible flame.

She pulled away a fraction, desperate to take one full breath.

"My lodestone," he murmured. "You are so beautiful. I can't believe you agreed to marry me. I am blessed—such a lucky dragon."

Gwenyth ran her fingertips over his cheeks, his bold nose, then his sensuous lips. The edges of his mouth tipped up in a smile, growing bigger and wider until she glimpsed his white teeth. Unable to resist, she fitted her lips to his. This time, their kiss was slow and tender.

It set her alive with urgent need.

"Leo," she whispered.

"Yes," he said and lifted her into his arms. He carried her from the sea and headed farther up the beach to a cottage she hadn't noticed earlier because it blended with the trees. It was part of the trees, she realized once Leo opened the door.

"Dry yourself off, my lodestone," he said, handing her a towel. "I'll grab our meal supplies and place them in the cool room. I will run," he added when she opened her mouth to protest.

By the time she'd toweled herself dry and explored, Leo was back with their basket of supplies and their clothes. He set the garments over the back of a chair and strode into a smaller room that she discovered was the kitchen. When he reappeared, his eyes glowed a warm amber. He stalked toward her, his face full of determination and a hint of lust. No, the emotion wasn't as harsh as lust but more urgency and desire.

His arms gripped her waist, and he swept her up. His long strides took them to a bedroom, and her pulse raced. She wanted him so much. The longing had crept up on her, taking her by surprise. With each passing hour, she'd grown to like him more and more. It was why she'd agreed to the marriage. Now that gentle attraction was taking on a life of its own. Leo placed her on the soft mattress and smiled down at her. Gwenyth licked her lips, shy and a little nervous, but wanting him, wanting this with every fathom of her being.

"I'm not sure where I want to touch first," he whispered, his gaze heated as it roamed her breasts. His chest was broad and muscled, no doubt from his constant flying, training, and his hard physical work to build his farming business. His biceps bunched as he leaned over to steal a kiss. Her gaze wandered farther down his body to his lean waist, his narrow hips, and the muscles of his abdomen. So sexy. She imagined licking his skin, her tongue running over the distinct ridges on his middle region. Lower still, his cock was erect, a clear portrayal of his desire for her.

During her perusal of his body, she'd ignored his dragon tattoo. His dragon stood, his legs asunder and hands planted on his hips. The instant the dragon tattoo noticed her watching him, he waved and blew a kiss. The way he did it with the knowing gleam had color racing to her face and sinking down her neck. His dragon ran his hand down his scales to rest on his groin and winked at her.

Gwenyth gasped.

"What's wrong?" Leo asked.

"Your dragon is crude." She said the words, although they didn't match the humor that was bubbling up inside her. She grinned at Leo, gaining confidence again. "Like any superb story, you start at the beginning. Touch me everywhere."

"An excellent plan," he said, and he dropped to the bed beside her. He combed his fingers through her damp hair. He kissed her, this time with purpose and skill. "You give me hope for the future."

When she tried to reply, to ask why, he stopped her with another kiss, this one passionate and all-consuming. She clung, craving more of his touch. Hungry for the physical act.

For the first time, Leo's big, competent hands wandered her body. He skimmed her breasts before cupping them and learning their shape.

Where his fingers went, his mouth followed with tiny bites of kisses that woke nerve endings and left her tingling with need. In return, she kissed Leo, tested the hard muscles of his arms and shoulders, and pressed herself close to his powerful torso. So good. So decadent. A gasp escaped her when he took a nipple into his mouth. He drew on the tight bud, and the sensation arced down her body to land between her thighs. She twisted in his arms, her legs splaying in a silent demand, a wordless enticement for him to do more.

"Leo," she gasped, her hands tugging at his hair. "I need you.

Please."

"Let me feast, wife. Let me explore and savor." His avid gaze met hers. *"Please."*

The yearning in his voice grabbed her, threw her into something unusual. She'd never experienced this desperate desire for another man—the need to become one, to get as close as possible. At least, it seemed new. Momentous.

She jumped as he released her nipple and ran his tongue down the middle of her chest. To her relief, he signaled his intentions by moving farther down her body. He explored her bellybutton, the irregular scar on her hip that she'd received the time she'd fallen off her bike as a child.

Yet another memory. It seemed as if time might heal the gaps in her mind.

Leo halted his explorations and glanced up at her. "What is it?"

"I remembered how I got the scar on my hip. The second you licked it, the memory appeared."

A strange expression came into his face. Was that a trace of fear?

"That's good, right?"

"I worry you might reject me, that all this has happened too fast," Leo said, still frowning.

His honesty was a slap to the face. But he'd shared his fears, and that brought warmth to compensate for the initial wallop.

Her heart squeezed out an extra-fast beat. "No matter what or if I remember things from my past, I will never regret you. Our marriage. You're a dragon worthy of knowing. My mind wants this marriage, wants you. My body aches for you, so I guess that means I wholeheartedly approve of this union."

"Since we're adults, we are free to marry where there are no impediments."

But what if there were obstacles? The notion drifted into her mind and took root like an insidious weed. Fear galloped behind.

"If you're uncertain, we can stop. We have time," Leo said.

"No." Her reply came swift and sure. "I want to celebrate our marriage. Being close to you in this way makes me happy. I wasn't joking when I told you I ache for you. That I desperately want to make love with my husband."

"Thank you," Leo said, his tone fierce. "I didn't know what I'd do if you wished to stop. I would've honored your request, but it would've been difficult."

Gwenyth smiled and held out her arms, a silent plea for him to return to his explorations.

"Just a quick taste," he said. "I want to memorize everything about you."

His words gave her pause and raised questions, but this time she didn't voice them. The last thing she wanted was to drive him from this bed.

Leo pinched her inner thigh, sending a jolt through her. "Pay attention. I want your mind and body focused on me and my dragon." He sounded strained, as if he was exercising impressive control.

So, she'd push him and break that control until they both burned in a joyous celebration of their marriage. Doubts and hesitation, she'd kick to the curb.

Leo breathed in and out, an audible expulsion of air that heated her feminine flesh. Every part of her stood to attention. She cupped his head until his gaze met hers. "Leo, you're taking too long."

"Making memories," he said, and an instant after he uttered the explanation, his tongue journeyed down her slit.

Her entire body jolted, and pleasure licked across her flesh. One touch and she lit up like a set of fairy lights. Once again, her mind supplied the comparison without a hitch, so she went with it, accepting the knowledge and embracing it.

"Do you like that?" he whispered.

"More than anything except how I imagine you'll feel inside me."

"Don't put too much pressure on me," he said with a trace of humor. "My dragon and I might fail."

"It's possible," she conceded, trying to appear thoughtful and failing because of the smile that kept slipping free. "But I know that the second time, you'd whop butt spectacularly."

He laughed, the joyful, musical sound widening her smile.

They had a connection, she and her dragon. Her trust and confidence in him had come fast yet naturally.

His tongue slid across her clit, giving her another one of

those jolts. Prickles of pleasure sizzled through her abdomen. Anticipation and impatience had her tilting her lower body upward and silently demanding more.

His chuckle told her he knew what she was doing, but he gave her what she craved. More touches. More pressure. More of those delightful sensations. Her hands went to his hair. She twisted and tugged the locks, urging him on.

Leo's caresses were halfway between soft and hard, the perfect touch to have her soaring high and fast. A moan escaped her and another when he pushed a finger inside of her. He licked and sucked and focused on the silent hints she offered him. *Clever dragon.*

"Leo," she said, his name a mere gasp. "Please. Please. *More.*"

He withdrew his finger then pressed into her a second time, equally slow and sensual. The drag of his digit against her inner walls ignited a burn that pushed all the right buttons. This time, her moan was loud and throaty, and when he sucked on her clit, the excitement burst. She shattered under his ministrations, intense pulses tightening and releasing around his finger.

A long moment later, he pulled away and rose up her body to kiss her.

She tasted herself on his lips, along with his deeper male flavor.

"Give me more," she ordered in a throaty tone. "But this time, do it with your cock."

Leo laughed. "I'd like that."

"Now," Gwenyth said.

He kissed her once more, this time slow and with tongue. Her breath caught at the exquisite pace of the kiss, the tenderness that assailed her. This dragon. Why hadn't she met him earlier in her life?

Another memory? She released the thought to concentrate on her husband.

Leo guided his cock to her entrance and pushed home with a stroke that left her gasping. It wasn't shock. It was more the rightness of the fit and the inner knowledge she'd found her one.

Leo released a growl of his own. He rested his forehead against hers for long seconds before withdrawing to the tip and pushed back into her.

"Magical," he whispered, resting again while fully embedded. "You feel hot and tight and perfect around my cock."

"Yes," she agreed. "But believe me, I'm certain it will be even better once you are moving and hitting all the right spots. That's when the magic will change into spectacular. I adore spectacular."

"Me too," he said, and he pulled back again before thrusting into her.

Gwenyth kissed his neck and found the perfect place to suck. Marking him felt right to her. A badge of their love.

Leo set up an invade and retreat, the drag of his shaft lighting her up again.

"Leo," she cried, gripping his shoulders and this time giving the soft skin of his neck a nip.

He seemed to enjoy that because he issued a tortured groan.

"More," he urged.

So she bit him again while his thrusts grew faster and erratic. His breathing turned ragged, his scent enticing. She opened eyes she hadn't realized she'd closed and spotted the ecstasy on his dragon's expression, the way his tattoo seemed relaxed and yet tense. Gwenyth stretched a fraction so she could reach where his dragon reposed, and she pressed her lips to the spot she could touch. A harsh groan escaped Leo, and it felt as if his cock pulsed inside her. Gwenyth kissed him again before wrapping her arm around her husband and giving in to the pleasure that shone like a beacon.

Leo plunged into her one last time, and stilled, his breathing hoarse. He sought her mouth, and the heat of his lips was blistering. It seared her lips and down her throat until she wondered if she'd implode. Then the heat changed to comforting and the faint tension in her released.

Another mini-series of spasms pulsed through her sex before trailing away to leave contentment and satisfaction.

"Gwenyth," Leo murmured.

"Leo," she replied. Instinct told her what had happened between them was magical and unique. Something special that she wanted to repeat again and again. Her hand went to Leo's dragon tattoo, and she patted the dragon's head. The tattoo moved into her touch and a hum slipped from Leo.

Gwenyth grinned. Leo's dragon was plain cute.

"Are you hungry?" Leo asked.

"I could eat."

Leo levered away and rolled to his feet. He extended his hand, and she noticed Leo's tattoo looked sleepy and content. Yep, so cute. She placed her hand in Leo's. Her stomach grumbled, and they laughed together.

"I'm drooling over the pie. It smells amazing."

"We can try that first," Leo said.

"It's dessert," she protested, a tiny voice at the back of her mind shouting that eating sweets first was wrong.

"There are no guidelines for food and my wife," Leo said with a smile. "We make our own rules."

"Works for me," Gwenyth said, a distant memory still refuting the meal order. No, not her, she thought. Someone else had insisted on preciseness in everything. She plucked at the information, and while her head didn't ache this time, the facts she sought remained elusive. Her mind was healing, though, and she thought that was a splendid thing.

"Are you happy with our marriage?" he asked without warning.

Gwenyth didn't hesitate. She wrapped her arms around him and settled in to show him how much she valued their marriage. The pie could wait.

CHAPTER 10

Leonidas, You've Brought Dinner

"**H**usband, there has got to be a better way of traveling with you." Gwenyth braced her trembling knees and leaned against Leo, who was still in his dragon form. She dropped Leo's bag of clothes on the ground and dragged a hand through her tangled hair. "That was a brief flight, and it scared me silly. I didn't think the second time would bother me as much. *Wrong*."

Leo's enormous, green dragon head turned to observe her, and her own eyes narrowed. Her husband of not even a day was laughing at her.

She poked him in the ribs. "Stop laughing at me."

"Leonidas, you've brought dinner," a masculine voice boomed across the giant field where they'd landed.

Leo released an amused grunt, and Gwenyth spun to skewer the recent arrival with her glare. He stood tall—at least six inches above her height of five-foot-nine.

Huh, she remembered her height. How weird was that?

She returned to studying the man, peeved at his stupid joke. His eyes were golden brown while his nostrils flared in a manner that told her he was testing her scent. Another dragon, then. A bushy ginger beard covered his lower face, and his dragon tattoo—an orangish-red in color—cocked his head to peer at her. His chest was a gathering of splendid muscles and bared to the elements. He wore a pair of tight black trews and black leather boots.

Jenny was safe with the minister's family, and they'd promised to watch her for as long as necessary, which meant Gwenyth was *the snack* in this scenario.

She studied the new arrival's grin and planted her hands on her hips. "Ginger, did you call me dinner?"

Leo snorted, a single ring of smoke erupting from his nostrils. He rubbed his head against her arm before nudging her farther away from him. Seconds later, he stood in front of them in naked splendor. Her gaze wandered his muscled body and his...ah...*undercarriage* before she thrust the bag at him.

Leo accepted the clothes and slung his arm around her shoulders. "Well met, Felix. Meet Gwenyth. She's my wife." Pride shimmered in Leo's words, and Gwenyth's irritation faded. Her husband beamed with satisfaction. A marriage of convenience with a human who was a stranger didn't faze him.

Felix's bushy brows shot upward, his eyes widening in surprise. "Married? But I thought you're betrothed to a dragon lass from Smoking Isle."

"You heard wrong," Leo stated.

"But she's due to arrive tomorrow," Felix said. "Her and her retinue."

Gwenyth shot Leo a searching glance but remained silent, deeming it best for him to take the lead since she was unfamiliar with castle protocol.

Leo sighed. "I had no inkling. Gwenyth, we'd better face my parents. We knew this wouldn't be easy." He opened the bag. "Hold this." He thrust his clothes at Felix and tugged Gwenyth into his arms. He kissed her, heat sliding from his mouth and into hers. A faint burning sensation bled down her throat. Not painful, but different. Pleasure roared through her on the tail of this heat, so she gripped Leo's broad shoulders and enjoyed the heck out of the kiss.

Felix spoke, reminding her they had an audience.

Aghast, she jerked away from Leo, but he contained her easily. He nipped her earlobe and whispered to her. It took her long seconds to make sense of Leo's words.

"I'm marking you with my scent again, reinforcing the traces of scent already present on your skin."

Gwenyth relaxed against him, finally comprehending the reason for the public kiss.

Leo kissed her once more, breathing more of that enticing heat into her before pulling back.

"I take it you're ready for your clothes now," Felix said in amusement.

"Please." Leo drew his black trews over his erection.

Gwenyth blushed on catching Felix's gaze. He winked at her, and the heat in her cheeks increased.

"Where did you meet your human?"

"I rescued her from the sea," Leo said without hesitation.

"I need to do more flying around the coast," Felix shared with her, his grin big and white. "How come I've never seen a beautiful lass during my flights? When did you marry? You never mentioned it last time I saw you."

Leo finished buttoning his shirt. "It's a recent thing."

Felix's eyes narrowed. "Your parents will question your timing."

"Too bad," Leo said emphatically.

Gwenyth allowed Leo to guide her from the training field toward the castle portcullis. Apprehension filtered through her when they crossed a moat and strolled beneath a fortified gate complete with gleaming spikes. Workers bustled around the courtyard beyond, and within seconds, the weight of stares brought a prickling discomfort. Ignoring them, she picked her way around a muddy puddle and wrinkled her nose at the blast of body odor.

Leo didn't stop to speak to anyone, instead continuing into a second courtyard, past a small chapel with a stained window. Their surroundings grew quieter and much cleaner, and she risked a full lungful of air.

"Stay close to me," Leo murmured as he led her up a marble staircase and through an impressive entrance with vaulted ceilings and gleaming floors. They climbed another set of cream and brown stairs, and Leo directed her along an equally impressive passage. Light sparkled off a chandelier hanging from the high ceiling and left dappled patterns on the tiled stone floor. As they passed open doors, Gwenyth received impressions of lavish rooms with expensive furnishings and paintings of men and women—perhaps dragons—who gazed down from the walls. Each bore a disapproving expression as if they knew she was a human and inferior and therefore had no business entering this castle.

Gwenyth had no right to Leo.

A tremor shook her fingers, and she curled her left hand to a fist to halt the show of nerves. Her heart palpitated, her breaths short and choppy while it felt as though sand filled her mouth. Repeated swallows failed to shift the dryness.

They walked for what seemed like hours but was probably ten minutes. The nerves dancing at the bottom of her tummy heightened her apprehension and exaggerated every worry. With Leo at her side, no harm would befall her.

She was safe.

He'd make it so. Of this, she was confident. *But he is one dragon among many*, a tiny voice whispered. Fear darted off, screaming through her until the horrified shout reached every nook of her mind. What if marriage to her ended in death for Leo?

"Don't worry." Leo grasped her right hand in a comforting squeeze. "Everything will be all right. We'll inform my parents of our marriage and leave. I have friends who will give us a roof for the night. Tomorrow, we'll fly to Perfume Isle and start our quest for the truth."

"I'm so nervous. What if they act first and don't listen to our explanations? All they need to do is embrace their dragon and breathe fire over me. I'll be toast before I can blink." Her voice took on an edge of hysteria while trepidation embraced her like a lumpy shawl on her shoulders. *This is ridiculous. Get a grip, woman.*

Leo laughed, amusement sparkling in his gaze. "That will never happen. No dragon breathes fire within the castle. We're a civilized race. We no longer allow our tempers or our dragons to fight whenever the instinct roars at us."

She lifted a brow, her gaze on him as she sought his reassurance. "No fire?"

"Not indoors. The last thing my parents wish is to destroy the home they and my ancestors have protected and beautified over the centuries. Damage of that sort would invite ridicule from their friends and acquaintances and destroy their standing within the community."

"Oh." Gwenyth sucked in a breath and let it ease out again. She was a ninny, bringing out her judgey hat. Just because they could morph into massive creatures in a blink of her eyes and blow fire, it didn't mean every dragon she encountered would attack. From what she'd learned so far, the dragon society was as old as the human one. Civilized. They had rules. Laws. "You're right. I'm sorry for acting so stupid."

Leo's fingers tightened on hers. "You're shaking. The worst thing you can do is let my parents witness your fear. Don't worry, my lodestone. Everything will be all right." Confidence rippled in his voice, his relaxed demeanor.

I hope he's right.

Leo guided her around a corner, and the first thing she noticed was the guard. The man—dragon, she presumed—stood taller than Leo while his scarlet tunic strained to contain his muscled bulk. A sword in a decorative silver hilt sat at his right-hand side, although she guessed it was more a statement than the guard's go-to weapon. The tension swelling inside her had a tremor rushing down her spine. Fear got ready to give a shout-out to the rest of her body, and she sucked in a fast, calming breath.

"Steady." Leo stopped and turned Gwenyth to face him. Tenderness shone in his face as he placed his hands on her shoulders. The corners of his eyes crinkled again, and she relaxed. "Gwenyth." He leaned in to steal a kiss. She stiffened when their lips met, then he licked the seam of her mouth, and passion roared to life in her. Her own hands lifted to clutch his biceps and draw him closer. A moan sounded, echoing down the passage.

Leo parted their mouths and pressed his forehead to hers for a long moment. "You can do this," he whispered. "We're married, and I can't wait to get to my room to celebrate in private."

"Me, too." Embarrassment emblazoned Gwenyth's cheeks, but she straightened and thrust back her shoulders at the faint dare in his gaze while ignoring her instinct to glance at the guard. "No pressure."

Leo offered her an encouraging smile and a nod of approval before he grasped her hand and led her toward the guarded doorway.

The dragon guard stiffened at their appearance, his hand going to the butt of his sword. His dark brown gaze roved them.

"Please tell my parents their youngest son Leonidas, Champion of the Skies, is here to see them," Leo ordered, donning an arrogant facade.

The guard relaxed at Leo's words, although his hand remained close to his sword.

Leo drew Gwenyth to a halt and appeared relaxed. His grip on her hand grew tighter, but she didn't complain. From the little he'd told her about his parents, they sounded scary and heartless, and she wondered how Leo had grown up to be such a decent man.

Another man appeared in the doorway. A familiar one. Telus, the snooty butler. Surprise flitted across the butler's face before cunning and haughtiness replaced his shock.

"Your parents are busy. They are preparing for your betrothed," Telus said, his long nose twitching with distaste as his gaze skimmed Gwenyth. "What is your bit on the side doing here? The castle is no place for a human."

"Telus, I would speak with my parents now," Leo said in an implacable tone. "Not later. Not tomorrow. Now."

Telus blinked, or at least she thought he did. His surprise faded beneath his concrete expression as he focused on Leo. "Your parents have enough to deal with at present. There is much to organize and contracts to complete. A betrothal is a delicate business and yours more so because of your parents' standing."

"Now, Telus." Leo advanced half a step to underscore his determination.

The guard tensed.

Telus sniffed and nodded curtly at the guard. "Very well. I shall ask if they wish to see you. Wait here." He marched away, his officious manner tickling Gwenyth's funny bone, despite the situation.

"Is he always like that?" she whispered to Leo. "He behaves as if he has a stick up his arse."

Leo snorted out a laugh. "His position holds significant prestige.

He won the position coveted by eleven other dragons."

"I see," Gwenyth said, although that was an overstatement. This world of Leo's was strange, and she'd felt far more comfortable with the minister and his wife.

She and Leo waited for a long five minutes.

"Do you think he's coming back? He wouldn't leave us here to make a point?"

"That's his style," Leo said. "Let's go."

He tugged her toward the open doorway. The soldier's hand tightened on his sword hilt.

"Don't," Leo advised him. "These are my parents. I won't harm them."

"There are rumors of someone wanting to take over the castle. To steal from your parents," the soldier, his voice full of thick gravel and bass.

"I have my property and have no intention of challenging for the castle. My older brothers are a different story, however. Watch them. Let us pass." Leo's implacable gaze bored into the dragon soldier, determination and strength emanating in a silent contest.

"Very well." He raked them with his gaze. "But if you injure Tudoarreo or Qille, I will make it my mission to hunt you."

"Fair enough," Leo said. "Come, Gwenyth. Let us greet my parents."

Gwenyth let Leo lead her into the room. Like the others they'd passed, this one was full of elegant statues, furnishings in luxurious silks of jeweled colors, and dozens of portraits and paintings hung on the walls.

One of a beautiful seascape drew her attention. The artist had captured a day of fun, but instead of humans, he or she had included dragons lounging on the sand, making the canvas appear whimsical to her eye.

Six chairs in a dramatic black-and-white formed a seating area around an enormous stone fireplace while drapes of a rich, lustrous ruby-red velvet framed floor-to-ceiling windows. A person could get lost in that fireplace. Gwenyth closed her gaping mouth.

"I told you to wait," Telus's voice boomed across the distance separating them.

"We don't have all day." Leo's face remained impassive, but a muscle twitching in his jaw told Gwenyth of her husband's fury.

"Gwenyth and I have things to do. Mother. Father." He offered his parents a respectful nod.

Gwenyth studied his parents. Both appeared young, not much older than Leo. Perhaps shifters aged slower than humans. She'd have to ask later.

His mother rose, as did his father. They were both tall like Leo. Unlike Leo, the garments they wore were of top quality. Gwenyth felt scruffy in her oversized black trews and baggy shirt, both handoffs from Leo.

"What is so important that you must interrupt our meeting?" Leo's mother asked. Her chin rose, her nostrils flaring as she glowered at Leo. After her first glance of distaste, she ignored Gwenyth.

"I'd like to introduce Gwenyth," Leo said in an even tone. "She is my wife."

Leo's parents stared at him, and his father laughed.

"Stop joking around, boy. You would have us believe you have married a human?"

"Gwenyth is my beloved wife," Leo repeated. "Telus knows this. Gwenyth told him the day he delivered your summons. Did he not divulge this information? You never gave me a chance to tell you about Gwenyth. As you can see, we are married." He lifted Gwenyth's hand to show them the ring he'd made himself and gifted to her to celebrate their marriage.

"You gave her a Marquess ring?" his mother demanded, her voice edging toward shrill.

"My Gwenyth is worth the price of an expensive ring," Leo replied. "She deserves much more."

"How could you afford a ring of this quality?" his father scoffed.

The frown broke on his mother's face. "It's a fake," she crowed.

Anger built in Gwenyth. She hadn't believed his parents were as awful as he'd described, but they were worse. She glanced at Leo but had trouble reading him. Although, he'd stiffened at the insult.

"I assure you this is a Marquess. I have the paperwork for the piece," Leo stated.

"Marriage to a human is impossible," his mother snapped. "We dragons do not marry humans. We take them and use them as they have destroyed us in the past. We fuck them for pleasure, but we do not join them in matrimony. Prove you're married."

"Don't bother," his father said in a snooty voice. "I don't care what you say. The betrothal to Nandag will proceed, and that is an end to it. Nan and her people arrive tomorrow to sign the official contract. The wedding will take place on the following weekend."

Gwenyth frowned. Leo had told her the betrothal and the marriage took up to a year. This seemed uncommonly quick. What was the hurry?

Leo was correct to suspect his parents' actions. Their plan reeked to high heavens.

"I am legally married to Gwenyth. I love her and do not wish to have another wife. Gwenyth is my other half."

His father puffed up, his shoulders expanding until his garments strained at the seams. A ring of smoke exited his flared nostrils. "The old tales of soulmates are rubbish. There is no such thing as a soulmate. I thought we knocked that nonsense out of you years ago."

Gwenyth had difficulty standing her ground and masking the fear that flashed through her. Leo's parents were scary. Their uncaring attitudes didn't signal reasonable or a willingness to listen to a convincing argument.

"This is not a discussion, Leonidas," his mother snapped. "We're not stupid. You married this human to place a barrier in our way. You have always been a tiresome child. Nothing like your brothers."

"Why must Leo marry Nan, The Strongminded?" Gwenyth blurted. "Why can't one of his older brothers get betrothed to her?"

"You dare to speak to our rulers?" Telus thundered.

Gwenyth froze, wishing she hadn't inserted herself into the conversation. She quivered, and Leo placed his arm around her waist. He drew her closer until their bodies touched. She took comfort from his proximity and pressed her lips together, so she didn't repeat her mistake.

"Gwenyth raises an excellent point. None of my older brothers are wed. Offer one of them as a match with Nan. Why does it have to be me?"

"Tudoarreo, The Dragon Lord, and Qille, The Taker of Life, do not answer to you," Telus thundered. "They are the absolute power in this castle, and your betrothal is their choice to make."

Leo's mother gave a contemptuous sniff. "Telus has the right of it. We make the decisions. Everyone follows our rules."

"I do not live here," Leo snapped. Neither his parents nor Telus deflated Leo's courage. "I have not lived at the castle for years."

"No, you prefer to dig in the dirt, despite your advantages," his father snarled. "You bring shame to our clan. Others laugh at your common activities. But runt, in this, you will follow our directive. You will sign the betrothal papers and you will marry Nan, The

Strongminded. The deal is struck, and nothing you do or say will make me change my mind. Are you clear?"

"Tell me why it must be me," Leo said, his voice cold and unfriendly. "You and Mother never pay me any mind unless you want something. Why must I align myself with Nan? Does her clan have something over you?" He pinned his parents with a determined gaze.

Gwenyth felt the exact moment when something clicked for him. Every muscle in his body tensed, and he seemed to go on alert.

"What have my brothers done? Which one has created trouble? You can't expect me to clean up the mess."

"The reasons are none of your concern," his father declared with regal hauteur. "You will follow our orders. Nan is a reasonable female. You can keep your human pet, although how you can bear to sully yourself with her. A weakling, she brings no advantages to your connection."

Indignation rose in Gwenyth. She might be human, but she was not weak. She was decent and hardworking and never shirked her responsibilities. A protestation struggled for release, but she bit her bottom lip to keep her words restrained. It was best to remain silent since she had no knowledge of castle life. The customs and hierarchy of dragons were beyond her. Although Leo had shared a little, there hadn't been enough time for in-depth explanations.

"Come, Gwenyth," Leo murmured.

"Nan arrives on the morrow," his mother called after them. "You will attend the welcoming ball."

Leo ignored his mother and kept walking. His arm was a heavy band around Gwenyth's waist, his inner tension communicating his anger at his parents. He hustled her from the room and down another passage she hadn't noticed earlier before he opened a door and urged her inside.

"Leo, this isn't—"

"Shush." Leo strode to a double door that led to a balcony. "We'll talk once we get outside and are among friends. I don't trust anyone here."

She nodded her compliance.

Leo disrobed and handed her his clothes. "Hold these. It's a quick hop to the battlefield."

She watched in fascination while Leo shifted. The transformation happened so fast she didn't get to appreciate his strong physique. His muscles. A shiver swept her and this time it had nothing to do with fear. She adored Leo. And after their wonderful time at the beach, she lusted after his powerful body.

Leo turned to face her, and a grin—no, a smirk—settled into place on his dragon features.

Gwenyth wrinkled her nose. "You promise it's a brief flight time. Right?"

"We'll arrive at our destination in mere minutes."

"Well, in that case, I can deal. I might even try to keep my eyes open this time." Then she shuddered. "Not my mouth though. I prefer to enjoy my protein."

"Our mate shows bravery," Leo's dragon said. *"Our parents were worse than usual."*

"Yes." Leo placed his talon around Gwenyth and flapped his wings to lift them into the air. They flew straight to the battlegrounds. When he landed, his old friend hailed him. Leo shifted to human form and accepted his clothes from Gwenyth.

"The castle is huge," she said, and awe shimmered in her eyes. "I can't imagine growing up here."

Leo scanned the sprawling honey-gold monstrosity with its towers and fortifications. "The best thing about the castle was the sheer number of places to hide from my three brothers."

Another of his friends, Jakab, strolled over to join them. A big dragon, he stood half a head taller than Leo. With his flowing jet-black hair, bulky body, and scarred face, the dragon intimidated some. Leo was curious how Gwenyth would react to his friend and in his friend's response to Gwenyth.

"Gwenyth, this is my friend, Jakab. We trained together, and now he trains younger dragons to battle."

"I'm glad to meet a friend of Leo's," Gwenyth said and extended her hand.

Leo grinned inwardly and wondered what his friend would do at the human action.

Jakab stared for an instant before taking her delicate hand in his enormous paw. "Great to meet you." His gaze caught on the ring Leo had given Gwenyth. "You're wed?"

Leo grinned, awe and pleasure winding through him. His dragon's hearty sigh echoed his satisfaction. "We are."

"Felix told me you went to see your parents. How did the meeting go?" Jakab asked. "You saw them?"

"We did, and our meeting went as I expected. They ordered me to set aside Gwenyth and treat her as my bit on the side."

A huff escaped Gwenyth, and Jakab sent her a sympathetic glance before he turned back to Leo. "What will you do?"

"First, I need to catch up on the castle gossip. Something is going on in the background. My parents have secrets, and they don't wish me to know the reasons for this hasty betrothal. Have you heard anything?"

"Nothing that might force a betrothal," Jakab said. "I'll keep my ears open, but if there are whispers, they're not making it to me. Have you visited the kitchens yet? Cook hears all the gossip."

"I'll do that," Leo agreed. "Cook will want to meet Gwenyth."

Jakab grinned. "Now, I know you're serious about your marriage to your human."

"Yes," Leo acknowledged and reached for Gwenyth. "My dragon and I agree."

"Oh yes, we are sincere," his dragon cooed. *"Tonight, we'll feast on each other. I cannot wait to taste her again."*

"If Gwenyth wishes the same," Leo cautioned along their private channel. *"I refuse to force her to do anything against her will."*

"She likes us in return. She stroked me so gooood."

Leo bit back his groan of agreement to concentrate on his friend.

"What is your next move?" Jakab asked.

"We require information." He scanned their surroundings and saw the other dragons were ignoring them, each of the five trainees busy with the exercises Jakab enjoyed setting to increase fitness levels.

"Have you heard any rumors regarding a break in the Dragon Isle's protective barrier?"

Jakab gaped enough for Leo to view sharp, white teeth. He shook his head and burst out laughing. "You jest."

"No," Leo said, his tone grim as he lowered his voice. "The last time I visited the castle, I left in a temper. Instead of returning home as I'd intended, I gave in to impulse and went for a flight across the sea. The barrier wasn't present, and I spied the mainland. That's how I met Gwenyth. I snatched her from the sea, and we barely made it back to our world. The barrier didn't snap into place immediately. It was like flying through thick soup. Once I forced my way through, the barrier was present, and the mainland invisible again."

"Where was this?" Jakab asked. "I fly parallel to the barrier most days and have never noticed what you describe." His gaze sharpened. "When was this? What time?"

"Three days ago, in the afternoon."

"Most of my training flights are in the morning. No one else has mentioned this. I've not heard rumors of a failing barrier. What do you think it means?"

"Could mean many things. Gwenyth and I will travel to Perfume Isle. I'll speak to our friends there and ask them if they've seen or heard anything."

"Your parents have paid the tithe to the druids?" Jakab asked, his hard frown making the bottom of his scar shift a fraction. "Could they have money problems? I see no signs of cost-cutting."

Leo shrugged. "I try not to spend much time at the castle. My family and the other inhabitants and hangers-on are a nest of vipers. I prefer fresh air, open skies and land, and choosing my way in the world."

"Likewise, brother," Jakab said. "I enjoy training dragons for battle, yet more and more, I dream of living a simpler life without all the bloody politics and jealousy that finds its way into my world. Do you intend to enter the next titanic battle?"

"I was going to," Leo said. "But now that Gwenyth is part of my life, I'm undecided." He smiled at Gwenyth, who'd been standing at his side, listening to their conversation. "I thought to discuss the pros and cons with Gwenyth before I made my final decision."

"Retire as a champion," Jakab said.

"Exactly."

"Back to the other, I'll make discreet inquiries. I might vary the times of my training flights too."

"Take care," Leo said. "Getting trapped on the other side might end up disastrous."

"I will heed your warning," Jakab said. "When do you leave?"

"As soon as I've spoken to Saffron about a better way to transport Gwenyth. She is not fond of flying clutched in my talons."

"I've been thinking about that," Gwenyth said. "All I require is goggles to keep the wind and the insects from my eyes. I can tie back my hair and wrap a scarf around my face to keep the bugs at bay."

Jakab cocked his head and considered Gwenyth. "Remember the fight where Chancery injured his head? The saw-tooth made him wear a helmet. I think it's still in the storage room. Gwenyth is smaller, but maybe we can adjust it to fit her needs."

"Would that work for you, my lodestone?" Leo asked.

"Anything is worth a try," Gwenyth said. "I don't understand why the bugs don't bother you."

"They do," Leo said. "But they seldom bite us because they have difficulty getting through our scales. Also, we fly higher where it's cooler with few bugs. I didn't want you to freeze."

"I could wear a thicker coat and perhaps gloves to keep my hands from freezing. Let's try the helmet combined with more clothes.

How long did you say the trip to Perfume Isle would take?"

"A minimum of two hours," Leo said. "It depends on the weather and wind levels. Sometimes, the trip takes longer."

"Is there somewhere I can purchase gloves and a warm coat?" Gwenyth asked.

"The coat should be easy," Leo said. "We might have to improvise until we can get gloves made to fit your hands."

"That's fine. I think that will—" Gwenyth broke off, her eyes going wide. "Who are they?"

Jakab and Leo shifted position for a better view.

Leo stiffened. "Soldiers."

"This is bad," Jakab murmured. "They're heading in this direction."

The group of ten soldiers marched toward them without hesitation. Their scarlet uniforms drew the eye and denoted their training and positions within the castle guards. These soldiers were his parents' guards.

The troop halted in front of them, and one soldier stepped out of line. He opened a coiled message and started reading in a pompous voice.

"Gwenyth, The Weak Human. I charge you with enticing Leo, The Younger Son, and distracting him from his formal duties. By order of Qille, The Taker of Life, you will be imprisoned, pending a public trial. Take her," he snapped to a soldier.

"No!" Leo roared. His dragon burst from him, his clothes

ripping at the seams. Before his change finished, a dart pierced his skin. The immediate numbness of the fast-acting drug had Leo staggering and collapsing. "Gwenyth," he cried, struggling to get to her side, crawling.

He was vaguely aware of Jakab's attempts to help, but the soldiers fired at his friend too. Jakab thumped to the ground beside him as darkness swooped at Leo's mind. His bloody parents. A fishy stench clung to the castle, and his parents were at the center. Leo fought the weakness of his limbs, strained to climb to his feet.

Gwenyth cried out, and even drugged and almost unconscious, Leo heard the terror in her scream.

"Gwenyth," he shouted, but the words emerged as an unintelligible croak. His eyelids grew heavy even as he continued his fight. Beside him, Jakab attempted to rise. His friend toppled back with a mighty thump. Leo groaned again. His parents had bested him this time.

There wouldn't be a next time.

He was done.

Once he discovered their scheme, he'd foil them. He'd seize their precious control and power. Leo might fill the position of the youngest son, but he'd become successful in his own right. The minute the drug released its grip on him, he'd rescue Gwenyth, and they'd leave this cursed castle. This was the last time his parents would use him to further their own ends.

The absolute last time.

CHAPTER 11

Things Take A Bad Turn

A dragon soldier snapped cuffs on her wrists, and once he'd adjusted the size to fit, he forced her away from Leo and Jakab.

"Move, human," he ordered.

Gwenyth didn't have to search his face to understand he'd enjoy applying more force. His satisfied expression told her he'd savor the physical violence. She trudged in the direction he shoved her, every part of her screaming for Leo. She craned her head, and tears filmed her vision on seeing Leo and Jakab lying on the field. Four dragons hovered in the air above the battlefield, the group of scarlet-clad soldiers having attracted their attention. Not one interfered with the soldiers, but once she and her captors left the grassy area, the dragons landed beside Leo and his friend to render aid.

Her breath eased out. They'd be okay. Their friends and fellow-dragons would look after them.

She was the one who faced danger.

Popsicles.

The word jumped into her mind when she'd rather have bitten off a robust mouth-pleasing curse. Instead, she remained silent and paid attention to her surroundings. The soldiers were heading toward the arched entrance at the front of the castle and the raised gate with myriad spikes. This was a nightmare.

Given what Leo had told her about his parents and what she'd witnessed, she should've expected a flat rejection of Leo's marriage. Their faces. They'd acted so icily toward Leo and treated him like a possession rather than a beloved son. Was that the dragon way? She had no idea, but given Leo's sweetness and determined protectiveness, she'd assumed his parents possessed a smidgeon of honor.

The soldiers marched into the vast courtyard that lay beyond the entrance. Other men filled the area, and from what she saw, she assumed they were training. Some fought with swords while another group pummeled each other with their bare fists. Those not fighting stood around, laughing and joking and critiquing performances. The scent of ash and body odor still perfumed the air.

The two soldiers striding beside her wheeled left and directed her into a dim-lit corridor. Each of the doors contained a barred window, and a few held prisoners since she saw them peering at her. One issued a sharp wolf-whistle and shouted an obscene comment that had heat crowding into her cheeks. *Eew!* A shudder of distaste rippled through her.

"She can share my cell," another shouted, cupping his groin as they passed.

Holy Hannah. Would they do that to her? Force her to share a cell with a strange man? Surely they wouldn't be that cruel.

When they reached the end of the corridor, a soldier opened a door. She started as a rat scuttled in front of them and disappeared through a crack in the wall. The soldiers didn't flinch. They escorted her through and down a set of steps into another hall. The prisoners' raucous cries were even more disturbing, and an icy wave prickled over her skin, leaving chill bumps in its wake.

She prayed even harder they didn't intend to make her share a cell.

The dragon prison was many levels deep and increasingly darker and colder. Fear and panic played with her mind, and begging words bubbled up, pushing for freedom. Luckily, the knot in her throat prevented them from spilling free. However, a croak of dismay escaped, and one soldier laughed.

"Wouldn't want to be in your shoes, human," he said.

They kept marching onward, and she and the soldiers strode

along another two corridors before her captors halted outside a door. A tall soldier opened it with a huge key—the sort one might see in an old movie or read about in a book. Gwenyth pushed at the thought, and her head throbbed, so she backed off.

The hinges on the door squeaked as it opened.

"In you go," one soldier shunted her through the doorway.

It was like entering a black hole. Somewhere in that darkness, water trickled from the ceiling, the steady *drip-drip-drip* bringing to mind dungeons in drafty castles. Oh, wait. This was a dungeon in a drafty castle.

"What have I done to deserve this?" The words burst from her, distinct this time.

Sympathy etched into one guard's face, but he didn't speak.

The other guard said, "Don't know. Don't care, human. We're following orders." He pushed her another two steps, backed up, and slammed the cell door shut. The key turned in the door with a scraping click.

"Wait! Don't leave me here."

The soldiers ignored her plea, the click of their boots on the stone floor receding. In the distance, a door opened. A few seconds later, it slammed, and Gwenyth pressed her forehead against the icy steel bars of the solitary window in her prison.

"Leo will find me," she murmured, the sound of her voice bringing minor comfort. The truth rattled in her brain, pressing against her temples in a pounding ache. How would Leo find her?

Her shoulders slumped.

That was if Leo recovered enough to realize the soldiers had taken her.

"Hey, human."

The quiet voice had her stiffening. Compared to the other prisoners they'd passed, he sounded normal. Gwenyth hesitated to respond. It behooved her to use caution and not trust anyone.

She bit her lip, wondering if she should reply before curiosity got the better of her. "Yes?"

"Why did they toss you in the dungeon?"

She considered and decided there was no reason not to tell the truth. "I married Leonidas, Champion of the Skies."

There was silence before the man barked out a laugh of genuine amusement.

"Yeah, that would do it. I doubt Tudoarreo, The Dragon Lord, and Qille, The Taker of Life, would accept their son's marriage to a human."

"How do you know I'm a human?"

"I can smell it on you."

"Oh."

"How did you meet the youngest son?"

"At the human village," Gwenyth lied.

"I've heard he does business with the humans and helps them if they require aid."

"What are Leo's older brothers like? Have you met them?"

Talking to the stranger, even if it was through a prison wall, helped to regain her equilibrium. Besides, her father always said information was power. He—

A gasp emerged, and she tentatively tugged the info that had popped into her mind unbidden. As usual, pushing and pulling to free the memory resulted in the recollection dissipating like Leo's smoke. Frustration brought misery, and she tapped her forehead against the bars three times. Each tap was progressively harder, but the outer pain jogged nothing free. She sighed. "Are you still there? Do you know Leo's brothers?"

"I know them." Bitterness surged in his tone.

Gwenyth caught her breath, waiting for more.

"They used to be my friends. We grew up on different islands, but our families visited often. Played together. Created mischief and mayhem."

"And then?"

"They took things too far. They raped a girl. The three of them with two of our other friends. I tried to stop them, but I was one against five drunken dragons."

"What happened?" Gwenyth asked.

"The girl committed suicide."

"You ended up in the dungeon?"

"The five ganged up together and accused me of the crime. I told the truth, but it was my word against theirs. The three oldest sons of the clan rulers plus two dragons of equally highborn parents. I never stood a chance."

Gwenyth got a sense of where this was going, but she asked anyway. "Who are your parents?"

"My father is highborn but lacks the standing of Leo and his brothers. My family is not as wealthy. Father is a scholar and teaches while my mother ran our pottery business. As part of his employment package, I received a decent education. My father thought the opportunity might help me advance and make valuable contacts."

"I see."

The man sighed. "I never had much to do with Leo since there is a seven-year age gap between him and his next oldest brother. I know his brothers teased Leo. Their mischief often tipped over into bullying. I hear whenever Leo didn't have lessons, he made himself scarce. No one knew where he went or what he did. His brothers didn't care."

"I know little of Leo's life. Only that he hates visiting the castle and prefers to live at his home rather than spend time with his family."

"I don't blame him. After a time, Leo left Hissing Isle and lived on another island. It shocked everyone when he returned and entered the annual battle. His brothers laughed and placed bets on him losing in the first round. The ultimate battle was something to behold. The current champion wore his arrogance close to the surface. He couldn't believe Leo dared to challenge him for his title." The man laughed, a deep bark of amusement. "Leo didn't muck around. He fought to win. That was three years ago now."

"His brothers don't bully him any longer," Gwenyth said.

"Not that I've heard. It was after the champion battle that I ended up in the dungeon."

Appalled, she said, "You've been here for three years?"

"Almost."

"They must feed you then."

"When they remember. A word of warning, no matter how hungry you are, try your food with caution. The guards find it amusing to add extra salt to make the prisoners thirsty, then they deprive us of water. Treat everyone with suspicion."

"Even you?"

"Especially me. I might spin you a lie."

"Why would you do that? I'm no threat to you."

"To gain your sympathy. From what I know of Leonidas, he will protest your imprisonment."

Leo would fight for her. The knowledge brought comfort.

"Do they let us out to exercise?"

He made a scoffing sound. "What do you think this is? A treat for the well-behaved and favored? I keep myself sane by exercising several times a day."

"Do they kill prisoners?"

He hesitated, and everything inside her pulled tight. Gwenyth wished she hadn't asked.

"Yes."

No sugarcoating his answer. "What is your name?"

"Martinos."

"Are you a dragon?"

"Yes."

"Can't you use your dragon to escape? Use your flames or something similar?"

"Such the innocent," Martinos mocked. "I wear a druid-made bracelet that keeps my dragon trapped. Without a druid's aid, I cannot remove the bracelet, short of chopping off my arm."

"That would be drastic."

"Yes. You didn't tell me your name."

"Gwenyth." As she said the name, it felt wrong, yet no alternative presented itself.

"Well, fair Gwenyth. I can't say I'm sorry to have someone to talk to. It gets lonely down here."

"What about the others in the cells?"

"They're on the upper levels, but this is the original dungeon. I've been the lone prisoner here for the last year."

"Oh." Gwenyth wondered how he remained sane. The prospect of staying here even one day filled her with trepidation. "How do you keep yourself sane?"

"Who said I was? According to those who put me here, I am a psychopath and capable of great cruelty."

"Are you?"

He issued another of those humorless laughs. "Wait and see."

"Apart from exercises, what do you do? It's so dark down here."

"You get used to the darkness," he said in a matter-of-fact tone. "Your eyes will adjust."

She hoped so. One light shone from the far wall—probably enough light for the guards to carry out their duties.

Martinos described his day. "Exercise comes first. If I ever get the chance to leave or fate allows me to escape, I want to seize the opportunity. Back when I was a free dragon, I used to paint. I'd made a name for myself and had a small shop. I specialized in portraits, but I also enjoy—enjoyed—painting scenery."

"When Leo and I walked through the castle to meet his parents, I noticed a large number of portraits. Most of those depicted seemed dour and disapproving."

She received another forced laugh from Martinos.

"I always thought so. I liked to paint mine with unique expressions. Some laughed while others held mysterious smiles. Some were serious and others thoughtful. It depended on their occupation or station in life as to how I tried to portray them."

"That makes sense. They should've hired you to improve on the portraits in the castle. I was half tempted to find a marker pen and do my own alterations."

"A crime," he barked. "One that would land you in the dungeon."

She fell silent at that. Her single transgression had been to meet

Leo and start falling for him, to agree to marry him. She hoped he was okay. His friends had watched what went down and had been moving to help Leo once the soldiers left.

"Has anyone ever escaped from the dungeon?"

"No," Martinos said without hesitation.

"There's always a first time." Gwenyth explored her prison. The room was the size of a bathroom. Enough room to lie down and attempt to sleep. Enough room to pace. Enough room to exercise—if she followed Martinos's advice. The walls consisted of solid rock. Her fingers ran over the rough, damp surface. A few stones held cracks, but not enough to allow a prisoner to escape. She scuffed her right foot and tripped over something on the ground. Not in time to catch herself, she shot off-balance, striking her knees on the rough cobbles. Gwenyth grunted, and tears shrouded her vision.

"You all right?"

"Tripped over the bed. You didn't think to tell me it was there?"

Martinos barked out another of his emotionless laughs. "Not your keeper."

She bit back another retort and pushed herself to her feet. Wetness dribbled down her leg. Blood, she assumed. She could feel it beneath her trews. Probably lucky she had a layer of fabric between her skin and the hard floor. She might have injured herself worse. As it was, she'd need to take care not to get an infection while in this hellhole.

"Anything else in here, I shouldn't trip over?" She'd thought her eyes had adjusted enough to see. Obviously not.

"Chamber pot. You'll want to keep that intact." Amusement sounded in his rough voice.

Gwenyth pulled a face. "Do the soldiers empty them?"

"Nope. There's a drain somewhere in your cell. Mine is underneath the bed."

Her eyes rolled. "This keeps getting better."

It was time for escape plan A. If that failed, she'd move on to plan B because the thought of remaining in this damp, cold cage was inconceivable.

CHAPTER 12

Big, Big Trouble

L eo came to slowly, his eyes flickering at the bright light shining in his face. He groaned, his mouth dry as he tried to recall how he came to be in this position.

"He's awake," someone said.

Leo didn't recognize the dragon's voice.

"Leo."

Another voice he *did* recognize.

"Jakab?" Leo pushed upright, and instead of the usual fluidity of his muscles, each part of his upper body groaned a sullen protest. He rubbed the back of his head, his fingers locating a lump. "What happened?"

"Your bloody family happened," Jakab snarled, his usually calm friend agitated and out of sorts.

Leo stiffened. "Where is Gwenyth?"

"They took her," the stranger said. He circled to a position where Leo could see him without straining his neck.

A younger dragon, and one he hadn't met before. One of Jakab's students.

"Tell me what happened," Leo said, his mind fuzzy.

"They shot you with a dart. Drugged you."

"Two darts," another student said as he joined his friend.

"That's why you've recovered slower than Jakab."

"Once they'd subdued you and Jakab, they escorted the woman to the dungeons."

"My bloody parents," Leo said. "I underestimated them. I thought Gwenyth would be safe with me. If they kill her, so help me." His hands curled to fists. "I'll visit them. Demand they release her."

"No," Jakab said. "Stay away from your parents. If they realize how much you care for her, they might issue a kill order."

A chill struck Leo as he considered his friend's declaration. Would his parents kill an innocent human? They hadn't before, although they'd ordered soldiers to run humans and lower dragons out of the castle. Killing a human... He paused, his brow wrinkling while he cast back his mind. He wasn't positive since his parents typically ignored him. His older brothers might have a better idea.

Not that facing them was more palatable than approaching his parents.

"Does anyone have a clue of why my parents want me to wed Nandag, The Strongminded? I don't understand why they're so determined on the betrothal. Why not one of my older brothers? They have far greater standing than me. The three of them live at the castle and involve themselves in various family money-making enterprises. That's the part of this that surprises me."

Jakab stroked his nose. "That's the thing. I've heard nothing. No gossip. No rumors. No speculation. I'm aware they're planning a ball, but the purpose never reached me. My sister works in the kitchen. She told me Telus informed them visitors were arriving. The butler issued each department with a list of duties and the various functions they were to prepare for. Secrecy surrounds Nan's visit."

Leo eyed the younger dragons who were loitering and eavesdropping on their conversation. He drew Jakab farther away. "This smacks of blackmail. That's the one reason that might force my parents to act in this manner."

Jakab tapped his chin. "Either that or Nan and her family have something your parents covet."

"I wonder if my brothers are involved," Leo mused. "The reasons don't matter. If I don't prize Gwenyth from the dungeon, our marriage won't mean a thing."

"You care for her."

"She is my mate, Jakab." Leo didn't explain further since he wanted Jakab to believe the bond between Leo and Gwenyth was solid. The last thing he needed was for everyone to discover their marriage was fresh, and their relationship tenuous.

Jakab stared at him, the gold of his dragon displayed in his widened eyes. "I thought mates were tales our elders told to make us careful in choosing a partner. A fallacy like pink unicorns."

"It's hard to explain. She fascinates my dragon half, and we both experienced the solid click inside when we first met Gwenyth. If we're with her, the world is better. Brighter." His brow wrinkled. "I sound like a sap but having Gwenyth at my side is pure magic."

"I heard mates can speak with each other via thought. That will help." Excitement flashed through Jakab, and he eyed Leo in clear anticipation.

"I've tried to communicate," Leo said. "My dragon and I hear nothing but silence."

Jakab scratched his chin. "Perhaps it's because she's a human."

"Or it might be the distance between us. None of the tales I heard about mates explained the finer details. We were given broad strokes."

"True. What are you going to do?"

"I'll visit the kitchen and the other castle departments where I have allies. Ask questions and gather information to come up with a viable plan."

"And if that fails?"

Leo straightened his shoulders. "If that fails, I'll rally an army and attack. I *will* get my wife back."

"And if anyone harms her, we'll tear them limb from limb." His dragon emphasized his thought with three rapid puffs of smoke.

Jakab barked out a laugh. "I take it your dragon is exerting his opinion."

"He is. I must go. Speed is of the essence."

"Wait." Jakab grasped his elbow to halt him. "If you require help, ask. I have men loyal to me. Dragons who know us both and will fight for what is right."

"Thanks. That means a lot."

"One more thing. My brother is a guard at the dungeon. He wasn't with the group who took your mate, but he'll know where they've imprisoned her. I'll visit him to learn what I can. Once you're done, return here to compare notes."

Leo's throat tightened, the offer of trust and friendship one that almost unmanned him. He managed a clipped nod before he departed. Leo hoped Jakab understood how much his friendship meant to him.

Several hours later, Leo strode to the battlefield to consult with Jakab. Although he'd met with his friends, he'd learned little.

Frustration tensed his muscles, and he had to concentrate on holding his human form.

"Let me out," his dragon roared. *"Now is the time to attack. Take them off guard."*

"We require a plan," Leo gritted out. He coughed from the surge of dense smoke that poured from his throat. "Quit it. You're wearing us out when we require every bit of cunning and intelligence to recover our mate. What would she say if she saw this tantrum of yours?"

His dragon paused, and it surprised Leo his other half was listening to him.

"You're right," his dragon said, his tone sulky. *"I will work with you rather than against. What is our plan?"*

"We'll hear what Jakab has learned first," Leo said.

"There you are! I've searched the castle for you."

Leo turned to face Telus. "Now you've found me."

"You're required at the tailor to have your fitting for the celebration ball tomorrow. Your mother is insistent you appear in the correct clothes."

"No." Leo turned his back on the butler.

"Your mother informed me if you ignored her orders, I was to send word to the head guard to mete out punishment to the human."

Leo froze. Telus's tone told Leo everything. The butler was enjoying relaying this message. Leo shifted to face Telus. "I see.

And what other tasks do my parents have for me?"

"I've written a list," Telus said. "Nan will arrive in three hours with her entourage. You will be present with your parents and brothers to help welcome her to Hissing Isle."

"I thought she was arriving tomorrow."

"The plan changed."

"Give me the list." Leo held out an imperious hand. Telus remained in place, and Leo snatched the papers from the officious dragon. Without another word, he stalked toward the battlefield.

Telus shouted instructions after him, but Leo's steps never faltered.

"I dislike that dragon. He has always treated us as if we were manure beneath his prissy feet," his dragon said. *"He doesn't or never used to treat your brothers like that. Why does he disrespect us? We've done nothing to upset him."*

"My parents and brothers treat us in the same way. It makes me wonder if one of my parents had an affair. I mean, our appearance doesn't stand out, but that doesn't mean we have both parents in common."

"How will we learn the truth?"

"Some of the old retainers might hold secrets."

"Will they talk?"

"Don't know," Leo said. *"Not that it matters. The most important thing is to free Gwenyth and spirit her away from the castle."*

"Priorities," his dragon replied with approval. *"I wish we could*

speak with her."

"Me too. Maybe we'll manage that once we make love to her again."

"Yessss," his dragon hissed in approval. *"I dream of our bodies joining."*

"So that's why I keep waking up with a stiff cock," Leo muttered.

His dragon sniffed. *"You want her."*

"More than anything," Leo agreed. *"She is our one. We cannot lose Gwenyth."*

"If anyone damages her, I shall go on a warpath," his dragon said, and it was a promise rather than a threat.

"I will be right there with you. Anyone who injures Gwenyth will not go unpunished."

Leo arrived at the battlefield to find Jakab hadn't returned from visiting his brother. While he waited, he observed the younger dragons training for an upcoming battle on Smoking Isle. The youngsters completed their exercises and landed. Once they shifted, Leo started talking.

"You," Leo said, pointing at a bright blue dragon with blue eyes. "You're taking the corners too wide. Streamline your limbs to avoid your body dragging against the air."

A green dragon sniggered. "You're overweight," Leo stated, shutting the youngster down. "If you drop some of that poundage and muscle up more, your speed will increase."

"What about me?" a small black dragon asked.

Leo grinned. "You need to eat more and build muscle. Work on your strength and endurance. Practice your turns. Even though I'm advising you to put on muscle, your smaller frame will allow you to turn faster. That will give you an advantage."

"You should listen to Leonidas," Jakab said from behind Leo. "He has experience and knows what he's talking about. We rarely have a champion such as Leo to offer tips."

"The Leonidas?" the green dragon asked, and he peered more closely at Leo. "I didn't recognize you."

"There's no reason you should. I have been focusing on things other than training and entering battles."

"Are you retired?" the black dragon asked.

"Not officially." As Leo uttered the words, he didn't feel the urge to test himself against other dragons. He'd achieved his goals. None of his accomplishments had changed his parents' behavior toward him. Something to consider.

"Be here tomorrow morning, and we'll practice those turns," Jakab said. "Bring your battle suits, and I'll arrange a battle with a few of my friends. That will show the difference a fast turn makes in winning or losing a battle."

"Yes, sir!" the three trainees chorused.

Leo waited until the young dragons entered the changing rooms and were out of earshot. "What news?"

"My brother says they have incarcerated her in the bottom level of the dungeon," Jakab said.

"In the old dungeons?" Shock filled Leo at the update. "That's where they detain the worst of the criminals. Why would they keep her there?"

"Because it's almost impossible to escape the lower level. No one has done it before."

"Almost?" Leo asked.

"Karlos, my brother, says the lower dungeon is in bad repair. Cracks are appearing in the walls and the cells flood during the rainy season. One prisoner drowned last year."

"And my parents thought to put Gwenyth in such danger?" Leo cursed, appalled at their treatment of his mate.

"Karlos also said he doesn't understand why they imprisoned your mate and placed her in the worst sector. Many of the soldiers are perturbed at her treatment."

"Perturbed enough to help her escape?" Leo asked.

Jakab glanced over his shoulder before giving a slight nod. "Karlos told me since the old commander left, routines and security practices have changed in the castle."

"If the dungeon floods, it must be nearer the river," Leo said. "I wonder if it's possible to dig into the dungeon?"

"It's not worth the risk. If you dug in the wrong place, you could flood the lower dungeon and the level above it. I had a thought during my return after speaking with my brother. The best time to strike would be when the group from Smoking Isle arrive. Either then or during the ball. If you follow your parents' instructions and attend the ball, they'll relax and think you're following their orders."

"No," Leo said flatly.

Jakab held up a hand. "Wait. They will split the soldiers. Most will be on security at the ball. If they behave as usual, the numbers left to guard the dungeon will be less than usual. That is the time to stage a rescue attempt. Even better, if some of those number left behind are sympathetic to your cause."

"But I can't be in two places at once."

"Which is where your many loyal friends come in," Jakab said. "Dragons and humans like you, Leo. You're decent and treat everyone with the respect they deserve. If you require help, ask."

"You'll be putting your lives in danger. Once I free Gwenyth, the chances are I'll need to move to Perfume or Smoking Isle to keep us safe."

"Build a large home and a battlefield," Jakab said with a broad grin. "Those who need to can seek sanctuary with you at your new place."

"You have it planned."

"Can you think of a better one?" Jakab asked.

Leo considered all that Jakab had said. "You're right about most residents not knowing what is going on. The more I learn, the more the events here at the castle worry me."

A junior servant trotted across the field to them. Leo and Jakab ceased their discussion once they spotted him.

"Yes?" Leo demanded.

The young dragon avoided Leo's gaze.

"You wanted something," Leo prodded.

"Mr. Telus bade me remind you of your appointment with the tailor. He said it was on your list."

"I have clothes," Leo snapped.

"Tell Telus Leo will be there soon," Jakab said and waved away the dragon. He waited until the servant had almost disappeared. "It strikes me the tailor's appointment might yield information. What else is on Telus's list?"

Leo pulled the forgotten list from his pocket and flattened it enough to peruse. "The tailor, the dance master." He rolled his eyes. "The barber."

Jakab nodded. "All tradesmen who visit the castle and ply their trade at the dragon township. Chat with them. You might strike gold."

Leo wrinkled his nose. "I do not gossip."

"Not even to save your mate?"

Leo sighed. "I'm off to my appointment with the tailor. I hope my parents don't expect me to pay for this."

"Do you know their financial situation?"

"I've never been interested," Leo said.

Jakab nodded. "I might seek a few of my fellow trainers and ask if they'd be interested in taking a trip to town this evening. I was thinking dinner at the Barbecue Shack and drinks at a pub.

Preferably one your brothers favor. Would you like to join us?"

"It's a plan." Leo decided a reconnoiter of the town and chatting with the locals, his old friends and acquaintances might bear fruit. He hated to think of the pain and fear Gwenyth was facing now.

And if the rumors were true, she'd be cold and hungry.

Terrified.

"If I can't get away, I'll send you a message."

Leo worked his way through his list of chores before it was time to meet Nan and her entourage. Frustration boiled in his gut, his anger growing as Telus inspected his appearance. The butler circled Leo before he gave his approval to the servant chosen to dress Leo for the meeting. By Lodar, he could clothe himself.

By the time Telus had arrived, Leo was ready to explode.

"You will do," Telus said. "When Nan arrives, stand with your parents and remain silent. Your father and mother will take care of welcoming speeches. You may speak with Nan at the ball tomorrow night."

By Lodar! What was going on here? His parents and Telus were moving him around like a piece on a chessboard. The parents who ignored him until it suited them.

"Will my brothers be present?" He forced a casual tone while tension roiled in both him and his dragon.

"They will be there," Telus informed him. "Everyone is meeting in the Flame room. Remain standing. I do not wish your clothes to crease. You must create a favorable impression."

"We resemble a stupid storybook prince," his dragon complained. *"The pants are so tight, we won't perform once we rescue Gwenyth."*

A startled chuckle burst from Leo.

"Laugh all you want, but our cock is an important body part."

"Was there something else, Leonidas?" Telus asked, not bothering to hide his smirk.

"No, nothing."

Leo wheeled around and departed. He increased his speed, and his long strides took him down the passage and around the corner. Only then did he slow to his usual pace.

"The more we learn," he told his dragon, *"the more I worry about the things we haven't yet ascertained and don't understand."*

"Yes," his dragon agreed. *"I vote we interrogate our brothers. We can manipulate them and acquire much of what we want to learn. Their arrogance and stupidity will play to our advantage. I hate that our lodestone is in the dungeon. She must be terrified."*

Leo considered all that might happen and increased his pace again. If he was lucky, he might have an opportunity to question those already present. His parents wouldn't arrive early, since they preferred to make an entrance. It was time to knock a few heads together.

CHAPTER 13

Orders and Obedience

The cold was insidious. It crept from Gwenyth's toes and up her legs and torso until she shivered in misery.

"How do you keep warm?" she asked Martinos.

"Keep moving. Jog on the spot. Run through my exercises. I've become used to the cold, but I remember how it was at the start. Is there a blanket on the bed? You should have one. Wrap that around your shoulders."

"Does your dragon help keep you warm?"

"Not when the druid bracelet binds him."

Gwenyth considered that. "Will he be all right?"

Martinos gave a bitter laugh. "We haven't communicated since the soldiers forced the bracelet on me."

Talking to Martinos helped Gwenyth to ignore the cold, to keep herself from worrying about Leo and what was happening outside the dungeon.

"What do you think they'll do with me?" she asked.

Martinos was silent for a long moment before he spoke. "I believe you'll be safe enough for now. They'll use the threat of your death to make Leo behave. After that..."

"Which means I'm safe short term." The regret in his words had tears pricking her eyes. She fought for composure and dragged in her next fetid breath with difficulty.

"What does your family do?" Martinos changed the subject.

Warning bells rang in her head. For all she knew, this dragon was a plant. She huffed out a breath. Such a vivid imagination. That came from reading too many books. *Huh.*

She pushed at the thought, and a face popped into her mind. Smiling lips.

Dimples. Beautiful brown eyes. Red hair.

"Are you there?" Martinos asked.

The memory popped as if someone had speared it with a sharp pin. Who was the woman? It was the first time she'd recalled a face.

A friend? Family? Or someone else?

It seemed as if her memory might be returning.

"My father is the baker in the village," Gwenyth said the first thing that came to her. "He makes delicious pies and cakes."

"And your mother?"

Was he acting nosy or making conversation? Gwenyth wasn't certain. "She works with my father."

"Do you have siblings?"

"No," Gwenyth said with finality. The less she needed to keep straight, the better.

"Do you work in the bakery?"

"I work behind the counter." Something about her words struck her as right.

A loud slam of a door had her starting.

"Interesting," Martinos drawled. "We're to have company."

"Another prisoner?"

"Quiet," Martinos snapped.

Gwenyth backed from the door, fighting her curiosity. Another door slammed, closer this time. Someone *was* coming.

"I can give you half an hour and no longer," a masculine voice spoke from outside Gwenyth's cell. "I will wait outside the locked door."

"Who is in that cell? I sense a presence." A demanding feminine voice.

Someone used to issuing orders and expecting obedience.

"The human woman who married Leonidas," the man said, sounding supremely uncomfortable.

The woman tittered. "Oh! What a fine jest. Let her out. I'll speak to her too."

"That is not a good idea," the man said.

"Open her cell door," the woman commanded. "I am paying you handsomely for this visit. A warning. I do not appreciate those who oppose me. I can handle my brother and a weak human. Open. The. Cell. Door."

A key turned in her prison door. Another scraped in Martinos's cell.

"Go," the woman instructed, imperious and regal. "I will knock on the door once I am done. Leave the torch."

The hairs at the back of her neck rose. *Danger*, it whispered in the air, and everything in Gwenyth stiffened. She didn't want this meeting the woman was forcing on her.

"Open the door and come out where I can see you," the woman demanded. "Both of you."

The contempt in the woman's tone had Gwenyth's knees shaking. At least she was no longer cold. Instead, renewed terror flooded her with the urge to flee. She inhaled and repeated the action until she'd steadied herself. After one final inhalation, she opened the door and stepped from the cell.

The woman wore a brown cloak with a hood that covered her hair and screened most of her face. She set the torch in a holder on the wall, and the light illuminated a larger area. The woman pushed back the hood to reveal her long black hair, her golden eyes, and her wicked smirk full of cruel amusement.

"What are you doing here?" Martinos demanded the instant he

stepped from his cell.

Gwenyth hadn't imagined what Martinos might look like, but she saw he was tall and lean in his ragged clothes. A black beard covered most of his face, but his golden-brown eyes glittered with anger. His eyes were the identical size and shade of the woman's. Gwenyth glanced back at the woman and her calm satisfaction. Her dispassionate demeanor.

"Brother, dear. Are you not pleased to see me?" she mocked.

Gwenyth shot Martinos a sharp glance but kept her mouth shut, not wanting to draw the woman's attention.

Too late.

The woman observed her, interest and a hint of malice filling her expression.

"And Leonidas's little plaything," she mocked. "What a pity I had to come along and spoil your party."

"Nan, stop," Martinos snapped. "Why are you here? What do you want?"

Nan? This was the woman Leo wished to avoid?

"Step closer, human. This light is appalling. I wish to better see you."

When Gwenyth hesitated, the woman darted closer and grasped her arm. Nan yanked her hard, and Gwenyth jerked three headlong steps.

"I don't appreciate having my plans disrupted," she spat. "I am Nandag, The Strongminded, of the lead clan on Smoking Isle.

You've already met my brother Martinos, The Shunned."

Martinos didn't react to the slur, and Gwenyth took her lead from him. It was best to remain silent and soak up info—anything to release her from this mess.

"I suppose you're attractive enough, even if you are a weak human."

Nan prowled around Gwenyth.

Gwenyth didn't move a muscle. She stood in place, apprehension pressing on her shoulders. Malice and calculation radiated from Nan, and Gwenyth knew, without a doubt, this woman was dangerous and would kill her without a blink. Leo was right to fight a marriage to Nan. He'd loathe everything about this dragon woman.

"Luckily for me, my spies warned me of the potential problems you might cause to my plans. The thing is," she mused. "Do I kill you now, or do I keep you imprisoned to apply pressure on Leonidas? Is he good in bed? Tell me that at least."

Gwenyth stared at Nan. Lord, she loathed bullies. People who told her what to do. She raised her chin. "He is a magnificent lover."

To her right, Martinos tensed.

Half a beat later, Nan struck her across the cheek. Gwenyth almost fell but caught herself. Her head rang with the blow as she straightened. Her gaze darted to Nan and away, but not before she caught the brief flicker to dragon in Nan's eyes.

"That is for daring to touch what is mine," Nan spat.

Martinos chuckled. "Do you intend to bitch-slap every woman in Leo's past? His league of women was legendary during his battle days."

"If I come into their direct path, they'll be sorry." Nan sounded calmer now, her smile one of beauty.

Gwenyth shuddered at the abrupt switch in her mood.

"I dislike those who impede my plans." Nan focused on her brother. "You know that already."

"I suspected you had a hand in my imprisonment," Martinos said, remaining calm, although tension slid into his frame. "Our parents spoiled you."

Their conversation gave rise to even more questions for Gwenyth. The politics and backstabbing in the dragon world had her longing for her peaceful home, the book from the top of her to-read pile, and a glass of red wine. The thought slid into her mind as if it was one she often acted upon. She hoped no one else ended up in these lands as she had. It wasn't for the faint of heart. Her cheek throbbed even though she tried to ignore the pain, and the dampness she guessed was blood.

Leo would come for her.

She sensed this with every particle of her being. Whether he'd charge to the rescue in time was another matter. In fact, now that she thought of it, she'd try harder to escape herself. It wasn't like her to stand back and accept her lot. She was a battler. Her mother had told her so. Her father had agreed.

Gwenyth paused, pleased with the random memories streaming into her brain.

"Once I am wed to Leonidas, you will both lose your usefulness. I will have no trouble consolidating my power and moving on to the next stage of the plan." Her eyes glittered with triumph.

Gwenyth wanted to check on Martinos's reaction to his sister's declaration but stopped herself.

Martinos's advice to say little or nothing seemed spot-on.

"My spies told me Leonidas keeps to himself these days. He has retired from the battle circuit and fights once a year to maintain his title. Having you slip into his life caused me several sleepless nights."

Gwenyth fought to remain mute. It was apparent Telus was one of her spies or someone in the butler's circle. She hoped Leo hadn't shared her story with his friends in case one of them intended to betray him.

"How long have you known Leonidas?" Nan demanded.

"I met him in the village."

"The human village. Bah! Leonidas lowers himself by dealing with humans. Once my plans come to fruition, I shall exterminate every human on the isles."

"Who would do the menial work?" Martinos asked.

Nan's expression darkened. "The lower dragons will work as they do now."

"And if they don't have the skills—what then, sister? As usual, you jump with two feet and never consider the consequences."

"You won't act so smart once I announce the day of your execution. I shall strike the killing blow myself."

Shock punched Gwenyth in the gut. Would Nan execute her own brother?

"Why would you do that?" Gwenyth blurted.

Fury turned Nan's golden eyes fiery red. She advanced on Gwenyth and slapped her hard across the cheek. The blow sent Gwenyth to the ground. Her head struck the stone floor, and everything went black.

CHAPTER 14

She-Wolf in Dragon Scales

N andag, The Strongminded, arrived three hours and
twenty-eight minutes later.

Her retinue had been late, but it had given Leo the chance to
interact with those assembled in the Flame room.

Leo watched the thunder of dragons as they appeared on the
horizon. Each dragon bore the same scarlet hide, apart from the
leader dragon. The leader was jet-black. The dragons around Leo
whispered behind their hands, expressions of awe and surprise
flowing from dragon to dragon. Black dragons were rare. Leo
hadn't thought to ask about Nan's color, but if this lead dragon

was in fact Nan, it raised even more questions.

Why would a rare black who could choose her consort want him—a standard green and the youngest son with no consequence? The answer supplied itself readily enough. She didn't want him. She was using him for secret gain.

Leo glanced at his parents and watched them exchange a look.

Interesting. They disliked this situation too, which meant Nan *did* have something over his parents.

Blackmail.

Jakab was right.

The thunder of dragons flew closer until Leo's superior sight read their expressions. The lead black dragon wore determination and a hint of smugness. *Bitch.*

Because it *was* Nan.

Every one of his instincts screamed this truth.

By Lodar, he prayed Jakab discovered a way to help free Gwenyth.

"This woman is a she-wolf in dragon scales," his dragon stated with disdain. *"The thought of touching her makes me feel nauseous. Do we have to act with politeness?"*

"We do," Leo said, even though he agreed with his dragon. Hidden trouble loomed, and frustration filled him because he couldn't unlock the puzzle of danger. Everything he'd learned of her told him anyone who mated with Nan would never have a peaceful existence. Hell, it was clear who'd take charge. However,

if the female thought to direct Leo's life, she should reconsider.

His mind slid to Gwenyth. At last resort, he could assemble a group of dragons loyal to him and storm the dungeon with force to rescue his mate. Of course, that'd mean losing everything he'd worked for on Hissing Isle. He and Gwenyth would need to leave. His farm, his home, and his property forfeited. Unless he challenged his parents and fought for supremacy.

Not the route he wished to travel.

This path would require him to deal with his three brothers.

Russays, The Magnificent, his oldest brother, hoped to inherit the position of leader. That was no secret. Russays would never stand aside and let Leo seize the spoils.

The visiting dragons landed, and Telus gestured at five servants dressed in scarlet-and-black livery. Once the visitors shifted to their human forms, the servants handed them cloaks to shield their nakedness.

Leo's father cleared his throat and pasted on a polite smile. "Nandag, The Strongminded, you are welcome to my home, and soon, we accept you into our family. Many have mentioned your beauty, and I see they have not exaggerated. Any of my sons would be lucky to have you as their mate. Leonidas, Champion of the Skies, is fortunate, indeed. Nandag, welcome. If you are ready, my head butler will escort you to your quarters. Later this evening, we will dine together and speak of the future. Does that meet with your satisfaction?"

Nan acknowledged the greeting with a curt bow of her head. His father was correct. She was a stunningly beautiful woman with her straight raven-black hair and creamy skin. Her eyes were an unusual pale golden-brown. While tall, she was curvy rather than lean in the way of most dragon women.

Despite her beauty, she radiated an arrogance and self-awareness of her worth. That she cast other women in the shade would be a source of pride to her.

"She isn't Gwenyth," his dragon whispered.

Exactly.

Gwenyth was the one who lit their world and made everything else unimportant.

"We have to rescue her," Leo told his dragon. *"I hate this standing around while our friends risk their lives by going against my parents."*

"We have generous friends."

"We would help them," Leo said.

"True."

Nan extended her hand to his father. Leo bit back his disgust as his father bent over her and brushed a kiss over her knuckles. Nan's gaze lifted and connected with his. Her lips curled, but it wasn't a smile. It was smug satisfaction.

What the hell was going on here? He hadn't managed to get any of his brothers alone to interrogate them. To his mind, they'd attempted to avoid him.

In the past, they'd made a game of taunting him. At least until he'd become Champion of the Skies, and Leo had decided the runt no longer accepted their teasing. His oldest brother had tried, pushing his luck.

Leo had knocked him down in two punches. Mostly, he avoided his family. It was time for him to stop running. Time to take a stand and demand respect.

"Any luck?" Leo asked Jakab, the moment Leo spotted him waiting outside the castle gate.

"Not here," Jakab muttered. "Come to my private apartments while I shower and change for dinner."

"My parents expect my presence, however I've decided not to follow their instructions to the letter."

The pair walked side-by-side, taking the narrow back alleys to get to Jakab's town apartment. The businesses that sprawled outward from the castle had closed for the day, and there were fewer dragons around to spot Leo. A fact he was grateful for. If no one noticed him, they'd be less likely to inform Telus.

The entire time impatience simmered through Leo, but he bit back his questions. They'd barely stepped inside Jakab's apartment when someone knocked on the door.

Leo scowled at Jakab. "Who's that? Have you set me up?"

"Truly," Jakab snapped, glowering at Leo. Jakab strode over to his door and opened it. "My brother is here. I asked him if he'd mind speaking with us both. He has information."

"I apologize."

Jakab slapped Leo on the back and squeezed his shoulder before he went to answer the summons. "You're worried about your woman. I get it." He opened the door. "Karlos, thanks for coming. You know my friend, Leo?"

Leo crossed the ground separating them and extended his hand. "Karlos, thank you for agreeing to help me. Have you seen Gwenyth? Is she all right?"

"Let Karlos inside first," Jakab protested. He closed the door and offered his brother and Leo drinks. Once they settled around a scarred wooden table, Karlos, at last, nodded at Leo.

"Your mate is alive. They have her imprisoned in the bottom dungeon. I was on duty today, and the head guard notified me a visitor would arrive to see the other prisoner incarcerated on the same level."

Leo cocked his head, wondering why Karlos would mention this visit. "Who is the other prisoner?"

"Martinos, The Rapist," Karlos said.

Leo released a surprised hiss. "Martinos hung around with my brothers. Although I'm younger, I have met Martinos. One time my brothers let me hang out with them, and we visited pubs. I saw no hint of danger in Martinos. He never showed temper or brutality. Yes, he was as young and stupid as the rest of us, but he never stepped over the accepted line with conduct. The charges of rape surprised me."

"What I didn't know until today is that Martinos is sister to Nandag, The Strongminded," Karlos said. "Did you realize that?"

Shock struck a blow in Leo. "I knew he visited with a group of dragons from Smoking Isle. No one ever mentioned a sister."

"Nan visited him today. I escorted her to the lower dungeons and stayed with her until she ordered me to leave. Before I left, she made me unlock your mate's cell too."

Leo half stood before Jakab grasped his sleeve and yanked. Jakab silently bade Leo take his seat and listen. Leo and his dragon obeyed, but not before a testy growl raced up his throat.

"Stop that," Jakab snapped. "Listen to Karlos."

"Sorry," Leo said. "Please continue."

"I eavesdropped from outside the main door. My feeling is Nan had something to do with her brother's imprisonment. Something about the situation reeked like old fish."

Impatience simmered in Leo, making him want to leap to his feet and protest. "How will this help me free Gwenyth?" All this talking was wasting valuable time.

Jakab sent Leo a warning glance, and Leo struggled to regain a smidgen of patience.

"Nandag knew about your marriage. She has spies at the castle."

"That was quick," Leo said. "I informed my parents of the marriage as soon as I saw them. Jakab knew, but I told no one else. I trust Jakab with my life." He cast his mind back over the events. "Maybe one of the guards who arrested Gwenyth. Or Telus. Telus knew. He's aware of most of the castle secrets."

"Knowing Telus, I'd believe anything. The dragon has always slithered like a snake," Jakab said. "The way he swans around the castle issuing orders. Nothing escapes him."

"He's very accommodating for my parents," Leo said. "I've never liked him, and the feeling is mutual. Our first battles came when I was a youngster."

Jakab picked up his mug of ale. "Do we know his island of origin? Is it possible he has ties to Smoking Isle?"

"I'm not sure who'd we ask without creating more of a furor. Back to Gwenyth. Are you certain she is all right? Nan didn't harm her?" Leo asked, tension sliding across his shoulders.

Something uncomfortable slipped across Karlos's face.

"What?" Leo demanded. "What haven't you told me?"

"Nan struck Gwenyth. Twice. I could do nothing to help her, and the head soldier appointed me as one of Nan's guards. I could not check on your Gwenyth. She was still breathing, though. Martinos protected her when Nan tried to kick Gwenyth in the ribs."

"Tell me everything," Leo ordered. "Miss nothing."

"I escorted Nan to the cell, and she had me unlock the cell for Martinos. Gwenyth made a sound, and Nan asked who was in there. I had to answer or draw attention to myself."

Leo leaned closer. "What happened next?"

"Once I opened the cell door, Nan ordered Gwenyth to show

herself. When Gwenyth hesitated, Nan threatened her. Gwenyth came out, and Nan acted all haughty. I could tell news of the marriage had reached Nan, and it interfered with her plans. I missed the bit before Nan struck Gwenyth. Martinos stuck up for Gwenyth and told Nan she was an innocent, but that incensed Nan even more. The second time, she hit Gwenyth so hard, your mate fell. I think she hit her head because she didn't move or speak."

"You should've intervened," Leo snapped.

Leo rose again, and Jakab grasped his arm, jerking him to a halt. "Use your brain, Leo. If Karlos had stepped in, all our planning would've been for naught. We need time to get our plan sorted and our people in place. Our best chance to rescue your Gwenyth is if we move during the welcome ball for Nan and her people. You know this. We've discussed it as the likely scenario."

"She was still alive when I left. I escorted Nandag to the office before returning to check on the prisoners. I'd locked the outer door so that they couldn't escape."

"You left Martinos alone with Gwenyth," Leo burst out. He leaped to his feet and grasped Karlos by the throat before he could escape. Jakab wrenched them apart and thumped Leo in the chest to force him to listen.

Karlos rubbed at his throat, more alert now than he had been on first sitting. He'd also moved his chair to place more distance between himself and Leo.

"He never hurt her. When I arrived back in the lower dungeon, he'd placed Gwenyth on the stretcher bed in her cell. Before he re-entered his cell, without my having to use a weapon—I might add—he told me Gwenyth hadn't regained consciousness, but she seemed to be breathing. I checked her and saw Martinos was right. Your mate should wake, and once she does, she'll have a cut on her face from where Nan struck her. Bruises too, but Gwenyth will recover."

"I'd like to wring Nan's neck myself," Leo growled. "I'm no closer to discovering why my parents appear to be jumping to her orders and handing me over like a prize. My brothers are avoiding me. I'm determined to hunt them down this evening."

Jakab rose to fill their tankards with more ale. "I wonder if Telus is related to Nan."

"I know how we can find out," Karlos said. "The head soldier is assigning me to the two lower dungeons this evening. I'll ask Martinos. Since Martinos is Nan's brother, he should be able to tell me."

"You couldn't have told me you will see Gwenyth tonight?" Leo bit out. His hand clenched his mug, and he imagined it was Karlos's neck.

Karlos pulled a face. "You wanted details of her meeting with Nandag. At least if I'm in charge of the lower dungeons, I can make sure your lady receives clean water, food, and another blanket. I can check on her and let you know when she regains consciousness."

Leo sucked in a harsh breath, then released it. "Thank you."

"Karlos, how many soldiers can we count on to look the other way, if we break into the dungeons tomorrow night during the ball?" Jakab asked.

"If you can offer them a bribe, I'd say at least half." Karlos glanced at Leo, his expression full of apology. "Your parents do not pay well."

"Organize it," Leo said. "Let me know how much you need. Getting my hands on money will not be a problem."

"All right," Karlos said. "I'll start my approaches this evening. Should I contact Jakab to let him know your mate is awake?"

"Please," Leo said, not as confident about Gwenyth's health as Karlos. This was the second hard knock she'd had. Humans were far weaker than dragons, and he prayed Nan hadn't damaged his mate beyond repair. Worry forced him to his feet and had him pacing the compact space in Jakab's apartment. "Thank you for your help."

"You're welcome," Karlos said. "I loathe the way they're treating your mate. Bullying is not right."

Jakab stood too. "Leo, your fidgeting is irritating. We might as well start our search for your brothers."

"What I'd prefer to do is storm the dungeons and rescue my mate," Leo said.

"That would rate as stupid," Karlos said. "Let your parents and Nan think you're going along with their plan. Ease their suspicions, at least until tomorrow. I'd suggest you try to disguise your appearance. Even better, send someone else you trust to gain the information you seek."

Leo glared at Karlos. "I can't sit back and do nothing. If it were your mate, you'd want action."

"Let's send some of my fellow trainers to locate your brothers and to collect any gossip that arises. We might be better to locate a copy of the castle plans. Find the exact location of the dungeons and the area around them. That might be the better way to release Gwenyth."

Karlos rubbed his chin. "Jakab is right."

Even though Leo chafed at the lack of physical activity, he saw sense in the suggestion. Secrets swirled around the castle as thick as mud. But given he was an outsider now, his time was best spent studying the plans and prodding at the castle's defensive weaknesses.

"Gwenyth," his dragon whispered. *"Hold on. We're coming for you."*

Leo set his jaw and followed Jakab from his apartment. He and his dragon were of the same accord. They'd do anything to save Gwenyth, even if it meant he needed to exercise patience.

It was a nightmare. Fiery dragons chased her, spurting blistering flames from their toothy maws. She couldn't tell who to trust, where to run for help. She was tired. So tired, yet she forced her exhausted body to keep moving. If she stopped, she was making her capture easy for the dragons. They'd sprung at her without warning, their red eyes full of malice. She'd run. Of course, she'd run.

Jagged shards dug into her head, her cheek, her chin. Her face blazed with heat and throbbing pain. Her eyes twitched in constant spasms. An old symptom of stress. She fought through physical agony, swam through the cruel darkness that surrounded her. Each breath came in a hoarse gasp, those excruciating too.

Every instinct shouted at her to open her eyes, to fight the lethargy, the raw discomfort. A pained gasp whooshed past her lips, and her body jerked upward. Her eyes opened this time, although her surroundings were poorly lit.

Where the devil was she?

She rose on trembling legs and thrust her hand out when she discovered her balance compromised. Her knuckles smacked against something substantial.

"Ouch," she muttered. Now something else hurt. Her head thumped in concert.

"Gwenyth," a male voice called.

It took Gwenyth's aching brain a while to comprehend and catch up, but her reality squeezed into a semblance of memories.

She was married to a dragon shifter, and because of this, his parents had chucked her in the dungeon.

"Gwenyth," the voice came again, this time carrying concern along with insistence.

"I'm all right, Martinos. Your bitch sister hit me and scrambled my brain."

He laughed, dusty and dry as if he hadn't used his throat much. "Tell me about it. I'm almost certain she was in collusion with Leo's brothers. Surprisingly, we don't have medical supplies for your face. The best you can do is collect the water dripping off the walls and use it to ease the swelling."

She gingerly fingered her sore cheek and her aching eye socket. "No wonder my head is pounding."

"I'm sure Leonidas is working to free you from the dungeon. With my sister's arrival, his task has become more difficult."

"Yes." Gwenyth accepted Martinos's assertion without hesitation. Leo was an honorable man, and he and his dragon would do their utmost to free her. She imagined he'd need to make a plan because failure at the first attempt would make everything worse. *Or maybe he intends to leave you here.*

No! That was Leo's prim and proper parents. He'd never do that to an innocent.

"What did your sister want?"

"To gloat over how low I've fallen. Nan informed me she has taken over the family business. According to her, it has become more successful than when I was in charge."

"Why does she require marriage to Leo if she's already successful?"

"Simple. She wishes to increase her wealth and power. Smoking Isle is smaller than this island. The land is rugged and unproductive, which is why our family became traders. We have a successful factory producing high-end ceramics."

"What do they do on Perfume Isle?"

"The volcano that formed the island is much older, and it has made the soil fertile and suitable for many crops. There are more arable areas too. The island boasts many farmers. Why do you not know this?" The words held suspicion. "I thought you grew up here on Hissing Isle?"

"My memory is hazy after your sister hit me." True. Her memory seemed on the same level as it had been after Leo saved her. Although a few strange things popped into her brain, some of which made no sense at all.

"I see."

A door slammed, and Gwenyth heard voices. More than one. "Lie down and pretend you're unconscious," Martinos murmured.

She followed his instructions and waited, scarcely breathing and her heart racing.

The outer door to their section of the dungeon opened. Bloody hell. It was Nan again.

CHAPTER 15

Leo, I Didn't Know You Cared

Leo ran down a copy of the plans in the library. While most castle residents socialized with the visitors from Smoking Isle, he'd ducked from the salon to visit Jakab.

Now, they were in the castle library.

Leo spread the old map over the desk in the far corner of the room. Books filled shelves on three walls, although his parents never read them.

"This isn't right. It's too new." Jakab pointed at the far-left bottom of the map. "See the additions to the ballroom? That's not part of the original footprint."

Frustration fueled Leo's temper, and he clenched his fists. This felt like a waste of time. Gwenyth might be dead for all he knew. If only they'd had more time to make that ultimate connection. Then, at least, there would have been a possibility of communicating. His inability to act and save her gnawed at him while his dragon paced, his tattoo zigzagging across his chest, ribs, and back. The unrest of his dragon tickled his ribs again.

"Cease," Leo thought to his dragon. *"I'm doing my best."*

"The inaction is bad. What if our Gwenyth is dead?"

"She's not dead," Leo snapped.

Jakab's head jerked up, and his friend stared at him. "She's not dead. Where else might the plans be?"

"Sorry," Leo said as he unrolled yet another set of plans. "I didn't realize I'd spoken aloud. Try the drawers over there at the bottom of the shelves."

Jakab strode over and jerked the top drawer open. "You're right," he said. "These look older."

Leo released the edge of the plans he was checking and stalked to Jakab. He'd plonked himself on the floor and unfastened the faded red ribbon on the first plan.

"This is them." Jakab's finger traced the line of the castle and the dungeons over to the side. He tapped the faded parchment. "We were right. Well, partly right. It looks as if there is a rear entrance to the kitchen."

"So the deliveries didn't disturb the castle residents," Leo guessed. "Likely, it was blocked during the period of riots when the common dragons sought equality."

"See this alley? It backs onto the dungeon too. It would've been the perfect way to drag in prisoners unannounced," Jakab said.

"I wouldn't put it past my ancestors. The record book is full of stories detailing their bravery. After the first few tales, I didn't have the stomach to learn more about my barbaric forebears."

"If we find this alley, we should be able to break into the dungeon with no one suspecting a thing. That's as long as this dungeon is where they're holding Gwenyth."

Leo jumped to his feet. "Let's investigate now. You know, my gut told me not to bring Gwenyth. I thought she'd be safe because I'd keep her with me. I didn't want to leave her alone at my home."

"*Should haves* offer no benefit," Jakab said. "We'd better shove all these plans back in a drawer. I'd hate to give anyone a heads-up."

With the plans tidied away, Leo and Jakab left the library. They took a route to avoid his family, their guests, and most of the servants. Or at least the servants loyal to his parents. Leo led Jakab down a set of stairs reserved for the servants and into a secret passage the old cook had shown him before she died.

He remembered the day since he'd raced through the castle to escape his brothers and ended up lost. The cook had found him, crying as he meandered through the original castle corridors.

Luck was not their friend.

"Damn and blast," Leo muttered. "What the hell is Telus doing here? He never lowers himself enough to visit the ancient rooms. If anyone requires something from this area, he sends a lower servant. This way." Leo directed Jakab into a cupboard.

Leo wrapped his arms around his friend and squeezed inside. He drew the cupboard door shut just as Telus exited the room he'd stood inside. Through the tiny gap, Leo spotted his second oldest brother, Nemyr, The Scary, leave the room. With a murmur too quiet for Leo to hear, the pair parted and went in opposite directions.

As Telus reached the cupboard where they hid, he paused. Telus sniffed the air, his nostrils flaring.

Every muscle in Leo tensed.

Telus sniffed again, shook his head, and departed in rapid steps.

For long moments, Leo didn't move. The last thing he wanted was for Nemyr or Telus to discover their presence. Telus had always struck him as sly and a dragon seeking to fill his coffers. As for Nemyr, his brother had killed a dragon servant because she'd refused to lie with him. Rumors had also reached Leo about the way Nemyr treated the human females if he trapped them alone.

Without warning, Jakab squeezed him. He made a kissing noise. "Leo, I didn't know you cared. Have you told Gwenyth of your feelings for me?"

Leo checked the corridor outside the cupboard and scanned what he could see of the room almost opposite before he inched open the door. Jakab bumped him, as cramped as Leo.

"Quit messing around. Telus and Nemyr almost caught us."

"Your brother?" Jakab asked. "The plot thickens and makes sense in a twisted way."

"How so?" Leo opened the cupboard and stepped into the corridor. "I think they've gone, but we'd better take care."

"You haven't been around during the last year. From the few things I've overheard, Nemyr resents Russays, The Magnificent. Nemyr believes he should be the heir rather than your oldest brother."

Leo shook his head. "The pair were close during childhood."

"That might be true, but it's when we reach adulthood that situations become more important. Things like status and race. We lose our innocence as we gain knowledge of the world."

That was true. He'd learned with life experience. "The best thing I ever did was leave my family and Hissing Isle," Leo said. "Gaining my independence from my family made me into the dragon I am today."

"What's with all the soul-searching?" Jakab's grin held teasing.

"I met my mate." Leo peered around the corner into another passage. A set of footprints showed in the dust. "It looks as if Telus walked this way. We'd better take care not to come face-to-face with him. The kitchen is up ahead. I don't understand what Telus is doing down here."

"A mystery for another day," Jakab murmured. "Gwenyth is our priority."

Leo led the way along the passage until he came to the kitchen door. Telus's footsteps, or at least he assumed they belonged to the butler, kept going. He made a mental note to check with Cook what was along that way. He didn't recall. Leo eased the door open.

Since the evening meal had ended, the kitchen was quieter. Cook was working on prep for the morning meal and was showing a junior maid the correct way to peel and prepare a jagger fruit. The honeyed scent of the pale yellow flesh filled the kitchen.

"Cook, could we have a word?" Leo asked.

The junior dragon squeaked and dropped her knife. She grabbed at it, sliced her finger, and yelped.

"So sorry." Leo grasped the adolescent female by the shoulders, intending to check on the cut. The girl screamed, and two male kitchen hands came running.

"It's all right," Cook said, her gray eyes flashing. "Nothing to upset yourselves about. Child, stop your blubbering, and let Leo tend your finger. I'll make tea. Take a seat." With that said, she bustled over to a range heated by a stone quarried on Smoking Isle. She lifted the lid to the range and huffed out a small but steady flame. The stone ignited, and with a satisfied cluck, Cook resettled the cover.

With her usual efficiency, Cook soon had a kettle of water heating.

Leo dealt with the first-aid, glad to have a task to perform. He fastened a special healing plaster around the female's finger. "It's not a deep cut," he said. "If you leave the plaster on overnight, the cut should heal by the morning."

"Thank you," the young dragon said.

Cook turned to her junior. "I hope you've learned your lesson, child. If you drop a knife, don't attempt to catch it. Away with you. I'll finish preparing the fruit."

"Thank you, Cook," she said with a curtsy.

Once she had gone, Cook turned to him. "Why are you skulking around the disused rooms? I almost leaped out of my skin when you jumped through the doorway."

Leo grinned at the older woman. She'd looked the same way for as long as he remembered with her vibrant red hair smoothed back in a chignon. He knew the name of the hairstyle because he'd asked as a youngster. She wore her baggie white trews and white coverall with a green apron tied around her waist. The apron color was the sole part of her uniform that ever changed.

Today's apron was the same green as the grass in the valley below his house.

"My mate is in the dungeon," Leo stated, anger pulsing through him afresh. "Her one crime is that she married me, and they're treating her like a dangerous prisoner."

Cook gasped and patted her chest. A smile bloomed across her lips until she was beaming. "My Leo has a wife."

"Gwenyth is not simply my wife, she is my mate," he said.

"A true mate?" Cook asked, astonishment replacing her

excitement at Leo's news. Then she frowned. "I heard your parents arranged a match for you to Nandag, The Strongminded. I thought to myself that this dragon was not the right one for you."

"My parents made the match without my approval. Gwenyth and I came to tell them, and they tossed my mate into the dungeon." Leo told Cook everything.

"Gossip tells me your brothers are friends with this Nan. They visited Smoking Isle last month, I think it was."

"Do you know how long they stayed or if they traveled elsewhere?" Jakab asked.

"No," Cook replied with a toss of her head.

"All right," Leo said. "If you think of anything useful, please let me know. How many staff are still working at present?"

"I was about to send the last two workers to their beds."

"Excellent. Once they've gone, do you mind if we knock a hole in your wall?"

Cook's brows rose. "Whatever for?"

"I never realized until I studied the original castle plans, but the kitchen is close to the old dungeon where they've imprisoned Gwenyth. An alley runs between the two, but I've never noticed an exterior entrance. I presume builders blocked it some time ago. Jakab and I think if we find our way into the alley, we can break into the dungeon with no one noticing."

"The guards aren't stupid," Cook said. "The dragon in charge is efficient. They might notice a hole in their wall."

"By the time they realize, I'll have Gwenyth safe," Leo said.

"Where do you intend to stash her?" Cook asked.

"I had thought to stay in an old, unused room until I determine a way to leave the castle unseen. But seeing Telus and one of my brothers loitering in the area has put me off that idea."

Cook's brows lifted, her surprise evident. "What were they doing there?"

"We don't know," Jakab said.

"You're best to free your mate and leave town. Or better yet, fly to a neighboring isle and make it difficult for anyone to follow you." Cook stood and brushed her hands over her apron. "You have little darkness available tonight. The castle walls are thick. It will take time and strength to break through them."

"She's right," Jakab said. "We didn't think to bring any tools with us either."

"There is an old door behind the pantry. It's locked, and I was told it led nowhere. The cook I took over from told me the builders made a mistake while constructing the kitchen. Instead of bricking it up, they placed the pantry in front of it to disguise their mistake."

"Why didn't you say so earlier?" Leo leaped to his feet, strode to the pantry and flung open the door.

"Do not make a mess," Cook ordered.

Leo ignored the demand and checked the walls. He shoved a heavy set of shelves aside.

"Leo," Cook said in a stern voice.

Leo didn't reply, the physical action tamping down his rising anger.

"He's not listening," Jakab said.

"Come and help," Leo ordered.

"At least try not to make so much noise. The last thing I need is someone coming to investigate. You'll get us tossed into the dungeon."

"Not with the delicious food you produce, Cook. You're safe." Leo manhandled another set of shelving away from the wall. "Found it," he said in satisfaction.

Jakab straightened. "Leo, we need tools to break through the dungeon wall."

"Not if we find a door. The earliest castle inhabitants required a way to get their prisoners in and out. It'll be there." Leo pushed confidence into his voice because he refused to consider anything other than success.

"Why are you here?" Martinos asked his sister.

"The human raises my curiosity since she bears none of my beauty. Leonidas no longer works on his reputation as a womanizer. He doesn't have a woman he visits to slake his needs. In theory, he should've been my easiest target. His parents assured me the marriage would go ahead. The plan is perfect on paper."

"You want to discover where you went wrong with your scheme." Martinos sounded disbelieving. "By Lodar, you're egotistical. Our parents spoiled you, and now you think everyone owes you."

"My scheme is perfect." Nan stopped speaking, and Gwenyth imagined her shrugging. She remained still and silent on the stretcher bed, listening to the dragon woman.

"Leo is spoiling everything," Nan said. "He is the perfect age for marriage and will gain more standing by affiancing himself with me. At least until he outlives his usefulness."

Gwenyth's mouth popped open at the sheer audacity of the woman. The way she was treating Leo like a possession—one she intended to mold to her specifications—was beyond ludicrous. She'd miscalculated because Leo had worked hard to become his own dragon. He followed the path he'd plotted for himself, and that was admirable. She wished Tony had—

Her thoughts halted amidst an arrow of pain that sliced through her sluggish memories. Who was this Tony person? She recalled the pale band of flesh on her finger, yet she didn't sense a male companion in her life. When she thought of a man, her thoughts raced to Leo. He was the one who consumed her. His kisses weakened her knees, and their last one had left her yearning for more. Privacy. A comfortable bed. Solitary time with Leo.

Gwenyth pushed her memories again, thinking the name Tony

and rifling through her mind for a face to go with the name. She came up blank.

"So get someone else."

Gwenyth frowned, her mind back on the conversation. What was Martinos trying to do? Make his sister angry?

"No." Nan snorted. "It wasn't as if I intended to keep Leo for long. He's the Champion of the Skies. So tough and sexy. It makes any red-blooded dragon woman wonder what he'd be like between the sheets. I want an heir and a spare, and then my reluctant husband is no longer necessary."

Shocked at the woman's callousness, Gwenyth scowled. Nan's attitude toward Leo was disgusting. Leo had feelings. He wasn't a lump of meat for Nan to fight over. Leo was her husband, dammit. Every part of Gwenyth wanted to heap abuse on this rude, despicable dragon woman. But she heeded Martinos's advice and remained silent. It wasn't the best idea to poke at the dragon since Nan had no problem making free with her fists.

"Are you certain she's still unconscious?"

"She's a weak human. Her body isn't as strong as a dragon's. You must come back tomorrow."

Nan sighed. "Tomorrow, I'm busy with ball preparations. I must massage my plan. While I haven't spoken to Leo yet, I'll seduce him without difficulty. Men don't resist me."

Sheer conceit.

Leo wanted her, not this dragon with an inflated opinion of

herself. The minister had married them, and Leo had assured her their marriage was legal. Nan hadn't considered that point.

Throwing Gwenyth into the dungeon wasn't enough. Nan needed to break the marriage before she could move on with Leo as her husband.

"It doesn't matter if she lives or dies. Easier for me if the weak human never wakes. That way, there is no impediment to me marrying Leonidas."

Martinos made a scoffing sound. "You're only now recalling Leo has a legal wife?"

"Bah! A human man of the church married them. I doubt that will hold up under dragon law. Telus suggested we resurrect the gladiator games to celebrate my betrothal to Leonidas. The human will be the climax of the show when she fights the other prisoners for her life."

Gladiator games? Gwenyth had difficulty remaining still, the urge to throttle the dragon woman so strong, her hands fisted.

"But that would be cold-blooded murder," Martinos said, and even he sounded shocked.

"Entertainment," Nan countered. "I thought you would make a worthy candidate to fight in the games. Make our family proud."

"You're a haughty bitch," Martinos snapped.

Nan laughed, her amusement like the tinkle of a pretty bell. The sound was incongruous coming as it did from this cruel, proud woman. "Something for you to consider during the next few days. I rather liked Telus's suggestion, and the gladiator battle will proceed. It will clear the dungeons and reduce the costs of maintaining them."

Martinos let out a growl and threw something at the bars of his door.

"Now, now, brother. It's not the time to have a tantrum. Save your energy for the battle to come."

CHAPTER 16

Our Mate Is Alive

The cracks in the dungeon's wall were many, but with a lack of tools and the heavy rocks, it would prove difficult for a prisoner to escape. Hearing the murmur of voices, Leo placed his eye to one crack and tried to look through.

By Lodar! What was Nan doing in the dungeon? She was talking to the male prisoner. Her brother. Wait, was that wolf fur draped around her shoulders?

Leo's breath caught, and for a moment, he thought he'd made a noise because Nan glanced in his direction. The fur *was* wolf, and it was an identical color to Jenny and her dead littermate.

A coincidence, true. But Leo wondered.

A betrothal took time to arrange. Nan's representatives would have approached his parents some time ago. It wasn't unusual for prospects to undertake a full investigation of an intended partner since with liaisons between dragons, sizeable amounts of money and property were factored into the decision. Leo thought back. The stranger who'd approached him to sell his property had come around six or seven months ago. Was there something he'd missed while perusing the property deeds? Something to check and research.

His parents had ignored him until they'd decided the betrothal to Nan was an excellent idea. He needed to learn what they were getting from the deal.

It seemed he'd underestimated this dragon woman. He'd assumed—wrongly—that Nan's parents had arranged the match.

Not Nan herself.

He pressed his eye back to the crack and focused on the conversation.

Gwenyth was still unconscious. That did not bode well. Worry speared through him, but he couldn't do anything until Nan left the dungeon.

This was her second visit, and it was unusual enough to cause speculation—Leo's and the prison guards.

About half an hour later, Nan departed, taking her torch with her and plunging the dungeon into darkness. It took a while for Leo to focus. He tapped his finger against his knee, wondering if a guard would check on them.

"We should be safe enough now," Jakab murmured. "My brother assured me he was on duty and responsible for the lower dungeons."

No sooner had Jakab spoken then another person entered the dungeon. The light illuminated their face.

Jakab's brother.

Leo froze. What did he do now?

Jakab never hesitated. "Karlos," he whispered.

Karlos's gaze snapped away from the cells within the dungeon. "Who's there?"

"Jakab and Leo."

Karlos strode closer to the cracked wall. "How? Wait. Never mind. What's your plan?"

"Leo!" a feminine voice cried out. "You're here."

"Yes! Our mate is alive," his dragon whooped with relief, and smoke poured from Leo's mouth.

"Of course, I came for you, my lodestone. I intend to dig through the wall and retrieve my mate," Leo declared. *Even if he had to do it with his bare hands.* By Lodar, Gwenyth was still alive. That was excellent news and rekindled determination surged through him.

"We need tools," Jakab murmured. "Dragon fire won't work. I have my dagger, but you'll need a crowbar and a strong hammer at the least."

Leo's shoulders slumped. Jakab was right. "All I have is my dagger. Perhaps Cook has something we can use."

"We shouldn't involve her," Jakab said. "Once your parents learn we gained access to the dungeon via the old kitchen entrance, they'll ask questions. She shouldn't suffer for our actions."

Jakab was right. The kitchen staff had seen them and could talk, given the right incentive. Frustration simmered through Leo as he juggled pieces of plans and decided what to do for the best. "We're running out of time. Let's retrieve tools and spring Gwenyth."

"Are you still planning to fly to Perfume Isle?"

"We'll be safer among friends," Leo said. "My house is the first place my parents will search. There and the human village. I feel stupid for not bringing tools."

"We didn't know we'd find a simple way into the dungeon. Karlos, we're coming back once we locate tools."

"The shift changes in one hour," Karlos warned. "My replacement kowtows to the head soldier."

A sense of hopelessness assailed Leo then. Obstacles faced him in every direction.

"I'll try to find something to help you from this side," Karlos promised. "I can't dig from this side, but I can pass the tools through a larger crack."

Leo pulled out his dagger and scanned the cracks in the wall. After choosing the largest one, he attacked the old mortar and stone.

Karlos left and returned with tools. "A bit of luck for you. My replacement is Georges. He's lazy and will spend most of his time playing cards with the other guards at the midway station. I doubt he'll bother checking down here."

"If you let us out of our cells, we could help dig from this side," Gwenyth said.

Leo heard the keys in a lock.

"Let Martinos out too," Gwenyth said. "He'll help."

They had accused Martinos of rape, and even though Leo hadn't considered him capable of the crime, he opened his mouth to demand Gwenyth stay away from the dragon.

"Leo, your brothers set up Martinos in collusion with Nan. Martinos will help us."

"Our Gwenyth is right," his dragon said. *"We must trust this dragon's will to escape is greater than his desire to injure our mate."*

Karlos unlocked the dragon's cell. "Stay inside until I return."

Leo wanted to protest, but both Martinos and Gwenyth remained in their cells. Leo dug at the stone and mortar, trying to widen the gap. He chipped a fraction of the cement away, but the constant grind of his blade against the stone blunted it fast. His frustration rose at the impossible task before him.

"Don't despair," his dragon shouted at him. Leo's shoulders slumped anyway. *"We will succeed."*

"Someone is coming," Martinos warned from inside his cell.

Leo stilled, ready to attack, only relaxing when Karlos strolled up to them.

"I gathered what I could find. Make sure you take them with you and discard them somewhere outside the castle. Each tool bears the castle mark for identification," Karlos said.

"We will do as you say," Gwenyth promised.

Leo's longing to hold her and kiss his mate had him digging faster. He almost cheered as a broken corner rock came free. The hole grew sizeable enough to pass a chisel through. Unfortunately, it was also big enough to warn any guards of an escape attempt.

Jakab returned quicker than Leo had thought possible.

"Cook was waiting for us in the kitchen," Jakab said. "She had tools ready since we hadn't returned straightaway. Cook pushed the cupboard back after I left. She doubts whether anyone will suspect her, but she didn't wish to risk questions."

"I love Cook," Leo said.

"Me too," his dragon agreed.

With the extra tools and the help from Martinos and Gwenyth, the hole grew larger.

"I think someone is coming," Gwenyth said.

"Keep digging," Martinos said. "I'll wait for whoever the visitor is and stop them if they try to alert the other soldiers.

Gwenyth gripped Martinos's arm for an instant. "Be careful."

A growl burst from Leo, but Jakab slapped Leo over the back, a silent reminder not to cause problems at this delicate stage of operations.

Leo showed his teeth at Jakab, but took heed and continued to chip at the stone. The added strength he applied to the chisel and hammer removed another largish piece.

The gap was now big enough for Leo to see Martinos at the dungeon door, his attention on whoever was coming.

"I heard things from Karlos about Martinos's trial. Karlos thought there was something questionable. I'm surprised they didn't execute Martinos."

"I believe he has been in the dungeon for several years. If they set him up, you're right. Why did they let him live?"

"Either he is useful to his sister or they have something on him that keeps him silent," Jakab murmured.

"Stop work for a moment," Gwenyth said.

Leo and Jakab stopped. The hole was sizeable enough now that any idiot would notice, and fine dust covered them all.

"It's all right," Martinos said. "It's Karlos again."

The door opened and closed, and Karlos stepped inside the cell. He closed the door behind him and pulled out more tools.

Jakab released a growl. "How are you going to explain this, Karlos? You'll lose your job and your freedom."

"My gut tells me of the rotten stench within the castle walls. I've sensed it for some time. I'll be leaving and not returning once my shift ends," Karlos replied. "Meanwhile, I might as well help."

"Can you hear the noise we're making on the level above?" Leo asked.

"It's no worse than the normal racket the prisoners make if they're riled up about something. Keep going," Karlos said.

With Karlos, Gwenyth, and Martinos working from inside the dungeon, and he and Jakab working from the alley, the hole rapidly increased in size.

"I think it's big enough now," Leo said. "Gwenyth, try to squeeze through."

"No, make it a little bigger, so Martinos and I can both get through," she countered.

Leo wanted to argue, but he'd already learned of his mate's stubbornness. And the truth, if she squeezed through the hole, the temptation to leave Martinos behind might get the better of him. The admission had him fighting shame. "We'll make the hole bigger."

It took another half an hour in which Leo stressed about the guard change and the rising of the sun. He still wasn't sure where to take Gwenyth. By the time they fought through the outer wall, the local tradesmen and other castle residents would've started their day. It'd make more sense to go to ground until the night. Fewer dragons to see them take to the air or witness their direction.

His parents would comb the city for them—that much he understood.

Leo pulled away another chunk. "Martinos, can you fit through here?"

"I'll make it," Martinos said.

"Gwenyth, you come first," Leo ordered.

She hesitated, glancing at Martinos and a wave of jealousy jabbed Leo in the chest.

"Go," Martinos said. "I'll follow you through."

"What next?" Jakab asked.

"Do you know a place we can rest and hide out until it gets dark?" Leo asked. "There are too many eyes during the daylight hours."

"True," Jakab said.

Leo watched Gwenyth wriggle through the hole. She came straight to him and wrapped her arms around his waist, pressing her face against his chest. He hugged her, relief making him dizzy. The light was dim in the narrow space between the kitchen and the dungeon. He wanted to study her face and check her for injuries. He wanted private moments without others present where he could touch her, kiss her, and reassure himself she was in one piece.

"Did they hurt you?" he murmured, keeping his voice low.

"I'm fine," she said. "Where are we going?"

He still didn't know.

"Jakab, do you think we could hide out at your apartment?" he asked his friend.

Jakab frowned. "If they learn Karlos is missing, they'll search his quarters. My sister and her husband have a property on the outskirts of town. They will give us food and shelter."

"If our presence doesn't put them in danger," Leo said.

"Francine is our half-sister," Karlos said. "Not many know of the familial relationship."

Leo couldn't stop touching his mate. His fingers twined with hers, the physical contact smoothing his apprehension. "Still, there's the possibility someone might learn of the connection. I'd hate your sister to suffer on our behalf. Martinos, your turn," Leo said. "Hurry, time is a precious commodity."

Despite his years of captivity, Martinos was bulkier than he looked. It took an effort to drag him through the space they'd dug, but finally, he popped free. Given his grimace, it must've hurt, but Martinos didn't complain.

"Thank you," he said, offering his hand for Leo to shake. "Your mate is amazing. You're a lucky dragon."

Leo agreed. He and his dragon had fallen under her spell. It appeared she'd worked her magic on Martinos too.

"Where will you go once we leave?" Leo asked.

"I'm coming with you," Martinos said. "I intend to help."

"No," Karlos said.

"Never mind that," Leo said. "Is Karlos coming through the hole?"

"No," Karlos said. "I'll exit through the dungeon and avoid the guards as much as possible. That will muddy the story for anyone who wishes to investigate the escape."

"Karlos, if you get captured, I'll come and kick your butt myself," Jakab declared.

"Hurry," Karlos urged. "Don't waste time talking. Go."

"How do we get out of here?" Martinos asked. "I had no clue the dungeon backed on to this area. I presumed it was deep beneath the ground."

"So did I," Leo said. "We're winging the plan. Bring the tools with us. We might need them to dig through another wall." He brought to mind the plan he'd seen. "This way."

He hoped the alley would emerge somewhere at the castle rear. Supposition led him to think the residents wouldn't want to watch deliveries so the entrance would be at the back, somewhere out of sight. He lifted the lanterns he and Jakab had brought with them. The light shone on Gwenyth's bruised face. One of her eyes was black, and her cheek was red and swollen.

"Did Nan hit you more than once?"

"I'll tell all once we're safe," she promised, and she squeezed his hand in reassurance.

"I'll kill Nan," his dragon snarled. *"How dare someone strike our mate? How dare they!"*

Leo tamped down his fury and gave a curt nod. "This way. Single file. I'll go first. Gwenyth, you walk behind me. Martinos next. Jakab will bring up the rear." A way of monitoring Martinos. Gwenyth might trust him, but Leo didn't have to—not until he learned more of the dragon.

Leo set a fast pace since someone could notice the escape at any time. The guard might not be as lax as Karlos assumed. The alley curved around a corner, growing even more narrow with a part of a wall collapsed. Leo squeezed through the gap, and Gwenyth followed without complaint.

"Our mate has spirit and determination," his dragon said, satisfaction in his tone.

"She amazes me," Leo replied. *"We are lucky to have such a brave woman as our mate."*

"We rescued her."

"It was fate," Leo replied as he continued to walk as fast as he could, given the limited light and the growing number of obstacles in their path.

"The sex was better than my imagination. Can we do it again soon?"

Leo barked out a laugh.

"What's funny?" Gwenyth asked from behind him.

Leo turned to grin at her. "I promise to tell you later once we reach safety."

Five minutes later, the alley ended, and Leo halted before a wall. Like the rest of the stonework, cracks were visible where the mortar had fallen away.

"What now?" Martinos asked.

Leo leaned closer to peer through the largest of the gaps. "We need to break through the wall fast with minor ruckus. Judging by the light, it's still early, but workers and tradespeople will be about their business."

"Once we get out, I think we should split up," Jakab said. "It will be harder for anyone chasing us if we go in different directions."

Leo turned to Martinos. "Do you have somewhere you can go?"

"I'll make do. I can't fly." He gestured at the bracelet encircling one biceps. "The bracelet holds a druid spell to stop me from taking my dragon form."

Leo stared at Martinos, unwilling compassion filling him. Although Leo didn't trust him, he sympathized with the dragon's plight. Imprisonment of his other half seemed a harsh punishment. "Does a druid need to remove the spell?"

"Yes," Martinos said, his tone devoid of the anger or frustration Leo imagined he'd feel at the suppression of his dragon.

"I have a plan for you. Make your way to the human village. It will take you a day on foot. Perhaps longer, depending on your fitness. Sleep in the rough to avoid detection. Head to the fishermen's cottages at the bottom of the village—the ones that edge the sea. Ask to speak with Henry and tell him I sent you. He owns a fishing boat and travels between the isles. If you're willing to work as crew, he'll give you passage to Perfume Isle. Sometimes, he travels as far as Smoking Isle. Tell Henry I'll pay him a boon during my next visit to the village."

"You'd do that for me, even though Nan is my sister, and she's trying to kill your mate and marry you?"

"I'm trusting my gut that says my brothers' involvement with your sister confirms shady dealings. I don't trust my older brothers." Leo picked up the iron lever he'd carried with him and began chipping away at the wall.

Jakab and Martinos helped him while Gwenyth started carrying the pieces they dislodged to build a barrier behind them.

"Where will you and Gwenyth go?" Martinos asked.

"It's best if we don't tell you," Gwenyth said from behind them before Leo could snap out a suspicious query of his own. "Otherwise, it defeats the purpose of splitting up."

"You misunderstand," Martinos said. "I've languished in the dungeon for almost three years, which has given me plenty of time to think about what happened. My sister wanted to run the family business. That's obvious. Your brothers, however..." He strained to remove a stone. "I've often wondered why they spared my life."

"My brothers forgot you," Leo said.

"They destroyed my honor, and I demand revenge. My dragon was taken from me, and the reasons are damn murky. I've racked my brain and can't fathom why."

"Where will you go after you get the bracelet removed?" Leo asked.

"I'll go home, keep a low profile, and investigate my sister and her tie to your brothers. It has to be something on Hissing Isle since this was where the crime they accused me of occurred. The soldiers captured me during a business trip, and the council incarcerated me here."

Leo pried another stone free and set it aside. The gap allowed a wash of early dawn light, and he scanned for pedestrians. None. *Yet.* Although the building blueprints remained in his mind, he still wasn't positive of their location. The single thing he was certain of was the alley had led them from the castle grounds.

He, Martinos, and Jakab continued to work in silence. As did Gwenyth, who cleared the area of stones behind them to give them more room in which to work.

"I think I could squeeze through the gap now," Gwenyth said. "Why don't I scout the area? At the least, I can give you an idea of our surroundings and where we are."

Leo wanted to protest. His dragon shouted a dissent because they wished to protect her from further harm.

"Leo," she said, coming close enough to place a hand on his forearm. Her touch seared through him, arrowing to his cock.

"Let us clear a few more stones, then you can go through," Leo said. "If anyone comes, run and hide. I'll come for you."

She opened her mouth as if to protest, then nodded. She continued with her rock moving, and when Leo glanced back, he was proud to see a hip-high wall of stone. Any barrier, no matter how flimsy, would offer them precious extra seconds in which to escape.

"Gwenyth," Leo said. "You should be able to fit through here."

She squirmed through without difficulty.

"Be careful," Leo ordered. "Stay in the shadows."

"I promise."

Watching her scurry away was the hardest thing he'd ever done. To stop himself from howling, he applied himself to making the hole big enough for all of them to pass through. His dragon chattered off his ear.

"We shouldn't have let her go. What if she gets captured again? The guards might notice our escape tunnel. What if that Nan revisits her brother?"

"Stop," Leo demanded. *"Gwenyth is clever. She won't get caught."* He applied force to a stubborn piece of rock, grunting as it came free without warning and almost planted him on his arse.

Jakab steadied him and yanked another bit from the wall.

"Martinos, you slide through the gap and leave," Leo said. "Once you're free, make your way to the human village."

Martinos nodded. "I'm serious about meeting with you again. Hopefully, we'll each have information we can share by that time."

"All right. Leave a message with the baker at the human village on Perfume Isle. Gwenyth and I will make our way in that direction."

"Thank you. I won't betray your trust." Martinos sent Leo a long look before nodding and squirming through the hole. Once through, he paused.

"I think we're near the entrance to the dungeon. Take care leaving."

Leo watched Martinos melt into the shadows.

"Do you trust him?" Jakab asked.

Leo shrugged. "Time will tell."

He put renewed energy into removing rocks, his worry increasing when Gwenyth didn't return. If the guards spotted her, all of this would be for naught.

CHAPTER 17

Survival Is My New Middle Name

G wenyth slunk through the shadows cast by the buildings. She approached a corner and slowed. Was that the clink of swords and the stomp of boots on cobblestones? She risked a glance around the corner and barely restrained her gasp.

They'd emerged right by a guard station. Gwenyth backtracked and wondered at the amount of activity given the early hour.

A blast of flame lit the road, and Gwenyth squeezed against the wall of the building at her back.

A black dragon flew overhead, giving Gwenyth a glimpse of power and beauty. Then the dragon disappeared over the rooftops and out of sight.

That wasn't the best direction for them to walk. She'd mention it to Leo. Gwenyth retreated, ghosting through the dim-lit areas and hugging the building walls. She had to wait for a man and an adolescent boy to exit their cottage. The pair walked in the direction of the guard station. The man noticed her, but Gwenyth made herself smaller and turned her face away, praying she didn't raise their suspicions. The instant he rounded the corner, she sprinted back the way she'd skulked earlier.

When she arrived at the hole in the wall, it was much bigger, and only Jakab and Leo were present.

"The guard station is that way. I'm not sure what's going on, but there's a lot of activity."

The two men exchanged a look and hastened their pace. A few minutes later, Jakab squeezed through the gap. Jakab hugged her and disappeared. Leo squirmed through the hole and dragged her into his arms. His kiss was way too brief before he snared her hand in his.

"Where will we go?" she asked.

"We'll make our way to the outskirts of town on foot and risk flying once we get to open ground." He pulled a dagger from his boot.

"It's blunt since I used it to dig at the wall, but it's better than nothing. Keep it hidden somewhere secure. Maybe in your boot. And my lodestone, remember this. Dragon scales are strong enough to deflect a knife blade. If you have to protect yourself from a dragon, go for the eyes or the delicate scales on the chest. Don't hesitate. Not for a second, because we're fast. Even better, hide if you can, but our sense of smell improves if we're in our dragon form."

"I'll keep that in mind," Gwenyth said.

"Act first. Don't give a dragon the opportunity to prepare and lose your chance to win. Let them think you're weak and inflict the most damage you can."

"I'm not sure I can injure another being."

"Promise," Leo said, his gaze so intent she'd swear she glimpsed his dragon in his eyes. "Gwenyth, swear you will act without hesitation."

She swallowed her unease and lifted her chin. "Survival is my new middle name."

He gave a clipped nod. "Let's go."

Leo dragged her down the street, his long strides meaning she had to trot to keep up.

"Slow down," she pleaded when her lungs threatened to explode from her half-breaths. "I can't maintain this pace."

"Sorry." He glanced at her, his expression darkening.

"What?"

"Nan doesn't get to hit you again."

"I won't have a problem sticking *her* with a dagger," Gwenyth muttered. "The dragon is a bitch. The second time she visited, she was wearing a fur wrap. It was the same color as Jenny."

"Are you sure? I thought the same, but you were closer."

"Oh, I'm positive. Is it possible she and her people have been lurking around Hissing Isle for longer than we think? She indicated an interest in your land."

"Now that makes sense. She must be part of the group who offered to purchase my land. I wonder if she met with my brothers." His steps slowed at the end of a rutted road.

Gwenyth halted at his side. A soldier wearing a scarlet tunic was tacking a poster on the wall of a cottage. A group of lessor dragons loitered, eager to read the contents the moment the soldier moved on to pin up the next sign.

Once the soldier pushed through the crowd and strode on, she and Leo eased closer to join the avid group of male and female dragons. No one paid any attention to them.

"What is it?" a woman demanded from the rear. "Read it out for all of us."

A chubby woman, who Gwenyth had noticed using her elbows to get to the front, cleared her throat, and began reading. "We hereby invite you to attend a special battle at the events arena to celebrate the betrothal of Leonidas, Champion of the Skies, to Nandag, The Strongminded. Prisoners will fight exotic animals and champion fighters in a battle to the death. Blood and gore guaranteed. A small donation will ensure your entrance to the arena. Doors open at dusk this evening."

Leo's arm, which had curled around her protectively, tightened to the point of pain. Horror rose up her throat, threatening to choke her. They intended to make Leo a widower and to marry him off to Nan. She tugged on his tunic, diverting his attention from the excited conversations around them.

He started, gave her a quick squeeze, and wove his way through the curious bystanders. The locals seemed more intent on discussing the upcoming battle while yet more newcomers struggled to get close enough to read the poster.

Leo led her down a quieter, residential street. He plucked a cloak off a washing line and a black tunic and a hat off another. He kept them moving at a brisk pace. They passed other huddles of dragons reading the posters. Several dragons stared at them but none spoke. Gwenyth was positive they'd recognized Leo, and she wondered how long it would be before the guards discovered she and Martinos had disappeared.

Around the next corner, the area beyond was more rural. A herd of goats sat in the shade of green trees. To their left, a dragon shifter plowed a field with two oxen.

"Put on the cloak," Leo said, handing her the cloth. "If it's too long, I'll hack off the bottom. We can keep the surplus fabric to cover your face while we're flying. Pull up the hood to conceal your hair and face."

He planted the hat on his head and exchanged his pale brown tunic for the black one he'd pilfered from the washing line. "Just over the rise, there's a field where I can shift. If we can get that far, no one will see me morph to a dragon. I'll skim the tops of the trees until the castle is out of sight before we gain height. Let's go."

Leo set a brisk pace, and she did her best to keep up. The farmer spotted them and waved. Leo waved back but didn't stop. Gwenyth's breathing became heavy, and a pain dug in her side. Her face ached while her head throbbed in tandem. She recognized her pounding temples as a symptom of dehydration. With the evening's excitement, she hadn't collected drinking water.

She swallowed and forced her legs to keep moving. Time to rest once they reached safety. She'd find something to drink later.

The brow of the hill seemed miles away, the incline like a cliff. Sweat beaded on her forehead and under her clothes. She wanted to thrust aside the cloak, but she persevered. One foot after the other. One foot. The other foot.

Up ahead, Leo disappeared. Gwenyth made a push, fear giving her feet wings. He wouldn't leave her. He wouldn't.

Panic roared through her, her breath coming in hoarse pants as she crested the hill. Relief, big and bright, struck like a spear to her heart. Leo was there, worry etched into his features. He took half a step in her direction, his face creasing into a smile on seeing her.

"I'm coming," she wheezed. "My legs are shorter than yours."

He offered her a brief hug of apology. "Sorry, my lodestone," he whispered. "We must keep moving. My parents and Nan want you to die in the arena. Since the fight takes place this evening, it won't be long before they realize you've escaped and I've disappeared too."

She acknowledged his words with a squeeze of his hand. "Lead the way and I will follow."

"You look exhausted. Once we reach the safety of the trees, we can rest."

"Will there be water?"

"You're in luck. A stream passes through the clearing up ahead."

The brief stop made resuming the trudge to safety even harder. Every muscle in her thighs protested while her head ached so much her vision blurred. She wobbled, caught herself, and managed another two half-strides before she dropped.

Leo cursed and returned. He scooped her up and set a brisk pace across an open field. The bubble of water reached her ears, her desire to dampen her mouth, and dunk her head into its coolness, forcing a moan past her dry lips.

"What's wrong?"

"Thirsty and so hot and achy," she whispered. "It feels as if I've caught the flu."

"An illness?"

"Yes." The croak of sound hurt her throat.

"Not far to go," Leo promised and increased his speed.

Gwenyth's eyes closed, and the waves of pain merged into one big ache. Everything hurt, and she drifted until Leo set her down.

"You must take a drink before we enter the trees, my lodestone.

I have no vessel to fill."

A blast of trumpets sounded in the distance. Leo stiffened as the blare repeated.

"Hurry," he urged. "They've discovered us missing."

When her brain refused to function, her body stalled in movement. Seconds later, mountain-cold water struck her in the face. She cried out, her eyes widening in shock.

"Sorry," he whispered, his eyes full of apology. "Drastic measures." He filled a cupped hand with water and held it to her lips.

The frigid water was the best thing she'd ever tasted. "I can do it myself," she said and suited actions to words. She drank three hands full of water before Leo cautioned her to limit herself. Aware he was right, she drank one more before washing her face and neck.

"Gwenyth, we need to seek shelter," he said, urgency lacing his words. "The guards will split up and fly in different directions."

Nodding, she stood. "I'm ready," she said and prayed it was true.

"Here's what we'll do. During our lovemaking, our scents combined, and you took on more of a dragon scent. That works to our advantage. We'll mask your scent with mud and find a place to hide. Hopefully, a safe refuge where we can relax since the more we make love, the better chance we have of our followers thinking we are two dragons. The change of clothes will have helped too."

"Sounds like a plan. Which way?" Despite the oncoming danger, the idea of making love with Leo filled her with joy and anticipation.

With Leo in the lead, they entered the trees, following a narrow animal-made track. When they reached a spot where the path crossed the stream, Leo stopped.

"Time to cover your face, arms, and legs with mud."

She pulled a face. "Do it."

A few minutes later, they continued along the path that forged deeper into the trees. It became darker with the tree canopies creating a roof over their heads. The click of insects and the tweet of hidden birds brought a comforting note of familiarity, a sense she'd walked through here or a similar place.

"Have you been here before?" she murmured once the path grew wide enough for them to walk abreast. Although her head still thumped, the water had revived her flagging body.

"I used to play here with my friends."

"Your brothers?"

"My brothers have never been my friends," he said. "The boys I met while working in the castle kitchen with Cook and the ones I trained with while learning how to battle. We drank water from the same stream."

"Do you have a hiding place in mind?"

"There are two possible ones. The second is a cave. It's farther away, but we'll push onward for as long as you can manage. This forest is large, and it will provide us with cover plus get us nearer to the sea and the closest point of Perfume Isle."

The trumpet blast sounded again, and this time, the signal was closer.

"They're coming this way," Leo murmured. "Tread silently. No more talking. If you wish to communicate, tug on my tunic."

"Okay," she whispered.

The trumpeting came nearer, and she glanced up in apprehension, positive they'd be visible to the dragons who were flying overhead. With her gaze upward, she stood on a stick. The crack came loud to her ears, her heart jolting in apprehension, but her mistake came at the start of another trumpet blast. She swallowed, almost lightheaded with relief.

"The trees are too thick for them to spot us, but I'd still like to put more distance between us and the castle. If they don't find us during the first sweep, they might hire the dog master from the human village."

"Dogs?" Gwenyth asked in a faint voice. She imagined rabid canine creatures with sharp teeth and frothy mouths. She pictured blood. Hers. A shudder passed through her. "They'd send dogs after us?"

"It depends on how determined my parents and Nan are to capture us. My parents dislike dealing with humans. The dog master loathes doing business with dragons, but he might at the right price."

"You know him."

"I and several of the other humans disapprove of the way he

treats his animals. He can be cruel."

"This island isn't human friendly. Why do they live here?"

"Humans have always lived here," Leo said. "It's their home as much as it belongs to the dragons."

"Do we have to stay here?"

Leo sighed. "I love my home, but it might be best to stay far from my parents and brothers."

"Did you speak with your brothers?" she asked, curious because of the things Leo had let drop about his siblings.

"I spotted one of my brothers with Telus. Nemyr. I decided it was best not to interrupt the pair."

"Do you know why your brothers dislike you so much or why your parents mistreat you?"

"No," Leo said. "It wasn't always like this when my grandparents were alive. We seemed happier and more a family then. I used to spend a lot of time with my grandparents and my Uncle Joharan. He and my grandfather enjoyed nature and farming. He taught me everything I know about the land. I was with them during the attack. We went on a picnic, and rogue dragons attacked our party. I fell early, struck on the head by a blow. Uncle Joharan, my grandparents, and their two servants died during the fight. I guess the attackers thought I was dead. My memories of the day are fuzzy."

"And your parents took over after your grandparents' deaths."

"Yes. Given my parents' attitude toward me, I've wondered if they organized the attack. I've never voiced my suspicions because it didn't seem wise. Uncle Joharan was meant to rule rather than my parents."

"You don't recall the attackers?"

"The dragons wore special paint that covered their natural color. It turned them bronze." His brow wrinkled. "Over the years, I've heard whispers, but I don't have proof. Just my suspicions. Shush," he warned. "They're doing another sweep of the forest."

For an instant, Gwenyth heard nothing, then a trumpet blast rang out above their heads. The sharp note reverberated, and panic froze her. A low whimper squeezed past her compressed lips, and Leo urged her face against his broad chest. She leaned into his strength, and he let her take comfort from him.

The trumpet blared, this time farther away, and Gwenyth sagged in relief. His powerful arms held her up, gave her support.

"Sorry," she whispered. "I can't go back in that dungeon. It was cold and wet. Horrible. And I don't want to know what the arena battles involve. I get the sense I wouldn't leave alive."

"No," Leo agreed, his voice grim. "Given my parents' determination, I'm not even sure Perfume Isle will be a haven for us."

"What will we do?"

"I plan to get there and reassess."

"We'll do that then. How far is the cave? We're both tired and could do with rest."

Leo squeezed her shoulders, pride shining on his face. "My lodestone," he murmured, and he stole a quick but gentle kiss. His touch seared her lips, and that fast burst of fiery heat warmed her inside out.

"The stream runs parallel to the track up here. We'll walk along the stream bed and try to muddy our trail should they follow us with dogs."

Gwenyth followed Leo and stepped into the stream. The water ran over the top of her boots, but she didn't complain. She slogged through the bubbling flow, placing her feet carefully on the slippery stones. The water level decreased, and she bent her legs backward at the knee to empty at least some of the liquid in her boots. By the time Leo deemed it safe to walk on the track again, fatigue nipped at her. Sheer determination kept her moving and the knowledge they'd rest soon. Her pace slowed, and she caught Leo frowning over his shoulder at her.

"Another half an hour," he murmured.

"I can do it," she said and crossed her fingers in the hope she was telling the truth. She made it another ten minutes before Leo came back and swept her off her feet.

He swung her onto his back, and she clutched his shoulders and wrapped her legs around his waist to remain in place, leaving his arms free to push back overhanging branches and other obstacles. Exhaustion tugged at her again, and her eyes slipped shut. She couldn't remember a time when she'd suffered this level of fatigue.

She searched her mind and found it blissfully blank. For once, the emptiness seemed comforting rather than scary or confusing.

"We're almost there," Leo said.

Gwenyth's eyes flicked open to study their surroundings. The tree canopy wasn't as thick here, which bothered her. "Why are we stopping?"

"Do you require a bathroom break? And more water?"

"Yes, to both," she said.

"Go behind those trees over there." Leo pointed out a clump of trees and bushes. "The stream cuts closer to the path just ahead."

"Oh, joy," she muttered.

Leo laughed. "Hurry. If the search team flies this way again, we'll be more visible."

The warning lent her feet wings, and she scuttled behind a trio of trees to take care of business. Leo was waiting for her when she emerged. They drank before setting off again. As Leo promised, they soon reached the cave. The trouble was a precipice lay between them and the cave.

"Can't we fly up?"

"The cave entrance is on the face of the cliff. The ledge isn't big enough to hold my body while I shift back to human. Climbing is the only way."

She sighed. "I guess that makes it safe from the dragons tracking us. All right. Let's do this."

"You ascend, and I'll follow you," Leo said.

Although she hated the plan, she followed his instructions.

"There's a place for your right foot here." He guided her boot into position. "Grip that rock with your right hand."

Bit by bit, Leo helped her to climb the cliff face. Once they neared the cave mouth, he rose to the same level as her and helped her crawl into the cave. She collapsed on the uneven rocky floor, her trembling legs refusing to function correctly.

"My sweet Gwenyth," he whispered. "Just a bit farther, then you can rest."

She dragged her body deeper into the darkness, taking courage from the fact Leo was at her back. Safe. For now.

Moments later, Leo joined her inside the cave, his large frame making the gloomy space shrink. He reached for her, and she went to him, trusting him in a way she didn't think—couldn't remember—trusting another man. Sometimes now, if she allowed her mind to wander or to relax, she sensed a presence. Someone who'd hurt her. Made her so angry, she'd wanted to stab with a weapon. But whenever she drew on the memory, seizing that sliver of her past, it dissipated into mist.

Had she hurt someone? Killed them?

Gwenyth pushed out a sigh. The hopelessness and frustration emerged harsher than she'd intended.

"Is something wrong?" Leo asked.

She avoided the real topic in her mind to pursue one of her other concerns. "Are we safe here?"

"I think so," Leo replied, his callused hands cupping her face.

She watched him in the twilight. Despite all that had happened, the betrayal of his family, and their flight from the castle, he seemed upbeat. Confident they could get to Perfume Isle, that they would escape Nan, and that they'd find answers with the help of his friends.

"This must feel like history repeating itself," she said.

"What do you mean?"

"You told me you left the castle before to escape your brothers' taunts and cruelty, your parents' disinterest in you."

His big shoulders moved in a shrug. "I guess I did, although they weren't trying to kill my wife," he said, anger highlighting his words. "The worst part is I don't understand why my parents are forcing me toward Nan. Or why Nan wishes to marry me when she thinks of me as nothing more than a bug beneath her shoes. You said she wants my land, but that won't be part of the betrothal agreement. It will still belong to me."

"She inferred she'd get rid of you once you passed your usefulness."

"Bitch," Leo muttered. "Then there is the barrier failure. No one understands how it works to keep our worlds separate. And Martinos. His sister and my brothers stood at his trial and accused him of raping the girl. My gut tells me there is a connection, but I don't even know where to start. For everything we learn, the mystery and the possible answers become more convoluted."

Should she tell him and add to his stress? "I think my memory is returning," Gwenyth blurted before she'd even answered her own question.

"What have you remembered?" His expression had gone blank, and she could merely guess at what was running through his mind.

"There's an ominous presence hovering in my memories. I can't decide if I'm scared or angry or something in between. This specter makes me uneasy."

Leo sighed and settled on the floor of the cave in a reclining position. He arranged her body until she sprawled on top of him, and they were face-to-face. "That word describes everything rattling around in my head. None of the clues are aligning and it's frustrating as hell."

"Yes." Idly, she played with the ends of his hair, smoothing and tugging the strands.

"The one agreeable thing in this situation is finding you," he said, and he kissed her.

The meeting of their lips, the sweetness, and tenderness in the exchange had everything inside her softening. A yearning grew and bloomed. One Leo seemed to share.

"I want to make love to you," he whispered. "If you're too tired, we can wait."

"No. I mean yes," she said, cupping his face. "As long as you think we're safe."

"For now," he said. "Few people know about this cave. I

discovered it while hiding from my brothers. They never found me."

Reassured, she kissed him, letting her actions do her talking. Each kiss, each caress was slow and unhurried. A silent exchange of what they'd become to each other. Languorous waves rolled through her as he kissed her neck and nibbled hard enough to spike both pleasure and pain.

"Gwenyth," he purred in her ear.

The stubble dusting his jaw dragged across her chest, and the upper swells of her breasts. She clenched her thighs together, wanting to hold onto the delicious tickle of heat.

Leo lifted her tunic, the pads of his work-roughened fingers dragging across tender flesh. The decadent abrasion had wetness pooling between her thighs. Her breathing went shallow, and the muscles of her inner legs clenched. She kissed Leo's cheek, his shoulder, and wished they could disrobe and explore each other without hindrance.

His fingers skimmed her breasts, and he lifted his head to kiss her. His tongue stroked hers, keeping time with the rub of his thumb over her nipple. She squirmed against him, rubbing her lower body against his rigid shaft. His masculine groan thrilled her and sent an answering tug deep into her belly.

"Gwenyth," he whispered, the longing in his voice bringing the sheen of tears to her eyes.

Her mind pushed at her, insisting—rightly—that she didn't

even know if she was free to love Leo and what if she became pregnant? The sane part of her shoved these worries away, locking it behind a barricade to stop it from spoiling this moment with her brave dragon. If the dragons hunting them captured her, she'd die. Right now, she chose to celebrate life.

"Let me remove your trews," she whispered.

His arms loosened, and he allowed her to move down his torso to straddle his hips. Without haste, she tugged the fabric up and away from his erection.

"Do dragons never don underwear?" she asked.

"The fewer clothes to discard when we shift, the better." The lazy gleam in his green eyes was apparent even in the cave.

"I like my underwear," she said.

"I adore your underwear. Pretty lace and silky fabrics. It's different from garments available in the human village."

"Hmmm," she hummed as she pulled down his trews far enough to gain access to his engorged cock. She lowered her head and licked the crown, sucking a little before lifting her head at his gasp. "Too much?"

"Too good," he replied. "I find myself with little restraint around you. I want you too much."

"And that's a dreadful thing?"

"It is since I want to spend hours making love to you."

She stroked his abdomen and pushed up his tunic to gain access to his ridged abs. Her fingers drifted across the delineation of muscle and over his flat stomach before she returned to his cock. As she explored his length with her hands and mouth, despite his assertions he wouldn't last, velvet tension grew in her, expanding and crowding away the uncertainty that kept assailing her. She focused on Leo, his beautiful body, and the tiny pulses and flexes of his muscles she drew from him with her touch.

She rose enough to drag her trews to her knees and teased her flesh to relieve or maybe add to the tension growing inside her.

Leo hissed as she stroked him too, the beads of moisture forming at the tip of his cock, telling her how close he was to his climax.

"Gwenyth," he whispered, his tone hoarse.

She smiled, enjoying her feminine power even though it was a double-edge sword, hacking and swinging at her willpower too. Gwenyth lifted her body, situated herself, and sank down, taking his shaft in one increment at a time. She watched her lover as his flesh filled her, pausing when fully seated. For an instant, she savored the fullness.

"Gwenyth." Her name was a ragged whisper, and it said everything. His hope for the future. The depth of his feeling for her. His enjoyment of what they were doing together.

She lifted off him and took him again, her pace slow to savor the thick slice of pleasure from each sweep of his cock against her inner flesh. With each invade and retreat, she shifted the angle a fraction until she hit a special place. Her head fell back with a groan while she slipped her hand off his hip to stroke her clit.

Slowly, she increased her pace and soft, needy sounds bubbled from her throat. It was delectable agony—this rush of pleasure and sensation. Each rise and fall pushed more excitement through her. Her pulse thrummed, her heart thudding.

Then, on the next downward stroke, she was soaring from her body before jetting back down in a series of rapid spasms. She ceased the strokes of her tender nub, the orgasmic buzz making her eyes heavy-lidded.

"Beautiful," Leo whispered. He gripped her hips, holding her in position and thrust upward.

She made a purring sound of approval as his cock reignited a sensitive place inside her. Her skin flushed with heat, and somehow, another mini-climax rocked her. Leo grunted, his hips jerking upward in one more thrust before he stayed buried deep inside her. Gwenyth collapsed, and Leo wrapped his arms around her. Their mouths met with a ferocious heat that seared right down her throat and into her lungs.

Once their kiss ended, Leo pressed her face into his neck, and she yawned her exhaustion. She sensed fatigue lurked in Leo too. She'd close her eyes for a few seconds before she moved and righted her clothing.

Leo nuzzled Gwenyth's neck, but she didn't stir. He didn't wake her, content with their intimacy, their bodies still connected.

"We might make a child," his dragon whispered, even though

Gwenyth couldn't hear this conversation.

Leo thought about a child. His and Gwenyth's and his heart beat a little faster. *"Not before we're settled."*

"You don't want a child with Gwenyth?"

"More than anything," Leo replied. *"But you heard her. She's getting flashes of memories. Making a child in these circumstances mightn't be the best thing."*

"This worries you. The return of her memories."

"The mate bond hasn't snapped into place as my grandparents described it to me." Leo smoothed Gwenyth's hair.

"She is our one," his dragon said.

"I agree, but there must be a reason the bond remains absent." Leo sighed. *"Right now we have far more to worry over. For my parents to arrange an arena fight—that hasn't happened in over one hundred years. A fight to the death would be bad enough for a dragon, but to subject a female human to this kind of punishment is barbaric."* Leo shook his head in disbelief. *"Why do my parents want to get rid of Gwenyth? Is it Nan? My brothers? Or heck, it could even be Telus. There are enough suspects to fill a novel."*

"We keep to our plan," his dragon said. *"Staying on Hissing Isle is suicide. We need to get to our friends and investigate once we reach relative safety."*

"I hate to say it, but it might be best if we get Gwenyth back to the mainland. At least she'd be safe."

"No!"

"What if something happens to us? If our parents decide we're expendable? What then? Gwenyth will have little chance if she's alone on Hissing Isle. We'll keep to our plan, but if we can return Gwenyth to her world, we must take the opportunity."

"She has no memory," his dragon argued. *"She'll be vulnerable on the mainland too."*

"But there will be humans who can help her. People of her kind who do not wish her ill. We must think of Gwenyth's best interests."

"I don't wish her to go."

"Me neither," Leo said. *"But if this is the only way to keep her safe, we must let her leave."*

His dragon fell silent after their conversation. Leo shifted positions, separating his body from Gwenyth's, a part of him breaking at the loss of their connection. Like his dragon, he'd fallen for this wonderful human woman. Every instinct told him they were mates, the forever mates as described to him by his grandparents, yet the bond hadn't snapped into place.

He wished the answers weren't such a mystery.

CHAPTER 18

Release Me. Let Me Go

"My lodestone," a deep voice whispered. "It's time to go."

Gwenyth groaned as a hand shook her awake. Every muscle protested the rattle of her bones at a second shake.

"Stop." Her eyes flickered open to discover Leo smiling at her. "It feels as if I've just fallen asleep."

"It's almost dark enough to risk flying over the rest of the island."

"How long will that take?"

"Around an hour until we reach the coast," he said. "It depends if we have to stop to hide."

Gwenyth pushed to her feet and stretched out her aching limbs.

"Did you sleep?"

"A little. I have enough energy to get us to Perfume Isle."

Gwenyth's stomach gave a loud rumble, and she clapped her hand across her stomach. "Sorry."

Leo pulled a face. "I'm hungry too."

"How will we do this?"

"I think the quickest way will be if you climb on my back, and I'll carry you down. Your eyesight isn't as good as mine in the dark."

"Let's do this." Gwenyth trusted him totally.

Leo lifted her into his arms before she could blink. Seconds later, he was climbing down the cliff at a pace that had her closing her eyes as she prayed for a safe descent.

"We're on the ground," he said, humor radiating from his voice. "I can't see anyone, but I'll need you to keep your eyes open and watch for anyone following or searching for us. Can you do that?"

"Yes," Gwenyth said. Swallowing a bug or two was nothing compared with keeping them both alive.

A loud screech had her leaping off the ground. She whirled around to peer into the trees in front of them.

"A night bird. An owl," Leo said.

"What else will we see or hear?"

"Maybe wolves or deer. Other birds. Hopefully, not a single dragon."

Leo stripped off his boots, then his clothes and handed them to Gwenyth. She rolled them up into a bundle, and plaited her hair to keep it out of her face, and tied the end with a scrap of cloth she ripped from the bottom of her tunic.

"Ready," she announced.

Leo stood back and morphed to his dragon. He nuzzled her arm before picking her up and taking off. Straight into a cloud of bugs. She gasped and made a choking sound, almost dropping Leo's clothing and boots in her attempts to get the icky bugs out of her mouth.

"Fly higher," she called.

He did, and while she could see nothing apart from tree silhouettes and old volcanic plugs, she didn't think others would spot them either. It was quiet flying this high above the forest, and she heard no birds or animals. Instead, the wind rushed past them, and a quick glimpse above showed stars peeking between ominous clouds.

Half an hour later, the moon slid into view, and she spotted a lake in a clearing in the forest. Still no dragons. Had they ceased the search?

Probably not.

There had been something about the determination in Nan and in Leo's parents that told Gwenyth this was not over. As she scanned the landscape below them, she considered the reasons his parents and Nan were so insistent on the joining.

Without warning, Leo swooped toward the trees.

Popsicles. While she'd pondered, she'd failed to spot the two massive dragons hovering in the sky ahead of them. The nearest dragon trumpeted a victory trill and arrowed toward them talons outstretched.

He or she let rip with a stream of fire. Leo dodged, but the heat of the flames seared Gwenyth's skin.

Since he was carrying her, Leo couldn't return their attack. He could simply evade.

"Go lower," she shouted. "When we're close to the ground, release me."

The two dragons split up while Leo hesitated, hovering in the air. Gwenyth turned her head and spied a dragon intending to attack from behind. The other dragon—a black—rushed them head-on.

"Watch out, Leo," she screamed.

Leo gave a hard flap of his wings and shot upward before either dragon could attack. He flew fast and strong, swooping low to the ground. When he reached a small clearing, he flew even lower before he dropped her. Even though she'd expected it, she hit the ground hard. For long seconds, she gasped for breath, the abrupt collision with the firm ground exploding the air from her lungs. Obviously, she was not designed for flying or leaping from a moving dragon.

The sharp *whop-whop* of wings forced her to haste. She shoved to her feet with an audible groan and raced for the trees. A shot of flames seared the ground right where she'd sprawled mere seconds earlier. Sparks shot through the dried grass, and a blaze soon danced through the spot where she'd landed. Gwenyth retreated until the trees acted as a protective umbrella. The flames grew larger and lit the foliage.

From where she stood, Gwenyth couldn't see Leo or the dragon attacking him. She scuttled through the waist-high undergrowth while trying to make the least amount of noise. She planned to find an alternative place to view the overhead struggle, and hopefully, she'd think of a way to aid Leo.

She crept to the tree line. Both of the dragons—the black and the green—were attacking Leo. They were taking turns and attempting to tire him.

Gwenyth spied several fist-size rocks and scooped one up to gauge its weight. Now to test her throwing skills.

Another random thought surfaced. She'd been on the rep softball team as a youngster. Time to put her skills to use. She mentally measured the distance and fired her first rock. *Bullseye!* It worked better than she'd thought. She fired at the black dragon since she knew for certain this one wasn't Leo. Her second rock missed, but the third missile struck the dragon's chest as it banked to rush Leo.

Gwenyth put muscle behind her fourth rock and took satisfaction at the dragon's screech of fury. She hefted the next stone and fired, missing because the creature wheeled and flew straight at her position. Flames flared around her, crackling and hissing as they fed on the undergrowth and trees. Gwenyth jerked back and sprinted deeper into the woods. She scooped up more rocks and slipped between the trunks until she found another vantage point.

When she was in position, she spotted Leo and the green dragon. The black dragon was nowhere in sight. Gwenyth stilled, peeking from behind the wide girth of a mature tree. She paused, wondering whether she should fire more rocks. No, she'd hate to hit Leo by mistake.

She collected ammunition, sneaking through the trees and avoiding the smoking area while keeping watch for the black monster. Had she injured the dragon enough to ground it?

Surely not. Gwenyth stilled and watched, scanning her surroundings. The skip of a small pebble along a clear spot of ground had her freezing in position. Where was that dragon?

A pale shape slipped between the trees over to Gwenyth's right before disappearing. She kept watching, and the shape darted closer to Gwenyth's position. Was that Nan?

The figure moved again, and Gwenyth weighed one of her rocks in her hand. Her chances of helping Leo increased if Nan remained in her human form. Gwenyth waited until Nan scurried closer before she fired her next rock. She struck the dragon's shoulder and took great satisfaction in Nan's surprised roar of pain.

Gwenyth scooped up two more rocks and darted to a new position. In her black tunic, she blended with the darkness while

Nan's naked body glowed in the moonlight, making her easy to spot.

"Stop playing silly games," Nan shouted. "You can't escape me."

Maybe not, but she could fire at least two or three more rocks and make Nan hurt. Gwenyth wasn't stupid enough to return Nan's shout.

Instead, she watched the dragon shifter and took pleasure in Nan's frustrated curses. The woman had a nasty mouth on her. Gwenyth took up her next position against a wide tree trunk and waited for Nan to show herself again.

She still had Leo's dagger in her right boot, but she didn't intend to venture close to Nan since she'd witnessed Leo's speedy changes. If Nan caught her, she'd shift and spurt fire. Gwenyth would be toast before she...

Ah!

There she was—the cocky dragon.

Gwenyth waited for a clear shot. *Now!* She flung her rock. It struck Nan on the shoulder, and the woman bellowed in pain.

"The instant I get my hands on you, I'm gonna rip off your arms," Nan snarled. "You think you're clever, but you're a useless human. Don't forget that. Mongrel humans don't have the pedigree to marry dragons. You can't fly, can't breathe fire or protect yourself."

Gwenyth listened to Nan's ranting but didn't react. Leo didn't agree. He appreciated her enough to marry her in a human ceremony. Gwenyth didn't know how the dragon marriage ceremony differed, but their marriage was real. Leo hadn't lied about that.

"Where are you?" Nan demanded. "Show yourself."

Gwenyth bit back a snort. Did she look stupid?

The battle sounds continued overhead. Gwenyth edged to a clearing so she could see what was happening while still keeping an eye out for Nan. The dragon made it easy for Gwenyth to keep tabs on her with her taunts and threats. Gwenyth stilled, a rock curled in her hand.

"I've had enough of this," Nan declared. "If I have to burn the entire forest, I don't care. I'll smoke you out and hunt you down. Leo will marry me, and that is final."

Gwenyth curled her lips in disdain. *Over my dead body.*

Nan stalked into the open, and Gwenyth pelted her with two rocks. Nan roared and rushed Gwenyth's position. Gwenyth kept firing rocks, some striking and others missing.

"Try running," Nan said. "You won't escape. I have your position now."

Gwenyth gritted her teeth, her mind sorting possibilities. Leo was busy, and she needed to save herself. She ducked to pick up more stones. Apart from the dagger, they were her best weapon. Nan couldn't shift back to her dragon if Gwenyth stayed beneath the trees. That gave Gwenyth an advantage. From what she'd already noted, Nan's temper and her arrogance made her stupid.

The dragon woman didn't believe she'd lose.

Gwenyth would emerge the victor or die trying.

Leo counted on her.

"You're hiding again," Nan snapped. "Come into the open where we can fight to the death."

Huh! And give up her one advantage? Not likely.

Gwenyth froze, scarcely breathing. Wait. *Wait.* Nan darted between the trees. Gwenyth aimed, fired. The rock flew in a straight line.

Bam!

Nan howled, and before the dragon woman recovered, Gwenyth flung another stone. This one clipped Nan on the head. Gwenyth didn't wait to witness Nan's reaction, but judging by Nan's aggrieved roar, she figured she'd done some damage.

"You're a coward," Nan shouted, the end of her sentence rising to a shriek. "Stop hiding and show yourself."

Why, when she was having so much fun? Gwenyth slinked through the forest, placing her feet with care to avoid standing on a stick and signaling her position. She gathered suitable stones as she slipped past trees and crawled through undergrowth. She peeked around a rough-barked trunk and discovered Nan a few feet away. The woman stood with her hands on her hips, swiveling as she sniffed the air.

Gwenyth ducked out of sight, convinced Nan would discover her.

Her heart thudded, panic icing her veins as she waited for Nan to pounce.

It didn't happen.

Instead, Nan tromped farther away.

Gwenyth peeked out and saw blood trickled down the dragon woman's cheek. Time to get serious. Once Gwenyth had a dozen stones collected, she crept from behind the tree and pelted Nan with rocks. One. Two. Three. Gwenyth kept firing, ignoring Nan's cries of pain and squawked insults. Once she was down to her last stone, she kept it in her right hand.

This was the perfect place with the trees growing close together and a thick canopy. Nan couldn't shift here without risking her wings or tail becoming hooked in the trees. And if she did that, Gwenyth would be ready.

"When I catch you," Nan roared, "I will rip you apart with my bare hands. I will chew on your bloody heart."

Gwenyth wrinkled her nose, her pulse racing from her exertions.

That sounded messy. Painful too. She was doing better than she'd expected against Nan, and that bolstered her confidence. Humans weren't useless after all.

A few more rocks. She'd aim for Nan's chest, face, and head.

Draw blood.

Hopefully enough to shroud Nan's vision.

Then, and only then, could Gwenyth risk attacking with the dagger.

Overhead, the two dragons battled with ferocious roars, their flames lighting the night sky. Gwenyth pushed aside her worry for Leo. He'd earned his title Champion of the Skies by beating every other dragon in aerial battle. But she'd bet this dragon didn't play by the rules.

Another trickle of worry speared her until she reminded herself she could best serve Leo by disabling Nan. Back to the plan.

Gwenyth glided through the trees, able to see and hear Nan's location because of the dragon's cursing. Then the woman fell quiet. Didn't matter. Once Gwenyth collected enough rocks, she'd stalk the dragon woman and disable her. No one ever accused her of a lack of ambition.

Gwenyth carried her ammunition in her hands. Ready. She peeked from behind a tree and discovered Nan three steps away. Gwenyth hadn't heard a thing. Nan let out a roar of triumph, and Gwenyth acted on instinct. She pelted her rocks at Nan's head, one after the other. Nan stumbled, raising her hands to protect her face even as she continued charging. The instant the last rock left Gwenyth's fist, she curled her fingers around the hilt of her dagger.

Blood ran down Nan's face and into her eyes. She backhanded Gwenyth and, in a lucky break, connected with Gwenyth's jaw. Gwenyth fell, striking her head on a tree trunk on the way down.

Gwenyth saw stars. Her head rang, but every survival instinct had her forcing her unwilling body upright. Nan released another of her triumphant howls and sprang at Gwenyth.

Instinct had Gwenyth reaching again for the dagger and plucking the blade from her boot. It came free in a clean arc. Gwenyth gripped the knife, holding steady while, triumph shining in her face, Nan forced her weight downward. The dagger slid into Nan's chest, the dragon woman releasing a shocked scream.

Nan struggled, but too late, she realized her weight was forcing her down onto the blade. She kicked and screamed, but Gwenyth refused to release the dagger hilt.

It was kill or be killed.

Nan thrashed, blood from her wound splattering Gwenyth. Gwenyth closed her eyes, still seeing stars. Then, Nan stilled, the fight fading from the dragon woman. Gwenyth shoved at the dead weight and squirmed free, not opening her eyes.

She took a shaky breath, her head pounding, the throbs—a *bang-bang-bang* almost too loud to bear. She groaned and pressed her hand to her temple.

"Joanna, turn off that loud music," she shouted. "I can't hear myself think."

When nothing happened, she opened her eyes, frowning at the trees, the greenery. This wasn't her bed in her apartment. There was no loud music. Where the devil was she?

With a groan, she turned over and pushed to her hands and knees. Her gaze focused on Nan. The knife hilt stuck from her chest and blood pooled on the ground beside her.

Memories whooshed into Gwenyth. No Elizabeth. *Liza.*

That was the name her friend Cherry and her half-sister Rena used. With her head still aching, she sprang to her feet. Joanna, her daughter.

Popsicles! How long had she been gone? She counted back—a few days.

That's all, yet so much had happened.

Dragons.

Not only were they real, but she'd married one.

Cripes, she was still married to Tony because her ex refused to release her without a fight. He declined to sign the divorce papers because her father had money, and Tony wanted a cut. Bastard.

She glanced at Nan, who was still and showed no signs of life. Liza crept closer. She reached out a finger to test for a pulse. Nothing.

Nan was dead.

A savage roar sounded in the sky above her.

Leo.

Liza stumbled away from Nan and along a narrow track until she reached the small clearing where Leo had dropped her. Two green dragons were still fighting, talons slicing and gouging. Flames lit the sky.

How could she help?

Heck, she wasn't even sure which dragon was Leo.

She collected another pile of rocks until she had thirty or forty. Her head still thumped, but the worst of the pain seemed to have passed.

If she could help Leo, the fight might end on a positive note.

Liza sucked in a deep breath and marched to the middle of the clearing. "Leo!" she hollered and prayed that he heard her. "Over here." She waved her arms and shouted again.

One dragon broke away. She cataloged the beast's wounds. It roared and attacked, spurting fire in her direction. An enemy, then.

The dragon opened its giant maw. Its big green chest expanded. Instinct told Liza to run.

She sprinted into the trees and barely dodged the blast of flames that rained down on the spot where she'd stood seconds ago.

Not Leo.

The dragon hovered, his colossal head twisting as he searched for her or perhaps Nan. The dragon bugled then listened. Yep, searching for Nan.

Too late, buddy. The weak human prevailed.

Liza tiptoed through the undergrowth until she reached her pile of stones. Softball champion. Yay, her! She waited until the dragon flapped its wings and flew closer before she launched her first projectile.

Bam! Take that.

Her other rock flew true and smacked the dragon in the chest. The dragon let out a screech of rage and swooped toward her. Liza scooped up several of her rocks at a run and darted under cover again. She exited the forest at a different point and lobbed more rocks. They didn't all connect, but it was enough to distract the green dragon and divide his attention.

Leo, bless the dragon-man, caught on to her gambit while she chucked rocks. He spewed fire and attacked from the rear. Around her, the forest crackled with flames. Dead branches and undergrowth caught fire and smoke filled the air.

Liza coughed, her lungs burning. The muscles of her arms quivered from firing all the rocks, yet she kept going, scooping up rocks and chucking them at the dragon, finding it easy to tell the difference between the two now.

Their strategy seemed to be working. Her rock clouted the dragon's snout. It roared, pain and fury filling the dragon's shriek. While she distracted the dragon, Leo attacked, tearing at the beast with his talons. Hunks of flesh dropped from the sky. Blood. At first, Liza thought it was raining, but no. She ducked away, grabbing more stones for the instant Leo backed up.

But that didn't happen.

The green dragon's shriek cut off mid-bugle.

Liza watched the huge beast shudder, then it dropped like one of her rocks.

She fled for the safety of the trees but didn't make it. The dragon crashed into the ground, the wallop of contact, shaking the land. Liza dropped to her knees, her heart beating almost out of her chest. Was the dragon dead?

Leo landed and shifted to his human form. "Gwenyth!" he

shouted.

"I'm here," she said, waving from behind a burning tree. "Is the dragon dead? I'll circle to meet you."

Leo scanned the clearing, his expression harsh and urgent. "Where's Nan? Where did she go?"

"Dead," Liza shouted. "I'll come to you."

Liza circled the burning trees and bushes. It took her longer than she'd thought to go around the fire. When she reached Leo, he was beating at the flames near him, and she helped, using her tunic to smother the flames until scorched earth and charred trees remained.

"Gwenyth," Leo said, long strides bringing him to her side.

His arms wrapped around her. He smelled of sweat and smoke and soot covered his limbs. Despite this, Liza felt the same sense of safety she'd experienced each time Leo held her. A tiny grin started and widened.

Dragons were real. Who knew?

Liza pulled away so she could see Leo's face. "My name is Elizabeth. My friends and family call me Liza."

Leo froze, his expression going blank. "Your memory has returned?"

"It has." Understanding his apprehension, she smiled and hugged him hard. "I still like you, Leo, and have much to tell you. My daughter is in danger. It's imperative to keep her out of my ex-husband's reach."

"You're married?"

"My husband and I separated when I was still in New Zealand, a country on the other side of the world. My husband learned my father is wealthy, and he wants his share of that money. He's refusing to sign the divorce papers."

"So we're not married?" Leo said. "Because you already have a husband."

"No, I consider myself divorced and free," she said. "That's not important. I have to get back to my daughter as soon as possible. We must discover how I got here so I can return to Joanna."

CHAPTER 19

The Past Returns

"She's on the mainland all alone?" Leo asked, horrified that he'd split up a mother and child, albeit unknowingly. "I'm not even certain crossing the barrier is possible again."

"My best friend Cherry and my half-sister Rena will watch my daughter. I can count on them to have my back. They know what my ex is like." She paused, her focus going to the immense dragon body. "Do you know the dragon?"

"My brother," Leo said. "Goticranth, Eater of Bunnies."

"Oh, Leo. I'm sorry." She frowned. "Bunnies?"

Leo sighed. "It's a lengthy story. I didn't want to kill my brother. I tried to stand back, but he refused my offer of a talk."

"Goticranth and Nan intended to kill both of us." Liza's eyes flashed in indignation. "Do we even know why? You refused to marry Nan, so she kills you. What sort of strategy is that?"

Leo shrugged, tired, physically, and mentally. His dragon hadn't uttered a word since Goticranth and Nan had attacked. The closest brother in age to Leo, now dead. Nan dead. The consequences would ring over their heads if they remained on Hissing Isle.

"Leo?"

"Gwenyth—I mean, Liza. I'm tired."

"Me too," she confessed. "As much as I want to discover a way to return to my daughter, neither of us can help her if we're so exhausted we can't see straight."

"There is a stream close by. We can wash before we find a place to rest for a few hours."

"Thank you." Liza placed her hands on his shoulders and stood on tiptoe to kiss him. Her lips lingered, and he held her tight and took the kiss deeper. Making the kiss hotter. Because he knew without a doubt that she was his mate. She'd fought at his side, and together they'd beaten Nan and his brother. He loved her, and she intended to leave the Dragon Isles.

"What if we can't discover a way to return you to the mainland?"

"We will." Her tone was fierce. Determined.

Leo led the way to the stream, allowing his senses to guide him.

Liza followed him. "How do you know which direction to walk? Have you been here before?"

"No, I've never landed this far out. Only near the cave. I can smell the water."

"Interesting. Nan couldn't seem to smell me. She kept spouting taunts to lure me out. Pure arrogance! She thought I'd fold like a pack of cards."

"I keep trying to think why Nan wanted to marry me, apart from the land. That couldn't be the sole reason. Why were my parents determined the marriage go ahead? None of my answers make the slightest bit of sense to me."

"Something was afoot. Martinos thought there was, but he didn't know either. Your brothers and Nan had trapped him into something he couldn't control. Maybe we'll find more answers," Liza said.

"I hope so. The why is going to drive me crazy until I learn more."

"Lots of random puzzle pieces that don't fit. Can you remember arguments or something else in the castle while you were growing up?"

"I was a child. My parents talked about Uncle Joharan, something about having a child with a common dragon, but I don't know any details. Not long before robbers attacked and killed my grandparents and my uncle, there was a falling out between them and my parents. You know, I'd forgotten that until now. My grandparents came to collect me, and my grandmother took me for ice cream while my grandfather and parents discussed something important."

"Who would know about this? Is there anyone we could question?"

Leo thought, trying to recall what had happened. "Telus has been around for ages. He's always part of any decision my parents make." He forced his mind back and shook his head. "I was a youngster. All I remember is trying to decide what flavor of ice cream I'd choose once my grandmother and I reached the shop."

"Telus flew to your cottage to deliver the summons. Is that normal?"

"No," Leo said. "I thought it odd, but there was so much going on. My parents' demands. Meeting you. Finding Jenny."

"The fact that Nan was wearing wolf fur means she or someone known to her trespassed on your land."

"Which means she and whomever else is part of this scheme have been watching me for some time."

"You never sensed them?"

"No."

"It might be unrelated."

Leo led her into a small clearing where the stream had widened to form a pool. "If it flies like a dragon and blows fire like a dragon, then it must be a dragon."

Liza flashed him a quick grin that made his heart race and longing creep through him. He didn't want her to leave, even though he understood her child must come first.

"Is the water safe for swimming?"

"Yes, but it'll be cold," Leo said.

"Not a problem. I have you to warm me up." She sat on a fallen log to remove her boots.

"Tell me about your daughter. Is she like you?"

Liza beamed. "She's six-years-old, and everyone says she looks like me. Her hair is long and straight and the same brown as mine. She loves school, and her favorite thing is painting. I can't draw a picture to save myself, but Joanna gets her artistic talent from her father. She enjoys reading and likes outdoor activities too. You and Joanna would like each other."

"You want us to meet?"

"Our marriage might not be legal, but I went into this with a rational mind. I could've said no. I didn't."

"So you're not leaving me?" Leo asked, and he felt his dragon stir, the rush of awareness he experienced when his other half took an interest in his human activities.

"I don't want to leave you. I'm not sure what we'll do, but my priority is getting to Joanna and making certain of her wellbeing." She stood and shimmied out of her remaining clothes. She'd discarded her tunic since it had holes in it after putting out the fire, but she still wore her underwear and her trews. "Are you swimming too?"

"Yes."

She'd saved his clothes and tucked them away under a tree, so between them, they had enough clothes to wear.

He held out his hand, and his heart did a brief blip when her fingers curled around his. His dragon purred, happier now that they'd established returning to her daughter didn't mean leaving them.

The water was every bit as cool as he'd expected. Liza froze when it reached her knees.

"If I wasn't so filthy and stinky, I'd flee like a scared baby girl," she shared.

"I'll warm you. I promised, and I never go back on my word."

"You're an honorable dragon, Leonidas, Champion of the Skies, and I'm glad we met."

"Even though my appearance shocked you so much that you drove your steel box over the cliff?"

"It's called a car. Besides, you rescued me."

"The best decision of my life. Come on. It's easier if we dive under."

"I know," she said with a grimace. "One. Two. Go!"

Liza screeched as he dragged her into the deeper water. He grinned and sank beneath the surface. When he bobbed up again, Liza's hair was wet. He scrubbed at the soot and blood on his chest and torso. Most of the wounds inflicted by his brother had already healed. He'd been lucky, and Liza's intervention with the rocks had helped him to win. A tiny part of him had hated hurting his brother, although that had passed when his sibling had no compunction in trying to kill him.

He wished he knew why. The why was eating at him, but now he had a list of suspects, most of them related to him. Something to worry about later.

Besides, he was with Liza, and they were alone and naked.

"*Yes,*" his dragon hissed, and relief stuttered through Leo at the arrival of his other half.

A few feet away, Liza was scrubbing at the black smudges on her upper body.

"Let me," he said, his voice emerging in a husk of want.

Liza's tinkly laugh amused him, his delighted reaction widening her grin to toothy and knowing.

"I recognize the glitter in your eyes, Leonidas, Champion of the Skies. You're feeling amorous."

"Copious sex," his dragon piped up.

"Yes," he admitted while mentally shushing his dragon. "I thought I'd lost you, but I couldn't search while my brother was trying to kill me. Dropping you in that way scared me to death."

"Hey." Her teasing smile faded. "We both had jobs to do. I might be a human, but I have strengths in the same way you do. We're a team."

"Always?" he asked, wishing he could bite back the words that reeked of insecurity.

"Always," she confirmed, closing the distance between them. She tugged down his head and kissed him, her hands and lips cool from the water in the stream. "Let's finish washing and grab some rest."

While it was an excellent plan, the last thing Leo wanted was sleep. "And if I prefer not to sleep?"

"I'm wired myself," Liza admitted. "We'll cuddle and kiss and do anything else that comes to mind. How does that sound?"

Leo took a step back while holding her gaze. He scrubbed his hand over his chest. "That is a fantastic plan."

Once they were clean, they joined hands and waded from the stream.

"This way," Leo said, leading her back into the trees. He stopped beside a green sliver of ground, a spot where the tree canopy covered their presence should anyone search for them. "This should offer comfort for rest."

Liza waggled her eyebrows at him.

"Your name suits you," he said. "Liza is mischievous while Gwenyth was more serious."

"Because Gwenyth had dragons chucking her in jail and trying to kill her." She paused. "Do you think Martinos made it to safety?"

"If he traveled as far as the human village." Leo cocked his head, his gaze intense. "Should I roar with jealousy?"

"No." Liza never hesitated in her reply. "I believe he's an innocent victim in this situation, as much as we are."

Leo nodded.

"Enough about Martinos," his dragon whined. *"Get to the enjoyable stuff."*

Leo barked out a laugh.

"What?"

"My dragon wants to cease the chatter and have sex."

Liza grinned, and Leo stared. He was coming to love her radiant face. Her sunny smile and the dimples that dug into either side of her mouth. She sashayed closer and placed her cool hands on his chest.

Her fingertips stroked across his tattoo, and a dragon purr echoed through Leo's mind.

"By all means," Liza said, then the teasing went out of her. "I hope Joanna is okay."

"You said your friend and sister would look after her."

"Yes, but Tony has legal rights because he's Joanna's father. Tony will seize the opportunity and make it difficult for Cherry and Rena. My daughter will be caught in the middle."

"I'm sorry, my lodestone." Leo drew her against his chest, his hand cupping her head. Her lips grazed his chest, right over his tattoo. His dragon released another rumble of a purr.

"We'll figure something out. Let's rest for a while," she said.

They stretched out together on the grass, which was even softer than he'd imagined. Now that he'd slowed down, the hammering blows his brother had landed on Leo's body ached. Fatigue weighted his muscles, but lying next to Liza soothed him. He reached for her face and guided their mouths together. Their slow kiss sent lazy satisfaction through him while his dragon cheered. The kiss started unhurried, but his dragon's excitement and Liza's proximity had Leo deepening the caress.

Their tongues tangled, and hands roamed with intent. He savored her silky skin beneath his palms, the catch of her breath when he mapped her body. He entered her, stroking into her hot core until they both gasped and strained for release.

The very second he climaxed, Leo felt the solid click within him.

Beneath him, Liza gasped and froze, her fingertips digging into hips.

"Leo?"

"Yes, my lodestone." He answered her in his mind and waited in breathless anticipation.

"Leo," she whispered.

"Talk to me in your mind."

Leo and his dragon waited again.

"Can she hear us?" His dragon ran out of patience.

"I'm not going crazy. I can hear you, and is that your dragon?" Liza sounded hesitant.

"Yes. Yes. Yes!" His dragon whooped, and Leo felt his tattoo battering his ribs in a weird dragon boogie.

"Well, this is a cozy threesome." This time Liza's thought held teasing and laughter.

"We're one," Leo whispered. "I'd heard tales of soulmates, and

I suspected you were the one for us, but when nothing happened, I doubted the old stories."

"Can we talk whenever we want without others hearing us?"

Liza shifted position and peered up at him, her expression intent.

"Not if we're in different towns or islands, but if we're in the same place, we can communicate telepathically. We can converse over short distances."

"So we're official," Liza said.

"Yes. Yes. Yes!" His dragon spoke for him.

"All right, dragon-man," Liza whispered. "You need to close your eyes and rest."

"I don't think I can. My mind is too busy. What do you say to starting our journey to Perfume Isle now? I'd prefer to avoid my parents."

"Put that way, I agree. There's no telling what their next step might be. What did we do with our clothes?"

"You left them by the stream," informed his dragon.

"Huh," Liza said. "That wasn't smart."

"I'll get them." Leo pushed to his feet and retraced their steps to find their clothes. On his return, Liza scrambled into her underwear and pulled on the pair of trews she'd been wearing.

"You'd better wear my tunic," Leo said. "We will fly high, so pull on the cloak too. It'll be colder than you've experienced so far."

Liza followed his instructions, then they walked until they

came to a larger clearing within the trees. There, he shifted. Liza approached Leo and waited for him to pick her up in his talons.

Seconds later, they were off, Leo's wings flapping as he lifted them into the air.

It was still dark, but the moon peeked from behind its scant cover of cloud and sent enough light for him to see their surroundings.

"How long before we reach the coast?" Liza asked him through their mind link.

Leo thrilled at the communication. *"About ten minutes, I think. The crossing to Perfume Isles will take between two to three hours. My friend's home is near the coast. Are you cold?"*

"I'll manage. Tell me about your friends. Who are they, and how did you meet them?"

"I went to school and first learned to fight there. My friends are Durgess and Rafael. They're the same age as me, and we trained together. Like me, Durgess and Rafael are younger sons. Their brothers are much nicer than mine. I look upon their brothers as my brothers. It's always fun when we get together."

"They'll help us?"

"Yes."

"My friend Cherry is like that. She and my sister Rena have my back against Tony and his shenanigans."

Leo flew over the forest, and soon a briny scent filled the air. His ears caught the rattle of pebbles as the waves rushed forth and receded.

"I wish I could see more," Liza said. *"The trees and mountains are so pretty. I love the scenery around your home."*

"Me too," Leo replied. He hoped his friends might have info since they often traveled to Smoking Isle for business. Once he and Liza reached Perfume Isle and rested, he'd fly toward the mainland. Liza wanted to get back to her daughter, which was understandable. The child was young, and with Liza's ex-husband causing trouble, of course, she wanted to return.

The troubling part was he wasn't sure where that left him.

Was there some way he could stay with Liza and travel with her?

His people had retreated to the Dragon Isles hundreds of years ago to escape persecution. Returning to the mainland would mean hiding his otherness and not flying whenever the urge took him. Leo wasn't confident he could handle that, but he couldn't lose Liza either.

"What are we going to do?" he asked. *"I don't want to lose you, but you want to find your daughter and ensure her safety."*

Liza sighed. *"I haven't thought that far ahead. I feel as if I'm getting tugged in dozens of directions and fighting to stay upright."*

Leo understood what she meant. *"If we can't find a tear in the protective barrier, we'll journey to visit the druids on Smoking Isle. They're responsible for keeping the shield in position, and each of the islands pays a tithe to them to ensure this happens. Each of the island rulers taxes their residents."*

"Has someone stopped paying their tithe?" Liza asked.

"That's a possibility."

Leo continued flying in silence. Then, because his curiosity itched about his mate, he asked questions, eager for information.

"You said you live in a village. What is its name? What do you do?"

"West Bansrston is the town where my sister, my friend, and I live. I work in a cafe. We sell tea and coffee and make cold drinks. We also sell food. I do a bit of everything—take orders, make coffee, waitressing if my boss takes a booking for a private function. Sometimes, I help in the kitchen. I might do the dishes or bake muffins. There are always tables to clear and customers to serve and chat with. Cherry, my friend, owns a bookshop. Occasionally, I'll help her if she's busy. I love to read books, which is how Cherry and I met. In fact, the reason I thought you were my husband when we first met and that we were on our honeymoon was because of the last book I read. A romance about a couple who'd recently married."

"Ah, I wondered why you'd assumed that. Now it makes sense."

"What else?" his dragon asked.

"In my spare time, I'm writing a book about dragon mythology. When I met you or rather when you rescued me, I was returning home after interviewing a couple. They told me the story of the last dragon ever seen in England."

"A distant relation," Leo said. *"A human killed him when all he wanted to do was rest after an arduous journey."*

"I'm so sorry. Humans panic when they see something they don't understand. Not that this excuses the actions of the human, but from what I hear, the dragon's sudden arrival scared the locals and the visitors at the village fair. They didn't understand the dragon required rest."

"You're not frightened of dragons," Leo said.

"No, but since I was researching dragons and collecting myths and legends, your appearance fascinated me. I forgot to watch the road—the reason my car flipped over the barrier. I was lucky the sight of a human didn't scare you. You saved me."

"Fate," Leo said, his words ringing with truth.

"Is it possible Nan and your brothers are responsible for the barrier malfunction?" Liza asked.

The notion had occurred to Leo, but he'd discarded it because his brothers would've gloated. They enjoyed lording it over their friends and acquaintances. *"I suppose it's possible, but I'm certain the rumors would've caught up with me."*

"I haven't been here long enough to learn the politics and the way each island runs, but I wondered if it would be an advantage for dragons to leave the Dragon Isles. How do you get your supplies? The things you can't make yourselves. Has there been a surplus of luxury items available?"

"Excellent points," Leo mused. *"I don't hang around the dragon village or the castle enough to know the answer to your question. Whenever I require food or supplies, I visit the human village."*

"*Have you noticed anything off there? That's another possibility,*" Liza said. "*Maybe some of the humans would prefer to move to the mainland instead of staying here. Or, a third possibility—maybe the druids in charge of things are open to bribes. Is there a head druid?*"

Another excellent point. Leo didn't have the answer. He kept flying, the trip going faster than he'd thought because of the tailwind and the fact he had Liza with him.

"*Is that... Are those dragons ahead of us?*" Liza asked.

Leo scanned the sky. While he'd flown, and they'd conversed, the sky had lightened. Liza was right, but the flight of dragons was too far away for him to identify.

"*How do you communicate between the isles?*" Liza asked. "*Is it possible these dragons are trying to intercept us?*"

"*I don't know. We should see land soon. If the wind is in the right direction, I get a hint of the spices that grow on the island. The fishermen take messages between us. That's all we've needed for communication.*"

"*So these dragons might have received a message from the castle. There are dragons behind us,*" Liza said, seconds later. "*Four. No five dragons.*"

Leo increased the pace of his wing strokes, trying to keep worry from flooding his mind. Nothing about this boded well for him and Liza. Exhaustion nipped at his heels, the battle with his brother and lack of rest slowing him.

"*I can see land,*" Liza said. "*How far away do your friends live?*"

"*A few miles inland.*"

"*Will we make it to safety in time?*"

Leo wanted to lie, but he couldn't. Not to his mate. "*I'm tired and not flying as fast as normal. It will be difficult to fight because I'm carrying you. I can't drop you again. We're too high. Last time we were lucky you didn't get hurt.*"

"*At the first opportunity, we'll talk to someone who can design a saddle or at least experiment with me sitting on your back. You must be free to fight,*" Liza said. "*That way, my hands would be free too. I could carry a weapon and help you.*"

"*I haven't heard of anyone doing this before.*"

"*We'll be the first,*" Liza said.

Leo studied the approaching dragons. A blue and two greens. He kept flying because there was nothing else he could do.

"*Do you recognize them?*"

"*Not yet.*"

"*What will we do?*"

Leo's heart soared at Liza's *we*.

"*I intend to keep flying toward our destination. In about five minutes, I should be close enough to the approaching dragons to identify them.*"

"*And the ones behind?*"

"*I think we can assume the ones following us are chasing with evil intent.*"

Fatigue swept Leo, every bruise and cut aching now that their destination was in sight. How the devil were they going to get through this?

Liza's heart fluttered against her rib cage, fear an itch along her spine. Her head angled back to spot the five dragons behind them who were gaining. The three dragons in front were closer.

"*Do you recognize them, Leo?*"

"*Friend,*" he said after a lengthy pause, his voice lighter than it had been earlier.

"*Plan?*"

"*Keep flying toward my friends and hope we reach them before those chasing catch us.*"

Liza wished she'd thought to grab a handful of rocks. Leo wasn't as speedy now, and she sensed his exhaustion. Frustration thumped her over the head since there was nothing she could do to help. She glanced back at the chasing dragons. They were nearer now.

"*They're flying in formation,*" she said.

"*Do they have sashes or breastplates?*"

Liza squinted through the constant rush of air. "*Yes.*"

"*Security. Either my parents or my brothers sent them after us.*"

"*How did they know where we were?*"

"*They might have discovered my brother's body or spotted the burned forest.*"

"*Your friends are closer than the soldiers.*"

Leo didn't reply but kept flying, his wings moving in a steady beat. When Liza glanced behind them again, she gasped. The soldiers had slashed the distance between them. They weren't going to make it.

Without warning, heat seared behind them.

Leo angled upward just in time, the flames missing them by inches.

"Leo, fly lower and drop me into the sea. I'm a powerful swimmer. I can make the shore by myself."

"No," Leo shouted, his reply a blast of deafening sound. *"I can't lose you."*

"If you keep holding me, you're at a disadvantage. You can't use your talons. Please, Leo. We have no alternative." Liza prayed the water was deep enough for what she intended. *"Leo, listen to me. If I die, I leave my daughter at the mercy of my ex-husband. I need at least one of us to survive. If something happens to me, find your way to the mainland. Save Joanna. Will you do that for me? Leo?"*

After a long moment, he replied, *"Don't die, my lodestone. Please. Without you, my world will have no light."*

"I'm expecting you to live up to your name and whop their butts. You hear me? Fight with your friends, then we'll find each other again. What is the name of the village where I will find your friends?"

"Travel to Maidstone village. Ask to speak to anyone at the House of Ghan. Tell them Leo sent you and you are my mate. They will help you. Are you certain about this?"

Leo's tension communicated itself in his voice. He hated her suggestion.

"Drop me to give us both a chance to survive." Liza hoped like hell she was speaking the truth. Leo had become vital to her in the scant time they'd known each other. He and Joanna plus Cherry and Rena and her dad were the ones who mattered. *"Now, Leo."*

As she spoke, he changed his flight path. He still flew toward Perfume Isle, but on a downward trajectory. As he flew closer to the sea, she tensed, certain this was a crazy idea, but unable to think of another way to ensure they survived. Those soldier dragons flying behind them looked mean, and they crept closer with every beat of their wings. They hadn't fought a battle to the death like Leo had and were fresher.

Panic seized her, every muscle tensed. The sea became closer and closer, the waves much bigger than they'd appeared from above. She had to do this.

"Are you sure about me dropping you? What if some of the soldiers follow you?"

"You won't let them." Of that, she was supremely confident. Leo would defend her with his last breath, and she could do nothing less.

"I love you, Leo. Now, go as low as you can and release me."

Still, Leo hesitated. For a moment, Liza thought they might both strike the sea, but Leo opened his talons. The wind whipped at her hair, and Leo's oversize tunic as she discarded the cloak she'd used to keep herself warm. Liza jumped from Leo's protective hold and was falling, falling, falling.

"I love you, my lodestone. Keep safe. I will come for you. That is my solemn promise."

Leo's heartfelt words flowed through her mind, and she had a flashback of her first glimpse of Leo, her shock and wonderment at seeing a dragon, then the freefall of her car. The remembered terror caught in her throat, a scream escaped, and she struck the water feetfirst.

The icy chill was a wakeup and jerked her brain out of her panic. Disorientation threw her, and for a dread-filled moment, she wasn't positive which way was up.

"Liza!" Leo's panic equaled her own.

Bubbles. She remembered her mother telling her once after they swam together at one of New Zealand's surf beaches and a wave had struck them both. It had been like a washing machine, sending her younger self every which way. She hadn't focused on anything except her next breath of air. And while her mother had explained bubbles wouldn't help in that case because of the churning water, if the waves weren't as rough, the bubbles always led to the surface. Liza kicked strongly, struggling a little with the surplus fabric of Leo's tunic. Her lungs protested, and all she could think of was her next breath. She kept kicking, following the bubble trail.

Finally, she burst above the surface of the waves and sucked in a huge breath.

"Liza!"

Liza floated on her back and gazed up at the sky. Although the sun hadn't risen yet, flames from several dragons made it seem daylight. From way down here, she couldn't tell which dragon was Leo.

"I'm okay," she told Leo. *"I'm heading to shore now. You need to concentrate on getting rid of the soldiers. Are you certain they are your friends? The ones coming from the direction of Perfume Isle."*

"Yes, my lodestone. I love your courageous spirit."

"Focus," she told him. *"See you soon."*

Liza took one last look at the dragons roaring and fighting overhead. Apprehension prickled in her, concern for Leo's safety. She turned toward the shore and gulped. This wasn't going to be a picnic for her either. Her arms already hung like heavy weights from her shoulders.

A pained screech cut through her thoughts of discomfort, and she trod water while her gaze shot upward. One dragon was falling, flames surrounding its massive body as it dropped like a rock. The dragon struck the water and created an immense wave.

Popsicles!

Liza gulped a huge breath and dove beneath the surface. The pull of the water tugged at her tunic top as she went deeper. Liza stayed down a little longer before surfacing again.

She counted the dragons. Well, at least Leo's friends had evened the odds.

Liza wasn't sure how long she swam, but by the time her feet could touch the seafloor, her breaths came in ragged gasps, and her limbs ached from overuse. She staggered from the water and up the sandy beach on legs that wanted to bend like pieces of rubber. Liza couldn't remember ever suffering such lethargy. She recalled the direction Leo had told her to walk, but to get started, she needed to climb a hill and forge a path through the forest that grew on this side of the island.

She fell and stayed seated to catch her breath. From her position on the beach, she could see and hear the dragons fighting. Three dragons flew over the trees beyond the sand, coming from an inland location. Their bugled challenges rang through the air, and with their arrival, some of the fighting dragons broke away and retreated toward Hissing Isle.

"Liza!"

"I'm resting on the beach, Leo. Getting my breath back after my swim. You okay?"

"Will be as soon as I can hold you."

Liza pushed herself to her feet, despite protests from her battered body. She spotted Leo's green form flying in her direction and waved her arms even though her biceps and triceps protested the action. Six other dragons followed him at a slower pace, and Liza stared in amazement, wanting to pinch herself.

Leo landed and shifted. Liza hustled to meet him halfway, and it was the best feeling in the world when his arms enclosed her, and he held her in his protective embrace.

"My lodestone," he murmured for her ears. "I promise never to drop you again."

"Twice in one day was terrifying."

"For both of us."

The dragons landed on the sand, each dragon shifting to reveal five males and one female.

"This is Liza, my mate," Leo said, and she thrilled to the possessive and proud note in his words. "Liza, this is Blaze, my battle companion, Rafael, and Griffith. They're brothers." He glanced at the other dragons in askance.

"Brigitte and Gattock," Blaze said. "Cousins."

The dragon men and woman all had light brown hair, some with blond streaks, brown eyes of various shades and the strong, fit bodies typical of the dragons she'd met so far. Luckily, they were also friendly.

"A human mate," Rafael said, although he wasn't a smartarse or rude about her human status. "Where did you meet?"

"Ah," Leo said. "It's a long story."

"Condense it," Rafael said in a terse voice. "I want to know why the guard dragons from your castle are attacking you and your mate."

So Leo told them about flying through the barrier and Liza driving off the road. Part of Liza thought they'd doubt Leo, but the men stared at each other. He told them of his parents arranging a betrothal for him and the subsequent events that had led him and Liza to flee to Perfume Isle.

"That's interesting. We were out here early searching for Sasha, our sister. She's missing," Blaze said. "She argued with our mother and went for a flight to cool off. She told Mother she intended to visit her friend. Three weeks ago now. No one has seen her since."

"Could that be the answer?" Rafael asked. "Somehow, she crossed through the barrier."

"Did she go flying in the afternoon?" Leo asked.

"Yes." Blaze nodded, his gaze intent.

"Same time as me. I was flying parallel to the mainland. After I plucked Liza from her steel box, I almost ended up trapped. The barrier grew thicker, and I had to force my way through. I don't know how long the barrier was down or if this has been happening for a while."

"By Lodar!" Rafael cursed.

The others shared a glance.

Blaze scowled. "If our sister is trapped on the mainland, that'd explain everything."

"My daughter is there too," Liza said.

"That's why we're here," Leo said. "We hoped you might have answers to help us get to the mainland or at least make a plan."

Rafael grunted and clapped Leo over the back. "No knowledge but dozens of questions. Come home with us, and we can talk further. I have to return to the House of Ghan tonight, but Blaze and Griffith will look after you. My parents will wish to hear your tale too."

"Thank you," Leo said. "Liza and I would welcome a safe place to rest."

Later that night, after a hot meal and repeated tellings of their story, Liza lay in Leo's arms in one of the many bedrooms in the Mountholden's family mansion.

"Can't sleep, my lodestone?"

"Every muscle in my body aches, but my thoughts won't cease scurrying around inside my head."

"Mine too," Leo said. "You heard what the Mountholden sire said. They have paid their tithe to the druids. The Mountholdens are as clueless as us,"

"Do you think the druids will help?"

Leo didn't speak for a while. "They're a strange bunch and keep to themselves."

"It's funny, but I suggested to my friend we take time off and have a vacation on Lindisfarne. The locals call it Holy Island. You can drive along the causeway if the tide is right. I thought it would be a suitable place to hide where Tony might have trouble locating us. Is it possible to get to the island from here? I'm desperate to hug my daughter."

"We, my lodestone. We will ask the druids if they'll allow us to pass through their world and onto Lindisfarne. Ask if this is possible."

"What if the druid's magic is failing, and that's the problem? I mean, do you understand how the magic works?"

"It doesn't matter as long as the barrier is functional."

"Perhaps dragons should've asked questions."

"Once we have an audience with the druids, we should have some answers, and our options will be clearer."

"I just want to hold my daughter," Liza blurted out. Tears formed behind her eyes, and the lump in her throat threatened to choke her. Repeated swallowing did little to shift the obstruction.

"I know." Leo stroked his hand down her spine. "We'll find a way. I promise."

Liza pressed closer to Leo and kissed his throat. "Cherry and Rena will do their best, but I know Tony will prove difficult. The lengths he's willing to go to get his way scares me."

"You have a valiant heart, my lodestone. Believe in your friend, your sister. They will do their part while we do ours."

"You make it sound so easy."

"I found you," he said. "My true mate. We will rescue our daughter."

"Our daughter?"

"Well, I hope to have more children, because our number one

daughter will require siblings. But you are my mate, so that makes Joanna mine. You are both mine to protect."

"I love you, Leonidas, Champion of the Skies. What about your parents and Nan's family? Won't they cause trouble?"

"Once we reach Smoking Isle, we'll investigate on the down-low. I'm positive the druids will create difficulties. We will require patience."

"Oh, joy," Liza said. "I'm not a patient person."

"Unfortunately, there is a protocol. If we meet with the older druids, they will insist on doing everything according to the old ways."

"Oh, joy." Liza said again, this time with a roll of her eyes.

"We will reunite with your daughter. This, I promise, since I will accept nothing less."

Liza kissed Leo, and he kissed her back, morphing their exchange into passion. Hands stroked, and mouths caressed. Bodies softened, and Liza marveled at how right this was between them. How easy yet exciting their relationship was. How happy Leo made her. She explored his sexy pectoral muscles, tasting his skin, his mouth. Leo groaned and rolled her under him. He licked and sucked and drove the passion between them higher.

She parted her legs in silent invitation, and he filled her, loving her long into the night.

Nothing had ever felt so good, so right, so perfect.

Liza loved her dragon-man with everything she had, and once

they discovered a way to retrieve Joanna, her happiness would overflow.

WANT MORE OF LIZA AND LEO?

Not quite ready to let Liza and Leo go? Yeah. Me neither. Get a glimpse of more in the bonus epilogue!

Learn how to receive your free bonus scene by visiting this website.

(https://dl.bookfunnel.com/7jw99jtqtp)

Are you ready to read Cherry's story next? This quiet bookstore owner is about to become the main character of her own real-life adventure story...

Learn more about *Cherry, Dragon Isles 2*, so you can keep reading this series today!

(https://shelleymunro.com/books/cherry/)

About Shelley

USA Today bestselling author Shelley Munro lives in Auckland, the City of Sails, with her husband and a cheeky Jack Russell/mystery breed dog.

Typical New Zealanders, Shelley and her husband left home for their big OE soon after they married (translation of New Zealand speak - big overseas experience). A twelve-month-long adventure lengthened to six years of roaming the world. Enduring memories include being almost sat on by a mountain gorilla in Rwanda, lazing on white sandy beaches in India, whale watching in Alaska, searching for leprechauns in Ireland, and dealing with ghosts in an English pub.

While travel is still a big attraction, these days Shelley is most likely found in front of her computer following another love - that of writing stories of contemporary and paranormal romance and adventure. Other interests include watching rugby (strictly for research purposes), cycling, playing croquet and the ukelele, and curling up with an enjoyable book.

Visit Shelley at her Website

https://shelleymunro.com

Join Shelley's Newsletter

https://shelleymunro.com/newsletter

Also By Shelley

Paranormal

Dragon Investigators

Blue Moon Dragon

Blood Moon Dragon

Black Moon Dragon

Snow Moon Dragon

Dragon Isles

Liza

Cherry

Rena

Sasha

Middlemarch Shifters

My Scarlet Woman

My Younger Lover

My Peeping Tom

My Assassin

My Estranged Lover
My Feline Protector
My Determined Suitor
My Cat Burglar
My Stray Cat
My Second Chance
My Plan B
My Cat Nap
My Romantic Tangle
My Blue Lady
My Twin Trouble
My Precious Gift
My Grumpy Wolf

Triple the Trouble
Shifter Shenanigans
Alien Shenanigans
Sexy Shenanigans
Threesome Shenanigans
Dragon Shenanigans
City Shenanigans
Holiday Shenanigans

www.ingramcontent.com/pod-product-compliance
Lightning Source LLC
Chambersburg PA
CBHW031203020726
47499CB00002B/473

*9 7 8 1 9 9 1 0 6 3 6 6 3 *